PRAISE FOR
THE INCORRIGIBLE CHILDREN OF ASHTON PLACE

"It's the best beginning since *The Bad Beginning* by Lemony Snicket and will leave readers howling for the next episode."

–*Kirkus Reviews* (starred review)

"How hearty and delicious. Smartly written with a middle-grade audience in mind, this is both fun and funny and sprinkled with dollops of wisdom (thank you, Agatha Swanburne). How will it all turn out? Appetites whetted."

–ALA *Booklist* (starred review)

"With a Snicketesque affect, Wood's narrative propels the drama. Pervasive humor and unanswered questions should have readers begging for more."

–*Publishers Weekly* (starred review)

"Jane Eyre meets Lemony Snicket in this smart, surprising satire of a nineteenth-century English governess story. Humorous antics and a climactic cliff-hanger ending will keep children turning pages and clamoring for the next volume, while more sophisticated readers will take away much more. Frequent plate-sized illustrations add wit and period flair."

–*School Library Journal* (starred review)

Also by Maryrose Wood

THE INCORRIGIBLE CHILDREN OF ASHTON PLACE,
BOOK I: THE MYSTERIOUS HOWLING

THE INCORRIGIBLE CHILDREN OF ASHTON PLACE,
BOOK 2: THE HIDDEN GALLERY

THE INCORRIGIBLE CHILDREN OF ASHTON PLACE,
BOOK 4: THE INTERRUPTED TALE

the INCORRIGIBLE CHILDREN *of* ASHTON PLACE

Book 3: THE UNSEEN GUEST

by MARYROSE WOOD

illustrated by JON KLASSEN

BALZER + BRAY

An Imprint of HarperCollins*Publishers*

Balzer + Bray is an imprint of HarperCollins Publishers.

The Incorrigible Children of Ashton Place Book 3: The Unseen Guest

For information address HarperCollins Children's Books, a division of HarperCollins Publishers, 10 East 53rd Street, New York, NY 10022.
www.harpercollinschildrens.com

Library of Congress Cataloging-in-Publication Data
Wood, Maryrose.
The unseen guest / by Maryrose Wood ; illustrated by Jon Klassen. – 1st ed.
p. cm. – (The incorrigible children of Ashton Place ; bk. 3)
Summary: Miss Penelope Lumley embarks on an investigation into the mysteries surrounding the Incorrigible children, Lord Ashton, the forests of Ashton Place, and her own past.
ISBN 978-0-06-179119-2 (pbk.)
[1. Governesses–Fiction. 2. Feral children–Fiction. 3. Secrets–Fiction. 4. Orphans–Fiction. 5. London (England)–Fiction. 6. England–Fiction.] I. Title.
PZ7.W8524Uns 2012 2011053315
[Fic]–dc23 CIP
AC

Typography by Sarah Hoy
13 14 15 OPM 10 9 8 7 6 5 4 3 2

❖

First paperback edition, 2013

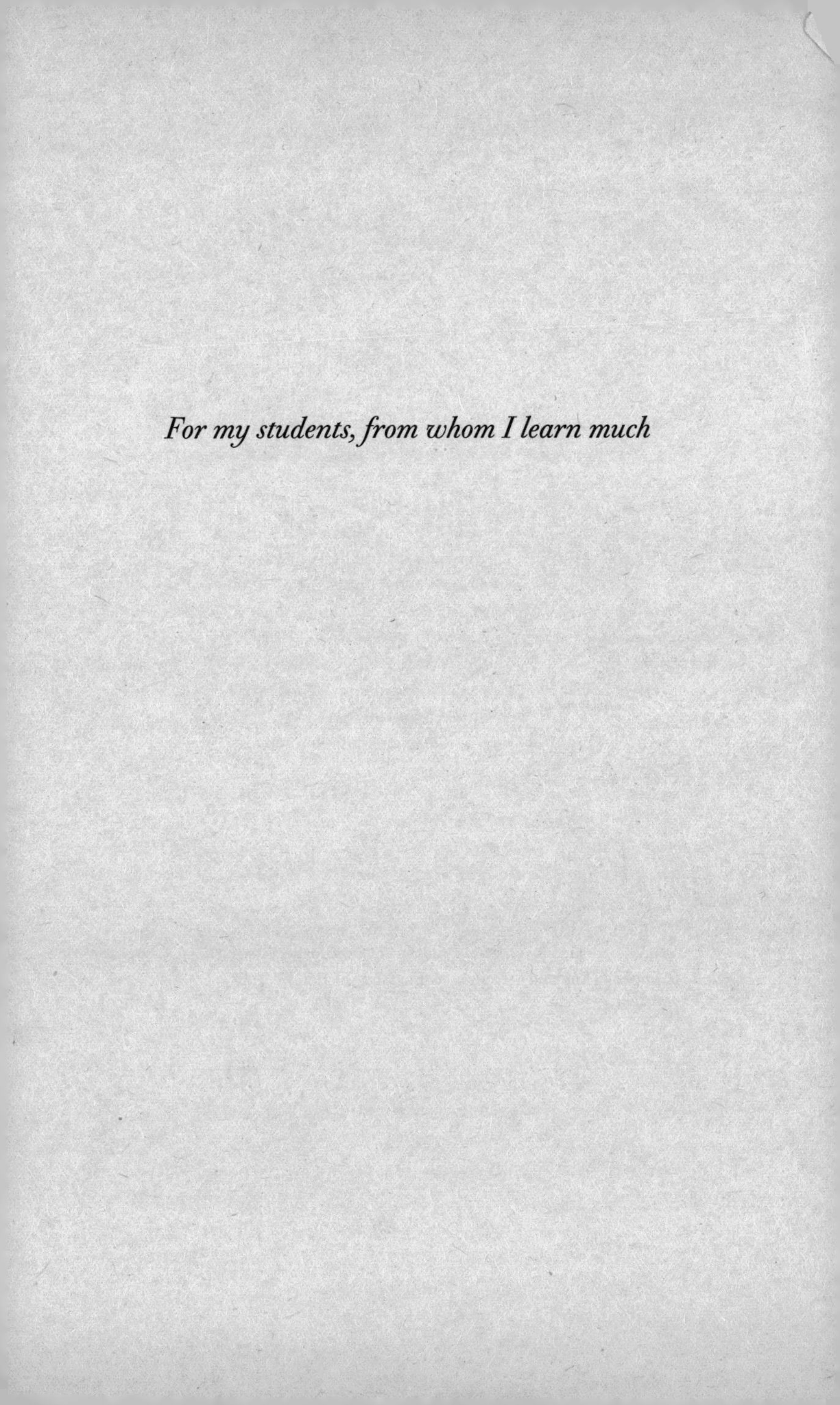

For my students, from whom I learn much

"The woods are full of surprises. But so is the house, miss. So is the land, and so is the sea."

The First Chapter

The nursery is becalmed, and Penelope reconsiders her position.

"Lumawoo, look. What bird?"

"That, I believe, is a nuthatch–Beowulf, do be careful!" Beowulf Incorrigible was leaning so far out the nursery window that his governess, Miss Penelope Lumley, was afraid he might tumble out.

"Nuthatch? Not warbler? *Awk!*" Beowulf's reply rose into a birdlike squawk as Penelope seized her student firmly by the ankles and returned him to a more secure position behind the windowsill. The bird in question—and on second glance, it did seem to Penelope as if it might be more along the lines of a warbler—cocked its head to one side, as if to say, "I know what I am, but what are *you*?" Then it pertly flitted off.

"Whether it is a nuthatch or a warbler is perhaps a matter for debate," Penelope said briskly as she shut the wide-open nursery windows and fastened the latch for good measure. "But you, Beowulf Incorrigible, are not any kind of bird. Under no circumstances are you to fly out the window."

"Sorry, Lumawoo." The boy cast a longing glance in the direction of the bird's departure, but he did not argue. Instead he retreated to the farthest corner of the nursery, where he began building tall, wobbly towers out of square wooden blocks that he then proceeded to tip over with barely a hint of satisfaction.

Penelope returned to her seat and tried to resume reading. But the nursery felt stuffy all at once, without the wonderful summer breeze that had been making the curtains billow and dance all morning. Beowulf's elder brother, Alexander, had spent the last hour pretending that the wind-filled curtains were sails on a ship. Their sister, Cassiopeia, had volunteered to act as a lookout against pirates while Alexander stood manfully upon the bridge of his imaginary vessel, happily navigating away with the shiny brass sextant that was now his favorite possession.

With the closing of the windows, that game, too, had come to an end.

"No wind," Alexander announced, wetting his finger and holding it in the air as a test. "We are becalmed. Drop anchor, mate."

"Aye aye, Captain. Seasick anyway." Cassiopeia obeyed but sounded glum. She was the youngest of the three Incorrigible children, and, it could be argued, the wildest. Truth be told, she had been rather hoping for a run-in with pirates, for she held a bit of a grudge against them ever since the Incorrigibles' recent trip to London, and was hoping to get "last licks," as they say nowadays.

(The theatergoers among you may be able to hum a few bars from *Pirates on Holiday*, the seaworthy operetta whose disastrous premiere the Incorrigibles and their governess had had the great misfortune of attending during their stay in London. If so, you will have some idea of why Cassiopeia felt the way she did. If not, it is enough to know that an intense dislike of pirates—especially singing pirates, which, luckily, are rare—had taken root in the child, and for good reason, too.)

Alas, there would be no swashbuckling today. The sails had gone slack, and the disappointed girl slumped in one of the cozy nursery chairs and clicked idly at the beads of her abacus: back and forth, back and forth.

Penelope noted the changed mood of her three students with dismay. Already she regretted closing the windows. She had done so to make a point about safety, of course, but upon reflection, perhaps a word of caution to Beowulf might have served just as well. For when the windows were open, the children had been happily engaged in educational pursuits: Beowulf was bird-watching, Alexander was navigating, and Cassiopeia had been making colorful threats against unseen pirates, which was good exercise for the imagination, not to mention the girl's rapidly growing vocabulary ("I'll fillet you like a mackerel, *woof*!" had been one of the choicer examples).

But now the three Incorrigible children were cross and at loose ends, a dangerous combination that could easily tempt any young person to misbehave, never mind three siblings who had been raised in a forest by wolves and were thus especially prone to mischief.

There was a *tap-tap-tapp*ing at the window. It was Nutsawoo, the bold and beady-eyed squirrel whom the children had improbably made into a pet. The furry scamp lived outside in the trees, as any sensible squirrel should, but he had become so tame that he often scurried along a low-hanging branch and made the heroic leap to the windowsill, whereupon Cassiopeia would spoil him with treats and try to teach him to do simple arithmetic with the acorns she had saved expressly for that purpose. Now the bewildered rodent could do nothing but press his nose against the glass and knock with his tiny, monkeylike paws as his bushy tail flicked to and fro with anxiety.

No one dared get up to open the window, of course. But the reproachful sound could not be ignored. There it was: the *tap-tap-tap*ping of a single, sad-eyed, snack-seeking squirrel.

Tap. Tap-tap. Tap-tap-tap. Tap-tap-tap-tap.

If you have ever sniffed at the spout of a carton of milk to judge whether the contents were drinkable, and then found yourself wondering if milk actually goes from fresh to sour all at once in a great curdling swoop, or whether it turns bit by bit, in little souring steps, and if so, at what point along the way the sourness would become evident to the human nose and whether it might not be wiser to have a glass of lemonade instead, then you will have some idea of Penelope's current predicament. By now she understood that the mood in the nursery had begun to curdle, so to speak, and that the cause had something to do with her shutting of the windows. However, she was not exactly sure how things had gone so wrong, so quickly. Nor did she know if the morning was already ruined, or if there was yet hope of turning things 'round.

She frowned and drummed her fingers on the cover of her book. It was not quite a year since she had become governess to the Incorrigibles. All three of the children had made remarkable strides regarding their own educations, yet there were many times that their governess felt she was still figuring things out "on the fly," so to speak. This was one of those times.

"Would anyone like to be quizzed on Latin verbs?" she asked halfheartedly.

The children shook their heads and sighed. Beowulf had given up building towers and was now gnawing on the blocks. Alexander idly poked his sister with the sextant, and Cassiopeia clutched her abacus in a way that suggested it might soon be hurled across the room.

"What shall I do?" Penelope thought, for she recognized a looming disaster when she saw one. "Should I reopen the windows and risk appearing foolish, as I have only just closed them? Or should I leave them shut and try to jolly up the children some other way? Perhaps they would like me to read to them. . . ."

But then she felt a sharp pang of guilt, for Penelope knew that the reason she had taken her eyes off Beowulf to begin with was that she had reached a particularly exciting part of the very book she now held in her hands and, as a result, had temporarily forgotten—just for a moment, of course—that she was a governess in a nursery at all.

The volume in question was one of the Giddy-Yap, Rainbow! series that Penelope was so fond of. In it, the tale's heroine, Edith-Anne Pevington, enters her trusty pony, Rainbow, in a pony-and-rider show. Once there, a comical mix-up involving lookalike saddles causes Edith-Anne to meet a boy named Albert, who also plans to take part in the show. His chestnut pony, Starburst, is as spirited and high-strung as Rainbow is gentle and sweet.

The confusion about the saddles is quickly settled, but the encounter with Albert leaves Edith-Anne flummoxed and unable to do anything but braid and rebraid Rainbow's already perfectly groomed mane and tail, if only to keep her mind off this distracting new acquaintance. *Rainbow in Ribbons* was the title of the book, and the pony show was the centerpiece of the plot, but this sideline business with Albert had captured Penelope's imagination in a way that made the book strangely difficult to put down, even when her own real-life pupils were climbing out of windows and so forth. For Albert reminded her of a recent acquaintance of her own—a perfectly nice young man named Simon Harley-Dickinson, whom she had met in London. She often wondered when she might see him again. . . .

"It *was* a warbler," Cassiopeia muttered to Beowulf as she fended off Alexander with her abacus. "Stop drooling and draw it."

Somewhat cheered, Beowulf turned away from chewing his blocks and took out his sketchbook. "For the guidebook," he announced, and got to work.

The word "guidebook" made Penelope feel yet another, different sort of pang—not only because she herself had recently lost a rather unusual guidebook that had been given to her as a gift (more about that later), but because Penelope had instructed the children to make a guidebook of their own, and this, too, was proving problematic.

The book was to be called *Birds of Ashton Place, as Seen from the Nursery Window*, but after three days of diligent bird-watching, even Penelope had to admit that only the most common and frankly uninteresting birds were so unimaginative as to spend their days lingering close to the house. Nuthatches, warblers, sparrows, and the occasional wood dove—perfectly acceptable birds all, to be sure, but where were the sage and mysterious owls? The soaring red kites, with their broad and tireless wings? Or the peregrine falcons, with their bladelike talons and darting eyes that could spot a tasty field mouse on the ground from hundreds of feet in the air?

Clearly, none of these noble specimens was likely to make an appearance at the nursery window. Yet bringing these three half-tamed, wolf-raised children outside, into the woods—surely that would be unwise? For who was to say how they would behave, if they wandered too far from the house?

Tap. Tap-tap. Tap-tap-tap. Tap-tap-tap-tap.

And then, silence. For even Nutsawoo, whose brain was no bigger than a medium-sized walnut, had found something more interesting to do.

At this point it should be noted that, although Miss Penelope Lumley was still two months shy of her sixteenth birthday, she possessed a great deal of wisdom for a person so young. For that she could thank her years at the Swanburne Academy for Poor Bright Females, which equipped her not only with a sound education, but also with the timeless good sense of the school's founder, Agatha Swanburne, who was known for her countless pithy nuggets of wisdom (nearly all of which are just as useful nowadays as they were back in Miss Lumley's day—a point to bear in mind).

Penelope drummed her fingers on the cover of *Rainbow in Ribbons* and tried to imagine what Agatha Swanburne would have to say about her situation. And in fact, the answer came to her. "Now I know just what to do," she thought. "For, as Agatha Swanburne once said, 'It is easier to change one's boots than to change one's mind, but it is far easier to change one's mind about whether or not to wear boots than it is to change the weather.'"

It was one of the grand lady's more enigmatic statements, but still, it had done the trick. Penelope rose from her seat and strode purposefully toward the windows. "Children, I have given the matter some thought, and I see that I was mistaken." She pushed aside the curtains. "First of all, I believe your guidebook needs a better title than the one I already suggested."

"*Birds of Ashton Place, as Seen from the Nursery Window*—no good?" Alexander asked, frowning.

"I believe it can be improved upon." Penelope undid the latch and flung open the windows more widely than before. At once the curtains filled with air and ballooned giddily into the room.

"*Birds of Ashton Place, as Seen with No Jumping Out Window*?" Beowulf offered as he batted away the dancing fabric that whipped playfully about him.

"That would certainly be a step in the right direction." Penelope inhaled deeply; the air smelled like lilacs, and there was a lovely low hum of bees and some very promising distant sounds of birdsong. "However, I think it is the bit about the window that needs changing."

Now she had all three children's attention. She folded her hands in front of her and faced her pupils with a solemn expression that was rather hard to keep up, for she could see (as the children could not, since now they had their backs to the window) that Nutsawoo had returned and was doing a skittering, celebratory dance along the tree branches. "I have reconsidered my position. Clearly, a guidebook written by looking through a window simply will not work. Instead, I propose we go outdoors and observe the birds in their natural habitat, so to speak."

"*Birds of Ashton Place That Live Outdoors*," Alexander

declared, rummaging about for his shoes.

"*Birds in the Fields and Treetops.*" Beowulf sounded very pleased.

"*Birds, Birds, Birds.*" Cassiopeia jumped up and down and flapped her arms like wings. "*Birds!*"

Penelope nodded thoughtfully. "These are all fine suggestions for titles. But I propose we call our guidebook *Birds of Ashton Place That Live Outdoors, as Seen Close Up by Three Clever and Obedient Children Who Will Under No Circumstances Run Off into the Woods.* Agreed?"

"Agreed," said Alexander, dodging back and forth behind the billowing curtain.

"Agreed, *ahwooooo*!" Beowulf howled, forgetting his words for a moment.

"Yes, *woof*!" Even more than her brothers, Cassiopeia could not help barking when excited.

Penelope suppressed a smile. Sour milk cannot be made unsour, but the three Incorrigible children were clearly made of different and more resilient stuff, and for some reason this made her feel deeply proud of them. "Very well. Let us take no more than three minutes to collect our bird-watching equipment. If we are in luck, we will find some interesting specimens before teatime."

"Hooray, hooray!" they shouted as one. The children set about gathering their supplies. For Alexander, this meant his sextant, notebook, and sharp pencils for recording the precise geographic location of each sighting. Cassiopeia swept up crumbs and leftover crusts of bread from the breakfast tray and tied them snugly in a linen square; with these she would tempt the birds close enough to be recognized. Beowulf packed up his sketch pad and pastel crayons; he was a talented artist and highly skilled at depicting each bird in all its beaked and feathered glory.

As for their governess, Miss Penelope Lumley: Her preparations involved making a trip to the kitchen for a flask of cold, fresh milk and a large supply of biscuits. Milk, because bird-watching outdoors was bound to be hot and strenuous work, and the children would soon be thirsty.

The biscuits were for her own use, in case the Incorrigibles themselves got carried away and needed to be lured back to more civilized surroundings. The children had always found the antics of small, edible creatures positively riveting and could scarcely take their eyes off them–clearly an advantage when bird-watching–but whether they could refrain from pouncing remained to be seen. Penelope had a great deal of faith in the children, but as a person who had recently made an error herself, and had gone to the trouble of correcting it, she knew better than to expect other people to be perfect at all times.

That is also why, despite a moment's temptation as she thought how pleasant it would be to read in the shade of an oak tree while the children scampered and sketched, she left her copy of *Rainbow in Ribbons* behind in the nursery. The plan was to go bird-watching; the children would require close supervision, and Penelope did not want to risk being distracted even for a minute. She was their governess, after all, and she too had learned a valuable lesson that day.

"Although I am frantic to know what happens next to Edith-Anne Pevington, that intriguing boy named Albert, high-spirited Starburst, and dear, sweet Rainbow, I will put aside my book until later and give my full attention to the task at hand," she thought, carefully tucking her bookmark ribbon in place so she could find her page again later on. "For to do two things at once is to do each one only half as well as one is truly able," she concluded.

That Miss Penelope Lumley had a knack for inventing catchy sayings was hardly surprising, given where she had gone to school. That she also had the ability to learn from her mistakes and replace a poorly thought-out plan with a better one—well, that, too, should come as no surprise to anyone familiar with the plucky young governess, or with her alma mater, either.

For, indoors or out, Penelope was a Swanburne girl, through and through.

The Second Chapter

It was not quite the bird
they were expecting.

As you may know, "*alma mater*" is a Latin phrase that means "nourishing mother." To nourish is to feed and make grow; therefore, a nourishing mother would be the one who has fed you and raised you so that you might grow up into the strapping young man or woman you are no doubt well on your way to becoming.

Nowadays, of course, "alma mater" is what people call the place where they went to school and, one hopes, were fed countless yummy bites of knowledge from a vast and scrumptious buffet of education. All of the poor bright females who graduated from the Swanburne Academy would consider the school their alma mater; some might even place small, boastful signs on the backs of their pony carts that read YOU HAVE JUST BEEN PASSED BY A SWANBURNE GIRL.

But Miss Penelope Lumley had no pony cart, much as she would have liked one. And to her, the words "alma mater" had always held a special, private, and, up until quite recently, altogether sadder meaning.

For Penelope had been enrolled at the Swanburne Academy as a very young girl, no older than Cassiopeia was now (that is to say, five or six at the most), and through all the long years since, she had not heard one word from her mater—that is, mother—or her father, either. Both Mater and Pater Lumley seemed to have slipped completely out of the picture the instant they dropped off little Penny at school. They never sent a present on her birthday or a congratulatory note after final exams (even when, year after year, their hardworking daughter ranked at the top of her class). Nor was there a get well soon card the time when Penelope had chicken pox and had to spend three days taking warm milk baths to stop the dreadful itching.

There had been no letters, no telegrams, and not a single picture postcard. There had been no word at all—that is, until Penelope's recent adventure in London with the three Incorrigible children. Just prior to the trip, Penelope had been given a guidebook by her former headmistress at Swanburne, the kind and elegant (and, as Penelope had also discovered, secretive and mysterious) Miss Charlotte Mortimer. The guidebook was titled *Hixby's Lavishly Illustrated Guide to London: Compleat with Historical Reference, Architectural Significance, and Literary Allusions,* though Penelope preferred to call it the *Hixby's Guide,* as there are only so many hours in a day. But instead of Big Ben and Buckingham Palace, the illustrations showed crystal-blue alpine lakes and edelweiss-covered meadows populated with snow larks, mountain hares, and other wildlife of that Swiss ilk.

(Some of you are no doubt wondering if elk are also of that ilk. Sadly, they are not. Elk have not been seen in Switzerland in many a year. In the interests of scientific accuracy, please strike the idea of elk from your mind. If you must, think of ibexes instead, a fierce and agile type of goat with great spiraling horns. Marmots will also do in a pinch, but under no circumstances should you think of elk. No. Elk. The elkless among you may now proceed.)

Despite its peculiarities, Penelope had grown fond

of the *Hixby's Guide*, for the pictures were charming and the brief descriptions were written in jaunty, if enigmatic, verse. Penelope had always had a keen liking for poetry. Alas, the book had been lost in a high-speed chase involving singing pirates and a howling parrot. (Again, please refer to *Pirates on Holiday* for details. The opening-night reviews were printed in the London *Times* and several other newspapers of record; they can be found at your local library indexed under *operettas, seaworthy*; *flops, theatrical*; or even *parrots, thespian.*)

Only after Penelope had returned to Ashton Place with more puzzles to solve than even Cassiopeia's abacus could keep track of did she receive a letter from Miss Mortimer revealing that the *Hixby's Guide*, had, in fact, been a gift sent by Penelope's parents.

Mater Lumley! Pater Lumley! Who would have guessed they could draw?

Even though the precious book was lost, Penelope's joy at knowing her parents were alive and thinking of her filled her heart with a deep and quiet joy. For a while. But then all sorts of troubling questions began to creep into the usually optimistic young governess's mind. For example:

If Miss Mortimer had been in contact with Penelope's

parents, why had she kept it a secret?

What was the point of all that alpine scenery, when what Penelope had really needed for her trip was a guidebook to London, which was a confusing city on foot and even worse if one needed to take the omnibus?

And the biggest, most heart-wrenching question of all: If the long-lost Lumleys were alive and well, then where, oh where, had they been all these years?

Where, indeed? For it is one thing to think your parents have not sent a birthday card because they are being held captive in a dungeon, or are journeying through untamed lands that lack an efficient postal service, or are, sadly, dead. Penelope had considered all these possible explanations over the years, and dozens more as well. But it is another thing altogether to realize that the whole time you were pining and wondering and shedding the occasional lonely and self-pitying tear as you soaked your chicken pox in the foamy slime of the milk bath, trying not to scratch, your long-lost mater and pater were romping through the edelweiss near a chalet somewhere, sketching flinty-eyed mountain goats and composing bits and pieces of, it must be said, rather mediocre poetry.

In short, now that she knew they were alive and well and fully capable of putting pen and paintbrush to paper, Penelope could not help being deeply angry with her parents, while at the same time missing them more than she had in many a year.

It was an unexpected development, to be sure. It left her feeling confused and a bit lost, like a person dropped in a strange city with only a useless guidebook to find her way around. A Swanburne girl does not mope, as Penelope had been taught countless times, and so she tried her best to put the whole subject out of her mind and think of other, happier things. But just as the instruction "do not think of elk" will cause great herds of the antlered beasts to come thundering through one's brain at inconvenient moments, the more Penelope tried to not think about her parents, the more keenly everything seemed to remind her of them.

Even now, as she escorted the Incorrigible children on their first-ever outdoor bird-watching expedition, she could not help noticing the small white flowers scattered throughout the lush grass of the parkland surrounding Ashton Place. It was not edelweiss, of course, for edelweiss is not native to England, but it was close enough to make Penelope's thoughts gain force and speed, like a velocipede flying down a hill.

"I will think of bird-watching and only bird-watching," she told herself sternly. "And absolutely no snow larks! Only your average, everyday English birds." But it was no use. Now that she was outside, away from the nursery and its chores and the useful distraction of Edith-Anne Pevington and Albert, the windows of Penelope's mind were flung open, so to speak, and all her cross and lonely feelings came billowing in freely, whether she wanted them to or not.

"Lumawoo? See bird!"

"We shall see some very soon, Alexander," she replied, but inside she was thinking, "Not only am I cross with my parents, but I am rather piqued at Miss Mortimer, too, for she has kept secrets from me. No doubt she would say it was for my own good, but surely I ought to be the judge of that. I am nearly sixteen, after all. And she has not replied to any of the letters I have sent since returning from London! I wonder why?"

"Is very large bird, Lumawoo. Not warbler."

"Many birds are bigger than warblers, Beowulf. A full-grown pheasant can be positively robust," Penelope said absently before returning to her train of thought, which was now zooming along like a Bloomer steam locomotive at full tilt. "And what of all those frightening things she told me about the children being in danger, with dire fates foretold, curses upon their heads, and so on? Not to mention her insistence that I keep my hair dyed this drab, dark color. 'Be on the lookout for unexpected events,' she said, but surely that is impractical advice. For unless one has the gift of prognostication, are not all events at least somewhat unexpected? Even when we think we know what is likely to happen, surprises tend to pop up willy-nilly—what? Wait!"

"Lumawoo! Ostrich!" Cassiopeia sounded highly excited. But Penelope was not looking in the same direction.

"Ostriches are native to Africa and are known for their lovely plumes; you may have seen some in Lady Constance's hats. But that, I believe, is a cuckoo. Beowulf, quickly; take out your pencils, you will want to get this down—"

"No cuck*ahwooooo*!" Beowulf howled insistently. The startled bird to which Penelope referred (it was a yellow-billed cuckoo, to be precise) flew off. Penelope turned to Beowulf with a frown.

"I know it is enjoyable to be out-of-doors, Beowulf, but you must try to rein in the howling, or you will get all the dogs in the county started—oh, my!"

"Lumawoo!" All three children gestured wildly. "Ostrich!"

"Lumawoo! Ostrich!"

"Yes, I can see that." Penelope was stunned, for before her stood what was indisputably an ostrich. The creature was nearly a foot taller than she was (to be fair, most of that height was neck and legs), and it had the most curious expression on its face—as if it were the giant bird that was shocked to encounter a young governess and her three young charges on the grounds of an English country estate, and not the other way 'round.

The ostrich tipped its head from side to side, and gave a little shimmy with its broad, feathered tail.

"Long way from Africa," Alexander observed. "Bad navigating."

"Need more paper," Beowulf said, for this was a great deal more bird than he had come prepared to draw.

"Big egg," Cassiopeia added admiringly.

"What on earth . . ." But before Penelope could say ". . . is an ostrich doing at Ashton Place?" the giant creature blinked and bounded off into the woods on its spindly legs at a truly astonishing speed. In a moment it was gone—as thoroughly and completely as if it had never been there at all.

Penelope's mouth hung open, but no words came out; there was so much to say that she hardly knew where to begin. What they had just seen was not merely unexpected; it was utterly impossible. And yet . . .

Cassiopeia reached down and picked up a long, arched feather that had fallen from the ostrich's tail. "Plume," she announced. She stuck the jet-black feather in her hair and began prancing around and chirping orders in a wicked imitation of Lady Constance Ashton. "Mrs. Clarke, get my tea! Margaret, get my dress!"

The boys giggled and bowed. "Yes, Lady Plume. Right away, Lady Plume." Under normal circumstances, Penelope would have scolded the children for being disrespectful, although the truth was that she, too, often found Lady Constance to be a rather silly person. But these were hardly normal circumstances, were they? If parents could disappear with no explanation, and children raised by wolves could tame squirrels and take up bird-watching as an educational (and so far, inedible) hobby, and a dedicated and well-trained governess could, not once but twice in the same morning, utterly fail to notice what was right in front of her—well, everything had gone topsy-turvy, and that was all there was to it.

"Ahoy!" Alexander had his captain's spyglass up. "Vessel on the horizon."

"Heavens, what can it be this time? A herd of elk?"

Penelope exclaimed, at her wit's end.

All four of them turned to look. Something—or someone—was coming up the path from the house.

"Is bird!" Cassiopeia pointed and waved her plume excitedly, no doubt hoping for another ostrich sighting.

"Is . . . train?" Beowulf said, confused, for the shape was fairly stout, although, to be fair, not nearly as stout as a steam engine would be, and of course there were no train tracks running along the path.

"No bird. No train." Alexander peered through the glass. "Is Mrs. Clarke."

Penelope took the glass and looked for herself. "It *is* Mrs. Clarke. And she appears to be trotting." She paused to rub her eyes, for if there was one thing that could have surprised her more than, say, finding a full-grown ostrich running loose on the grounds of Ashton Place, it would be the sight of Mrs. Clarke out for an afternoon's jog.

The approaching rhythmic *jingle-jingle-jingle* of a great ring of keys banging against ample hips confirmed it: It was Mrs. Clarke, the head housekeeper of Ashton Place, chugging toward them at a slow but steady speed. Her waddling gait was a snail's pace compared to the ostrich's swift departure, but for Mrs. Clarke it was remarkably quick. Penelope and the

Incorrigibles watched in amazement as she plodded across the grassy field and came to a stop before them.

"Miss Lumley! Miss Lumley! There you are. My, that was brisk!" Mrs. Clarke was mildly out of breath, but she bore a pleased expression. "What a lovely day it is! If there wasn't so much work to do in the house, I'd take a nice long ramble outside myself."

"Mrs. Clarke . . . ." At this juncture Penelope might have said any number of things: "We have just seen an ostrich" or "Would you like to join us on our bird-watching expedition?" or even "Is there any hope of having lemon tarts with tea today?" But instead she blurted, "It appears you have been exercising."

The older woman's cheeks were already pink from exertion, but her proud blush shone through nevertheless. "Why, yes, I have, here and there, I must confess! I was complaining about feeling winded on the stairs, you see, and Old Timothy gave me some advice about how to fix it. He said I ought to do what he does when a carriage horse goes lame and has been off work for a while. You build up its strength bit by bit. Short trips at first, and then a bit longer, then add a bit of weight in the carriage, until soon the beast is better than new. And faster, too."

She pounded herself on the chest. "I'm not quite

ready for the Derby, mind you, but I'm picking up my pace, to be sure. And look at you children! I scarcely recognize you, you've grown so big. You boys will be wanting new trousers soon; I spy a bit of ankle peeking out. And where did you get that pretty bit of plumage, Cassawoof?" (Mrs. Clarke was the only person besides her brothers whom Cassiopeia let call her by her nickname; she would have let Penelope call her that as well, of course, but Penelope felt she ought not encourage too much woofiness in the children, and therefore always used their proper names.)

"Ostrich," the girl replied, pointing in the direction of the bird's exit.

"Fell out of a ladies' hat, did it? Well, it suits you, dearie. But speaking of ladies"—and now Mrs. Clarke's cheerful tone changed to a more anxious one—"Lady Constance is in an awful tizzy, Miss Lumley. That's why I came toddling out to find you and the children, so you can prepare yourselves."

Penelope felt a wave of relief: At last, here was a piece of news that was completely unsurprising. "Thank you for your concern, Mrs. Clarke, but you needn't worry. The children and I have survived Lady Constance in a tizzy before."

"Not like this one." Mrs. Clarke took the opportunity to stretch out her calves. "A messenger showed up at the door with the news. It seems we're to receive a very important guest, and Lady Constance is in a state of fuss and bother the likes of which I've never seen before and hope I never see again. If only Lord Ashton were home!"

Penelope could think of only one person important enough to cause such pandemonium in the household, but a visit from Queen Victoria seemed altogether unlikely, despite the fact that Her Majesty and Penelope had recently exchanged some pleasant correspondence. "Still, it would be a delightful surprise," she thought, and was about to ask if it was, in fact, the Queen of England who was on her way, but Mrs. Clarke had finished stretching and went on.

"We are receiving Lord Fredrick's mother. Goodness, how long it's been! It must be ten or twelve years since we've seen her. She'll be staying for dinner and who knows how long after that. Why she couldn't let a poor housekeeper know ahead of time is beyond me; the kitchen is in an uproar! I shouldn't be surprised if you and the children will be expected to make an appearance. I'd advise you to hurry back to the house at once and scrub up a bit, just in case."

"We certainly shall. Thank you for the warning, Mrs. Clarke. I wonder if you could tell me: Why has Lord Fredrick's mother not visited for so long?"

But the portly housekeeper was already chugging back the way she came. She gave a wave good-bye without turning 'round, and the *jingle-jingle-jingle* of her keys quickly faded into the distance.

Penelope was glad to see Mrs. Clarke so full of pep, but she wished the housekeeper had paused to answer her question. Lord Fredrick Ashton was a strange fellow, and Penelope had grown deeply curious about some of his odder traits: for example, his fascination with full moons, the dates of which he kept meticulously circled in his almanac, and which seemed to coincide with unexplained disappearances and fits of barking and scratching. "They say that the apple does not fall far from the tree. Perhaps meeting his mother will be instructive," she thought. To the children she remarked, "Look at her go! Mrs. Clarke may well be ready for the Derby before long."

At the mention of a horse race, the children began snorting and rearing up like three spirited ponies. Mrs. Clarke had been quite right to notice how much the Incorrigibles had grown—less than a year had passed, and already Alexander had gained an inch and a half.

Seeing him paw the ground and whinny only served to emphasize how leggy and coltish he had become. Beowulf had also gotten taller, and even Cassiopeia had lost a touch of her baby plumpness about the cheeks.

"An ostrich cannot fly, but time certainly does," Penelope thought. "How sad it is that my three pupils are growing up so quickly, and yet their true parents are missing it all."

Just . . . like . . . mine. The words seemed to come from outside her, but it was only a whippoorwill offering its plaintive, three-note cry.

Whip-poor-will!

Whip-poor-will!

Elk, elk, elk–missing parents seemed to crop up at every turn. Penelope shook off a lonely pang and said, "You heard Mrs. Clarke, children. That is enough bird-watching for today. We are needed back at the house."

"But, Lumawoo! Only one bird."

"Given its size, I should think an ostrich would count as three birds at least. Now, my fine ponies, how about a race back to Ashton Place? The first Incorrigible to set hoof in the house gets an extra biscuit."

That was all she needed to say. The children eagerly galloped ahead. In their haste to be first, they failed to notice a tree sparrow and two different types of finches in the trees just to the right of the path, but Penelope felt it was better not to risk further distractions and said nothing. Besides, after coming face-to-face with an ostrich, anything short of a dodo was bound to be a letdown.

(As you may know, a dodo was a comical-looking and utterly defenseless sort of bird that even in Miss Lumley's day had been extinct for more than a century. Imagine a fifty-pound pigeon with the feet of a turkey, the beak of a toucan, and the prehistoric charm of a rhinoceros. Dodos could not fly; they could not run; apparently they did not taste very good, either. With so many disadvantages, you may think it a wonder they survived as long as they did, but the extinction of the dodo was not caused by natural predators, inclement weather, or even a plague of contagious dodo disease. No; it was the carelessness of people that did them in. Some wrongs can be made right by a heartfelt apology and a sincere effort to do better; alas, this is not one of them, for no matter how sorry one feels about it, there will never be dodos again. It is a great disappointment to bird-watchers, to be sure, but far, far worse for the dodos.)

As for Penelope, even as she jogged along, trying in vain to keep the galloping children in sight, the "do not think of elk" principle was in full force.

"So, Mater Ashton is paying a call at Ashton Place," Penelope mused as she bounded over the rocky paths. "It seems that even Lord Fredrick Ashton gets an unexpected visit from his mother now and then. Perhaps the Incorrigibles and I will also be so fortunate, someday." Then she called, "Children, not quite so fast! Whoaaaaaaa!"

The Third Chapter

Lady Constance plays a game of hide-and-seek.

If your sister Lavinia takes the last biscuit from the biscuit tin and leaves you nothing but crumbs, you might very well feel mad as a hornet, but if you are wise as an owl, you will stay cool as a cucumber and sweetly ask your mater to bake a fresh batch. Happy as a lark, you will take the oven-warm biscuits up to your private tree house and, hungry as a horse, devour them all yourself. Then it will be Lavinia's turn to be mad as a hornet–unless she discovers your clever scheme and, gentle as a lamb and sweet as a kitten, somehow persuades you to share.

Why comparisons to insects, animals, and even vegetables are so often used to discuss matters that have only to do with humans is a question that philosophers have yet to answer. Consider the expression "dead as a dodo." Dodos, as you know, are extinct; therefore, this rather gloomy phrase means that the thing being described is not merely dead. It is very dead; in fact, it is extremely and permanently dead, and likely to remain so.

Granted, the differences between "dead," "very dead," and "extremely and permanently dead" are not easy to comprehend. What is clear is that, in Miss Lumley's day, as in our own, dodos are as dead as, well, dodos, but the carelessness of humans is far from extinct. Scaling a slippery, snow-capped mountain without the proper equipment can lead to a gruesome end, no matter how thrilling the scenery. And many fine poems have been written about shipwrecks, but only a foolish captain would knowingly set sail into stormy seas.

Certainly no one of good sense would sail headlong into the whirling, tornado-like temper of Lady Constance Ashton, if it could be helped. When highly agitated, as she was now, Lord Fredrick's young bride had a regrettable tendency to blow over anything in her path.

"I cannot *believe* that the very first time I am to meet my mother-in-law it is with less than an hour's notice, and of course Fredrick is not even at home! How is it possible that the Widow Ashton could arrive with no warning? Or did she write to Fredrick, and he simply forgot to tell me? If that is the case, I may scream from the sheer frustration of it all! Margaret, *what* is taking so long?"

It had fallen upon poor Margaret, the good-hearted and squeaky-voiced housemaid, to help Lady Constance change into a fresh gown and fix her hair so that she might receive her unexpected guest. But Lady Constance would not stay put; she raced from window to window and peered out to see if the Widow Ashton's carriage had arrived.

"It'll go quicker if you hold still, ma'am."

"How can I hold still at a time like this? Wait—do you hear something? Do you suppose it is her? Why are there so many trees by the windows? I can scarcely see a thing!"

"Patience, m'lady. Like my old mum likes to say, a watched pot never boils."

No doubt Agatha Swanburne would have agreed with this homespun wisdom, but the advice went unheeded, for Lady Constance had just reached the same conclusion that Penelope had come to that very morning. "This is absurd; I cannot tell anything from looking out the windows. Follow me, Margaret!" Clutching a powder puff in one hand and a container of face powder in the other, Lady Constance ran out of her dressing room, down the stairs, and out the front door of Ashton Place. Breathless, she scanned the property, first in one direction, then in the other. "She is not here yet," Lady Constance cried, throwing her arms wide in despair. Every time she gestured, she left a trail of rose-scented powder. "Oh, it is torture! If she truly is coming, I say she ought to get here at once and put an end to this dreadful waiting."

Margaret took her frantic mistress by the arm. "My lady, if you please, come inside and stand by the mirror so I can pin up your curls in the back."

On most days a mirror would have been an excellent way to focus Lady Constance's attention, but today was not most days, for when Lady Constance saw her reflection she shrieked.

"Eek! I look like a ghost!" In fact she had powdered herself into an otherworldly pallor, which she now tried to fix by powdering herself even more. "Margaret, you must do something about my face. To look at me, anyone would think I was a bloodless old crone of twenty-five."

"I will, in a moment, my lady. First I must get your hair put up properly. And your dress is not even fastened."

"Face, hair, dress—why is it all so complicated? If I were a bird, I would wear the same feathers every day and no one would think less of me for it." Lady Constance batted at her face with the puff until she all but disappeared in a perfumed fog. "What if she hates me, Margaret? Men can be very attached to their mothers; at least, that is what I have heard. Perhaps the Widow Ashton will speak meanly of me to Fredrick and turn him against me."

"I hope not, ma'am." Margaret had nearly gotten all the wayward yellow ringlets pinned into place, but at her well-intended reply, Lady Constance spun 'round in a panic and the pins went flying.

"You hope not? You *hope* not? Why? Do you actually think there is the tiniest shred of possibility that Fredrick's mother might find me . . . unappealing?"

"No, of course not, my lady."

"Of course not is right. It is ridiculous to worry. I am lovely and charming; everyone says so. *Ah-choo!* Oh dear, the powder is all up my nose. *Ah-choo! Ah-choo!*"

"Take my handkerchief, ma'am."

Lady Constance did, and blew her nose into it noisily, talking all the while. "On the other hand, who knows what sort of person Fredrick's mother is? She might be perfectly dreadful and dislike me for no reason at all. Fredrick hardly speaks of her, but Fredrick hardly speaks of anything, *ah-choo!* Did you know, Margaret, the woman did not even attend our wedding? I find that terribly rude. *Ah-choo!*"

"If my lady will let me get at these buttons . . . I am sure my lord's mother must have had a good excuse—"

"Oh, she had a fine excuse! Apparently the Widow Ashton has been in deep mourning ever since Fredrick's father was killed in some sort of gruesome accident, many years ago. I ask you, is that a reason not to attend your own son's wedding?"

"Killed in an accident, *tsk tsk*! Poor Widow Ashton, what a sad and lonely life she must have." Margaret whizzed through the buttons on the back of the dress and tied the sash at the back of the skirt into a floppy bow.

"Do you really think Fredrick's mother is sad?" Lady Constance's look of surprise was made comical by her clown-white face. "To lose one's husband in a gruesome accident is a serious misfortune, I suppose. If anything as horrible as that were to happen to me,

I would do nothing but cry for a week, at least—but no! Fredrick is going to live a long, healthy life." She stamped both her feet for emphasis, as if trying to squash an elusive bug. "I will have to insist upon it, for it would be dreadfully dull if he did not. Wait, what is that noise? Someone is coming, it must be her, and I am not ready, not *nearly* ready—"

"I see biscuit!"

"No, I see biscuit!"

"Giddy-yap, giddy-yap, Rainb*owooooo*!" Just as their governess had instructed, the Incorrigibles had raced the whole way home until, laughing and breathless, they reached the door at nearly the same time, with both boys claiming first dibs on the winner's biscuit. Cassiopeia was a fierce competitor, too, of course, but her legs were the shortest; also, the plume in her hair had fallen out at one point, and she had to run back to get it, thus costing her valuable seconds.

In the excitement of their galloping, the children had slipped far ahead of their governess, who at the moment was nowhere to be seen.

"Eeeeeee!" Lady Constance shrieked as the three children burst into the house and skidded to a stop at her feet.

"Ahwoooooo!" the children howled, for they were

equally startled to find themselves in a near collision with what appeared to be the ghost of Lady Constance.

"*Ahwoo*, you say? *Ahwoo?*" Lady Constance tiptoed backward in horror until her back was pressed flat against the wall. "What will Fredrick's mother say if she finds the three of you here, drooling and barking and *ahwoo*ing away? Why, she will think I am a fool to harbor such uncivilized creatures in the house that still bears the proud name of Ashton! Miss Lumley, you must conceal these Incorrigible children at once." She ran outside, searching. "Where is Miss Lumley? Monstrous creatures! What have you done with your governess?"

Beowulf discreetly wiped his mouth (for the exertion of the race had left him drooling, just a bit) and gestured toward the path. "Lumawoo coming," he said.

Alexander peered through his spyglass. "Slower than ostrich, faster than Mrs. Clarke."

"Do you like my plume?" Cassiopeia waggled it in front of Lady Constance's face. It tickled the lady's nose and brought on more sneezes that sent hairpins flying every which way. Margaret scurried to gather them up.

"*Ah-choo!* You are quite mad, all three of you. *Ah-choo!* I don't know why Fredrick insists that you live here. As soon as he returns I am going to put my foot down, once and for all–"

"Pardon me, but there is a carriage coming up the drive, my lady." Margaret rubbed Lady Constance's cheeks with her sleeve to remove the excess powder, but the sneezing fit was already under way.

"*Ahwoo!* I mean, *Ah-choo!* Oh, I am all confused! I simply cannot greet Fredrick's mother with the three of you standing at the front door as if you belonged here. *Ah-choo!*" A wicked look came over the lady's face. "Children, do you know how to play hide-and-seek?"

Lady Constance had never suggested a game to the Incorrigibles before; in fact, she scarcely spoke to the children at all if it could be helped, so they were not sure how to respond.

"Gesundheit, and pardon me, your gracious ladyness." Of the three Incorrigibles, Alexander was the most adept at the socially useful phrases Penelope had taught them. "We do not know hide-and-seek. Is it a good game?"

"Why, it is the very best game of all!" Lady Constance made her eyes grow wide in that false, excited way that grown-ups sometimes do when talking to children. "Hide-and-seek is when the three Incorrigible children run very far away and stay there, quiet as mice. And sooner or later, somebody just might come out to find you! *Ah-choo!* Doesn't that sound fun?"

"No run in forest?" Beowulf asked dubiously, for he recalled Miss Lumley's instruction from earlier in the day.

"*Yes* run in forest." Lady Constance clapped her hands in exaggerated delight. "Yes, yes, yes, you *must* run into the forest, just as far away as you can. Can you do that, children? For I think it would be quite an adventure for you, and I would much prefer you to be out of sight and out of mind and *absolutely* out of the house for the duration of the Widow Ashton's visit."

She smiled hugely, baring her pearly white teeth in what could only be called a wolfish grin. "I will give you the loveliest present if you could scamper off and not come back. A nice, crunchy bone, perhaps?"

The children looked tempted. But before they could begin to play this interesting-sounding game, the clippety-clop of hooves and the clattering of carriage wheels announced that it was too late.

"She's here! Oh, my hair! My face! My nose! *Ah-choo!*" Lady Constance wailed.

"Ma'am, your buttons have come undone!" Margaret squeaked.

"Hide," Beowulf suggested to his siblings. No doubt he was still thinking about the possibility of a bone, for he dearly loved to gnaw. But Lady Constance misunderstood.

"Hide? *Ah-choo!* Very well, then–if you three will not, then *I* shall hide! After all, Fredrick's mother cannot dislike me if she has not met me." And with that, Lady Constance kicked off both of her pretty silver shoes and began to haul herself into the low, spreading branches of a nearby tree.

At the sight of her mistress shinnying up the gnarled trunk, Margaret, whose voice tended to rise in pitch when she was nervous, let out a squeak that only bats could hear and raced into the house to get help, thus leaving the three Incorrigible children alone to greet their guest.

As anyone who has ever eaten a box of Cracker Jack caramel-coated popcorn already knows, life is full of surprises. On a good day, one might find a colorful plastic top that spins; on a great day, the rare and much-coveted secret decoder ring. Alas, not all surprises are so pleasant. Long-absent parents send puzzling, alpine-themed gifts, and enjoyable bird-watching expeditions are cut short by the arrival of guests.

That life's unexpected plot twists are not always to our liking should never be cause for despair. Even Agatha Swanburne, who had never tasted Cracker Jack in her life, once said, "Better to make the best of a bad situation than to make the worst of a good one." Surely the secret decoder ring would be a more thrilling prize to find inside the box than yet another uninteresting sticker, but either way, one can still enjoy the popcorn.

Yet there are times when even the pluckiest among us fail to follow this sage advice. Instead of muddling through and making the best of things, we pull the blankets over our heads and hope that whatever is troubling us will simply go away and leave us alone. This is called "burying your head in the sand," and the expression comes from a widely held but mistaken belief about ostriches. You see, somehow the rumor began that when the giant birds wish to hide themselves, they burrow their heads into the sand and assume that if they cannot see their enemies, their enemies cannot see them, either.

It is true that ostriches have exceedingly tiny brains relative to their size, yet even ostriches are not quite as dim-witted as all that. And no doubt the brain of Lady Constance Ashton was far bigger; however, it seemed she did put some stock in the idea that if she fled the scene, she could prevent the Widow Ashton from seeing her and therefore from disliking her. But a shoeless, whimpering lady in a half-buttoned gown dangling from the branch of a tree is hardly inconspicuous. It was only the Widow Ashton's inability to see objects clearly without her pince-nez that prevented her from spotting her daughter-in-law the moment she climbed out of her carriage.

(A pince-nez was a sort of eyeglass popular at the time. It had no earpieces, as modern eyeglasses do, but stayed on by means of a pinching mechanism that tightly gripped the bridge of the wearer's nose. No doubt this was just as painful as it sounds; nowadays the pince-nez is as extinct as the dodo. In the case of eyeglasses, at least, progress does have its advantages.)

The three children stood at attention as the Widow Ashton approached. She was a tall, handsome woman no older than sixty, dressed in a black crepe gown with a crisp white collar and cuffs, and a veiled cap pinned on top of her head. She swooped toward the house, arms stretched wide. "Freddy!" she cried. "Oh, my Freddy, someone show my boy to me at once; it has been much, much too long!" She gave a cursory glance to the children–and then a second, far sterner look. "Three, already? Horrors! It seems I am too late." She peered forcefully through the pince-nez. "But wait; Freddy has been married less than two years. Even you–yes, you, the littlest one–are older than that, are you not?"

"I estimate five," said Cassiopeia, who believed it was important to be accurate when speaking about numbers. By now she had slipped on Lady's Constance's grown-up lady shoes and was feeling quite fancy in her ostrich plume and pretty silver heels.

"You are not my Freddy's, then. Who are your parents?"

Cassiopeia turned to her brothers. The boys exchanged looks and shrugged.

The Widow Ashton frowned. "You do not know who your parents are? That is peculiar, to say the least."

"I'll tell you what's peculiar." A distinguished-looking gentleman with white muttonchop sideburns strode around the back of the carriage. He wore khaki trousers tucked into tall leather boots, a safari jacket, and a pith helmet. His walking stick was topped with the carved head of a lion frozen in midroar, but he seemed to use it more for effect than as something to lean upon, for his step was quite spry. "Blast! You won't believe this, Hortense! Bertha is missing."

"Missing? How is that possible, dear? I thought the cage was locked." She turned to the children. "This is my friend Admiral Faucet." She pronounced it *faw-say*. "He is a famous explorer. Although if you don't know who your parents are, I don't expect you've heard of him, either."

"Alexander Incorrigible, at your service," Alexander said with a gracious bow.

"Beowulf Incorrigible. How do you do?" Beowulf clicked his heels together neatly and added a little hop to make it even more special.

Admiral Faucet did not reply; his gaze was fixed on Cassiopeia. "What on earth?" he exclaimed. With a sudden swashbuckling gesture, he used the lion-mouthed handle of his cane to snatch the plume from Cassiopeia's hair.

"Mine!" she yelled, and began pummeling him on the leg. The thickness of his tall boots must have absorbed the blows, for the admiral did not seem to mind or even stop to acknowledge his tiny attacker. He was too busy examining the feather. He stroked it, held it up to the light, and even gave it a sniff.

"Where'd you get this plume, little girl?"

"Grrr." Cassiopeia disliked being called little, for in her own mind she was just the right size.

"Never mind, then; I don't talk to children who growl." He turned his attention to Alexander. "You look like a sensible lad. Answer me, yes or no: Have you children seen my ostrich?"

Alexander hesitated, for the admiral's question was poorly phrased and therefore difficult to answer without sounding rude. For yes, the children had seen an ostrich, but Alexander had no way of knowing if it was the exact bird that the admiral considered his own. "I don't know," he said, squirming. "What did it look like?"

The admiral scratched at his whiskers. "Let me see. It's about six feet tall, and it's a bird. Does that narrow it down for you, laddybuck?" He pounded his cane into the ground. "It looks like an ostrich! How many ostriches a day do you see in this place?"

"Don't lose your temper, Fawsy dear. They are only children." The Widow Ashton lowered her voice to a loud whisper. "They must not be very well educated, either. They don't even know who their parents are."

The Incorrigibles could hear her, of course. Beowulf in particular took offense, for he was quite serious about his studies. To prove it, he recited the first lines of a poem that Penelope had begun teaching the children after their interest in birds had taken a firm hold.

"Once upon a midnight dreary, while I
pondered, weak and weary,
Over many a quaint and curious volume of
forgotten lore—"

Still cross about the plume, Cassiopeia fiercely chimed in:

"While I nodded, nearly napping, suddenly there
came a tapping,
As of someone gently rapping, rapping at my cham-
ber door."

Not to be outdone, Alexander finished the verse:

"'Tis some visitor,' I muttered, 'tapping at my
chamber door—
Only this, and nothing more.'"

Using their fists and feet, the three children started tapping and rapping and rapping and tapping. Alarmed, the Widow Ashton took a step backward. Admiral Faucet held out his cane, ready to strike.

Luckily for all, it was at that very moment that Miss Penelope Lumley arrived. She held one shoe in her hand and began calling from the end of the curved driveway that led to the front of the house.

"Children, there you are! As you see, I broke the heel off my shoe running over the rocky path and had to hop the rest of the way home." She hopped once, to demonstrate. Then she noticed the visitors. "How do you do, ma'am? Sir?"

The Widow Ashton looked Penelope up and down through her pince-nez. "Are you my son's wife, then? Lady Constance? You are obviously energetic, and sensibly dressed, too, if a little plainly. No silly froufrous for you, I see! I admire that in a young lady."

Penelope stood on one leg like a stork and did her best to curtsy. "Thank you, but I am the children's governess, ma'am. My name is Miss Penelope Lumley. I work for Lord Ashton, and these three children are his wards. Do I have the pleasure of speaking to Lord Ashton's mother?"

The Widow Ashton nodded. Admiral Faucet waved his walking stick in the air. "Ashton's wards, eh? And what have these three moppets done with my Bertha? They took one of her plumes, see?" He narrowed his eyes at Cassiopeia, who, despite being only a quarter of his size, narrowed her eyes right back.

Penelope turned to the admiral. "Pardon me, sir. Who is Bertha?"

The admiral's cheeks turned ruddy with anger, which threw his white muttonchop sideburns into bold relief. "My ostrich! My ostrich that I shipped at great expense all the way from Africa! Do you have any idea how difficult it is to catch an ostrich? They're mean and stupid but faster than a Thoroughbred. That's why I want to import them to England. For racing. It's a business venture that simply cannot fail. That is, unless my Bertha is lost."

"We did see an ostrich on our walk, sir. It . . . I mean, she–Bertha–ran off into the woods," Penelope explained. "She was remarkably fast. And quite a lovely bird," she added, to be polite.

"Nicest ostrich we've seen," Alexander agreed.

The answer seemed to calm the admiral. "She is a beauty, isn't she? Well, that's all right, then. I was afraid she'd gotten lost at the dock, or someplace along the road, but it sounds like she just wiggled out of her cage a bit earlier than planned. Bit of exercise will do her good. I'll have to round her up somehow. Blast, why couldn't you children just say so?"

"Fawsy darling, be sweet. Didn't you hear the governess? These are my son's wards." The Widow Ashton gave each child a dewy smile in turn. "Alexander, was it? Beowulf–who could forget a name like that? And what are you called, dear?"

"Cassa*grrrr*," Cassiopeia muttered, for she was still cross about the plume. "How d' you do."

The widow slipped her arm through the admiral's. "See how polite they are, Fawsy? I would have expected my Freddy to marry a flighty, silly sort of girl; that was always his type–but anyone who could raise three such well-behaved children must be of a more substantial character. What a relief! Now, Fawsy, give Cassagurr back her feather. It looked so pretty in that lovely auburn hair, didn't it?"

"All right, sugarplum. You know best." He chuckled and held the ostrich feather out to Cassiopeia. "Take your plume back, little growler. We might as well be friends. After all, if all goes according to plan, I'll end up being your grandpapa."

"Grandpapa Admiral?" Alexander asked, confused.

"That's right, dear." The widow nervously tugged at her veil. "Admiral Faucet wishes us to wed. I have not yet given him my answer, of course, for I would never agree to remarry without Fredrick's blessing. That is why we have come home, to Ashton Place. That, and this ostrich-racing business–but Fawsy, perhaps we ought not to speak of these things until Fredrick is present. I wonder if he is at home?"

Weeeeeeeeee!

The Widow Ashton peered around her through her pince-nez. "Miss Lumley, what is that dreadful squealing noise? Do you keep pigs?"

"Not in the house, my lady." It might have been a screech owl, but owls were nocturnal and therefore would not be out in the daytime. A frightened pig was also a fair guess, yet Penelope could swear the sound was coming from the treetops, which ruled out pigs completely. (As in the case of ostriches and dodos, the inability of pigs to fly has been well documented.)

Weeeeeeeeee!

The Widow Ashton winced and stuck her fingers in her ears. "It sounds frightfully close. Perhaps Fredrick has ordered a roast suckling for dinner in honor of our visit."

"Blast, I hope so." The admiral patted his stomach. "On safari you live on beef jerky and canteen water. Not very appetizing."

Weeeeeeeeee!

Eeeeeeeeeek!

Crack–thump–

With a final crash, followed by an *"ow,"* the source

of the squealing was revealed: It was Lady Constance, now sprawled on the grass like a broken doll. During the entire conversation between the Widow Ashton, the Incorrigibles, the admiral, and Penelope, Lady Constance had clung bravely to her branch. Somehow she managed not to make a sound: not when she learned of an ostrich running loose on the grounds of Ashton Place, nor at the absurd praise heaped on the Incorrigible children by the Widow Ashton. Even the scandalous news that her supposedly grieving mother-in-law seemed to be on the brink of remarriage did not force a peep from the precariously balanced Lady Constance.

But then came Nutsawoo. Naturally, the lady's unexpected presence in the tree had attracted the squirrel's attention, and being nearly tame, the hungry scamp had come right up to her to beg for treats. Lady Constance had held on desperately while Nutsawoo perched not six inches away from her face, gazing pleadingly into her eyes.

That was when Lady Constance began to squeal. It was not until Nutsawoo tapped her on the nose with an acorn to make his request for a snack perfectly clear, like so:

Tap. Tap-tap. Tap-tap-tap. Tap-tap-tap-tap.

Lady Constance had clung bravely to her branch.

that her *weeeeeeeeee* turned to an *eeeeeeeeeek*; she lost her grip on the branch and tumbled to the ground in full sight of all. Nutsawoo was dragged down as well. After freeing himself from the nest of yellow curls on Lady Constance's head, the surprised squirrel leaped onto Cassiopeia's shoulder for a quick nuzzle and a biscuit crumb before skittering away.

"Stop that vicious rodent!" Lady Constance yelled as she rolled on the grass, for what was left of her dress was tangled all 'round her. "I will have it made into a collar at once!"

No doubt Cassiopeia would have objected strongly to that remark had she had the chance, but the Widow Ashton spoke first. She peered down through her pince-nez. "Who on earth is this dirty, uncouth, and uncivilized creature?" she demanded.

Penelope gulped. "May I present your daughter-in-law, Lady Constance Ashton."

Lady Constance looked up and smiled. There were leaves in her hair, rips in her stockings, and dirt smudged across both cheeks. "Mother Ashton," she trilled, spitting out a piece of bark and extending both arms upward, as if offering an embrace. "I am so happy to meet you at last!"

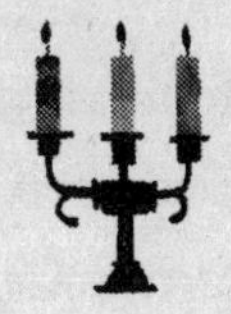

The Fourth Chapter

Rhetorical questions are asked, but other questions are not.

It was scarcely an hour after this incident that Lord Fredrick returned to Ashton Place. He suffered from the same poor eyesight as his mother, only much worse, and it took some energetic squinting before he realized who she was. At that point he simply harrumphed and said, "Well, look what the cat dragged in." Luckily, his mother's joy at seeing him so overshadowed the unfortunate first impression made by Lady Constance that, after a few joking remarks about "wives growing on trees" and so forth, the story of

Lady Constance's tumble from the branches became a source of merriment.

At least to the gentlemen it did. Once introductions had been made, the entire party settled in the drawing room. While the Widow Ashton fussed over the children—she would not hear of them going back to the nursery but insisted on keeping them near her on the settee; she even requested tea and cakes to be brought in, though it was not yet close to teatime—Lord Fredrick and Admiral Faucet slapped their knees and exchanged tree-themed puns.

"Ashton, I think your wife was out on a limb, har har!"

"Don't be a sap, Faucet. Her bark is worse than her bite. Ha!"

"Maybe she ought to pack her trunk and leaf. Ho ho!"

"A'corn she will, knock on wood!"

Lady Constance endured the teasing with a frozen smile. "I was only playing hide-and-seek with the children," she explained. By this time she had been hauled back to her dressing chamber by Margaret to bathe and change all over again and had emerged looking more like her usual doll-like self, if a bit scratched about the arms and legs. "We were having such fun, weren't we, children? But those three naughty imps forgot to come looking for me! Why, I could swear they left me in that horrid old tree on purpose, with nothing but filthy squirrels and birds for company."

Penelope sat with her hands folded, in a narrow, straight-backed chair. Under normal circumstances she might have objected to letting the children stuff themselves with cake before dinner, but the prospect of eavesdropping on the Ashtons was so deliciously tempting, she let it pass. "Perhaps Lady Constance will not be the only surprise to tumble out of the Ashton family 'tree,'" she thought, unable to resist a leafy pun of her own.

(It should be noted that puns are easily spread from one person to the next, much like the common cold. To understand why, consult the Law of Contagious Puns, a little-known corollary to Newton's First Law of Motion, the scientific principle that explains why an ostrich in motion is likely to remain in motion, at least until the bird gets tired. To understand why plump housekeepers jog faster when heading downhill, consult Newton's Universal Law of Gravitation. To understand why slices of plum cake placed on a tray in front of three hungry children tend not to remain on the tray for very long, one need only have a taste.

Clever as he was, Isaac Newton never got around to discovering the Universal Law of Cake, which remains in effect to this very day.)

"What kind of bird?" said Alexander, opening his notebook.

The question took Lady Constance by surprise. "Why, a *bird* bird, of course. With wings, and feathers, and a . . . what do you call it? Beak." Her giggle cut shrilly through the air. "What other kind is there?"

All three of the Incorrigibles leaped up to answer.

"Warbler. Nuthatch. Robin. Shrike," said Beowulf, counting on his fingers.

"I believe Lady Constance meant that as a rhetorical question," Penelope interjected, but the children's enthusiasm for the topic had already taken over.

"Finch. Wren. Blackbird. Owl."

"Not just owl: barn owl, screech owl, snowy owl, great gray owl . . ."

"Hawk. Osprey. Eagle. Gull."

"Ostrich!" shouted Cassiopeia, climbing on top of an ottoman. "Kiwi. Emu. Dodo!"

Alexander held up a hand. "No dodos." The three children sadly shook their heads.

The Widow Ashton clasped her hands together. "Such clever children, knowing all those complicated names. And how I miss playing hide-and-seek! Do you remember, Freddy, the jolly times we had when you were just a wee little nearsighted boy? You always had to be the one who hid, since you could never see well enough to seek for anyone."

"Quite so," Lord Fredrick mumbled, rising. "Say, Faucet old chap, come join me in my study for a cigar. Too much chitchat going on in here, what?" Without a backward glance, the lord of Ashton Place strode from the room. Admiral Faucet nodded to the others and followed. The Widow Ashton sighed to watch them go.

"My son has changed a great deal in ten years, and yet I know that deep inside he is still my Freddy. Isn't it nice that he and Fawsy are getting along so well?" She offered more cake to the Incorrigibles, who accepted with glee. "I do so love children, don't you, Constance? What happiness they bring to a home!"

Lady Constance nearly dropped her teacup but recovered. "How right you are, Mother Ashton. Not a day goes by but I think of how our lives were changed the instant my Fredrick took these three ferocious, I mean adorable, children under his wing. I only wish we had three more just like them."

Cassiopeia mumbled something in reply. Her mouth was full of cake, so the word was hard to make out, but

Penelope thought it sounded like "mayhem."

"Quite so," the widow agreed. "It broke my heart that I had only my Freddy. How I would have loved a bigger family, and especially a sweet little girl to spoil, like Cassagurr! But that would have been unwise." A shadow flitted across her face; then she brightened. "Miss Lumley, you and the children will join us for dinner, I hope? After so many years away, I long for the whole family to be together at the table."

"If you wish," Penelope replied, glancing at Lady Constance.

"Of course they will join us," her mistress said through gritted teeth. "I never take dinner without my sweet little Cassawoofy-woofy-woo." Stiffly she patted Cassiopeia on the head.

"Careful of my plume," Cassiopeia warned. But then she smiled at all the unexpected attention. For what child does not like being treated kindly by an adult? Even a silly, cross, and not entirely truthful adult like Lady Constance Ashton?

As Miss Lumley would later explain to the Incorrigibles, a rhetorical question is one that is asked, but that no one is expected to answer. "For what child does not like being treated kindly by an adult?" is a rhetorical question. So is "Why, it seems I've taken your saddle by mistake, Miss Pevington; how could I be such a dunce?" Not to mention the old standby, "Do bears live in the woods?"

There are countless such examples, but to catalog them all would take weeks, and who has time for that? (Note that "Who has time for that?" is also a rhetorical question. The curious among you may feel free to search for more instances within these pages, if you find that sort of treasure hunt enjoyable. And who doesn't?)

Yet about one thing there was no question at all. In a few hours' time, Penelope and the children would have no choice but to join Lord and Lady Ashton, the Widow Ashton, and Admiral Faucet for dinner. This was hardly a regular occurrence. The children nearly always had supper in the nursery with Penelope, who would read aloud to them as they ate. Most recently they had been enjoying a poem called "The Raven," by Mr. Edgar Allan Poe. This was the poem they had begun reciting to the Widow Ashton earlier; it was about a man who keeps a gloomy talking bird as a pet. "Nevermore!" the bird was prone to cry, at frequent, rhyming intervals. "Nevermore!" Every time the raven cried "Nevermore!" the children would toss their peas in the air and try to catch them in their mouths. Professional educator that she was, Penelope was proud to have devised a way to combine the study of poetry and the eating of vegetables into a single enjoyable lesson.

But that was in the nursery. How would the Incorrigible children fare in the dining room, where they would be expected to sit still between courses, eat their vegetables straight off their plates, and remain quiet and attentive as the grown-ups droned on about prime ministers, the trouble in Burma, and whether the price of gold was going up, down, or sideways? Even an ordinary child who had been raised indoors and was used to the strange ways of adults would find such a meal intolerably dull. The last time the Incorrigibles had attended a grown-up dinner party had been at Christmas, and on that occasion, well . . . to put it delicately, all squirrel had broken loose.

Penelope tried to be optimistic. "Even without 'The Raven,' there will be no shortage of stories to keep the children amused," she told herself. They would all be eager to hear more about Bertha, the runaway ostrich, and the admiral's many thrilling adventures in far-off lands. "And surely Lord Fredrick and his mother will have a great deal of 'catching up' to do," she thought.

"He hardly said a word to her earlier, in the parlor, before heading off with the admiral. I wonder why? Did the shock of seeing his mother again leave him speechless? Was there so much to say, he simply did not know where to begin? Or are there other reasons he did not wish to engage in 'chitchat,' as he called it?"

There were other questions she might have asked, too. For example: How would Penelope react if *her* parents showed up at the door, bearing bouquets of edelweiss and perhaps a bottle of celebratory schnapps? Would she weep with grief, or whoop with joy? Would she stand there shyly, clutching her favorite book of German poetry for comfort? Or would she become tongue-tied at the prospect of saying those unfamiliar words "mother" and "father" and have to fall back on the same socially useful phrases she had taught the Incorrigibles to use when making polite conversation with strangers? "A pleasure to see you again after all these years, Mrs. Lumley—or shall I call you Mater?"

Precisely what Penelope would do, how she would feel, and what she would say if it were *her* long-absent parents who turned up at the door, with piles of overdue presents and many apologetic remarks about how terribly, terribly sorry they were about missing the last ten or so years of her life—well, these were questions Penelope was in no hurry to ask. To do so would only make her disappointment that much worse when, day after day, the longed-for guests failed and failed and failed yet again to arrive.

An unasked question was hardly the same thing as a rhetorical one, as Penelope well knew. But neither sort was likely to be answered anytime soon.

DINNER WOULD BE SERVED AT eight o'clock, as was the Ashtons' custom. This was perilously close to the Incorrigibles' bedtime. Penelope had implored the children to take naps in the afternoon so as not to be grouchy later, but their excitement made sleep impossible. Instead Alexander wrote lists of questions to ask the admiral about latitude and longitude, the best kind of compass to use in a damp jungle climate, and other navigational topics, and Beowulf busied himself sketching a portrait of Bertha, which he intended to give the Widow Ashton as a gift.

Cassiopeia was both pleased and embarrassed at being singled out by Lady Constance, and this confusion made her even more agitated than her brothers. She tried on every dress she owned to see which would go best with her plume. In the end she could not choose and asked Beowulf to gnaw marks into a pair of acorns so that she might roll them as dice and decide that way. She also demanded a pair of silver-heeled shoes like the ones Lady Constance had worn earlier, but there were none in her closet; all she had were her usual sturdy lace-up boots and her party shoes from the previous Christmas, which she had already outgrown. She stared glumly at the boots until she got the idea to paint them silver with some of Beowulf's paints and set about doing that.

Penelope had less trouble deciding what to wear, for she spent more of her governess's salary on books than clothes and saved the rest in accordance with Agatha Swanburne's wise financial advice: "Nest eggs do not hatch unless you sit on them for a good long time." Shortly before eight she slipped on her best summer dress (which was very much like her everyday summer dresses, except for a bit of lace around the collar). She undid her hair, brushed it out, and rewound it into a neat, freshly pinned bun.

She sighed as she did so, for the dark, drab color of her hair was the same unappealing shade she had worn all through childhood–a shade she had only recently learned was the result of the Swanburne hair poultice that Miss Mortimer insisted she continue to use at regular intervals. That Penelope's natural hair color was the same vivid auburn as the Incorrigibles' had been revealed when she had briefly stopped using the poultice; why her hair color ought to be hidden was yet another pressing question left unanswered by Miss Mortimer.

"Perhaps she will explain when she answers the many letters I have sent. Best not to think about it until then," she told herself, briskly tugging down her dress sleeves and giving her hair a final smoothing. One might say she had chosen to bury her head in the sand about the whole thing, but in any event it was time to go to dinner. Cassiopeia's boots were now so soggy with silver paint as to be unwearable, so Penelope advised her to cram her toes into the too-small party shoes and leave her heels hanging out the back like slippers, and off they went.

They were met just outside the dining room by Mrs. Clarke, who offered the children more helpful advice. "Take some bread so you don't get peckish, but save your appetite for dinner. It's rude to ask personal questions, but show an interest in the other guests. When in doubt, smile! Without baring your teeth, of course; people might take it the wrong way. Just be yourselves, dearies. But on your best behavior! And whatever you do, *don't be nervous.*"

She might as well have told them not to think of elk. By the time the butler opened the heavy double doors to the dining room and gestured for them to enter, the Incorrigibles were panting with fear. Penelope, whose own tummy had begun to do flip-flops when she realized she had forgotten the difference between consommé, crudités, and crème brûlée, any of which might potentially show up on the dinner menu, had to give the children a gentle shove before they dared go in.

Ivory-colored place cards with names written in elegant script showed where each person was supposed to sit. The great wooden dining chairs were as big as thrones, but someone had thought to put pillows on the seats intended for the children, so at least they had some hope of being able to see their food. Cassiopeia had just mustered the courage to climb up and reach for a breadstick when the doors opened once more. The butler announced in a booming voice:

"May I present Lord Fredrick Ashton and his mother, the Dowager Lady Ashton. Admiral Faucet and Lady Constance Ashton. Dinner is served."

"But we *know* who they are," Cassiopeia blurted. Penelope shushed her with a finger.

"That's 'faw-say,' my good man. Not 'faucet,'" joked

the admiral. He gave his walking stick a twirl. "Do I look like a piece of plumbing to you? Though I've been known to smoke a pipe now and again. Pipe, har har!"

Lord Fredrick took his place at the head of the table; Lady Constance sat at the opposite end. The guests had been arranged boy-girl, boy-girl, with the Widow Ashton, Alexander, and Cassiopeia on one side, and Beowulf, Penelope, and the admiral on the other. Servants lit the candles and the soup was brought in, followed by a savory pudding, a fish course, and finally the main dish: six brace of pheasants arranged on a silver platter, served with roasted turnips and a chestnut puree.

The children found it all quite tasty and did not ask for ketchup once. During the meal, Lady Constance made bright, careless remarks about shopping and the weather, and the admiral told manly tales of exploration and danger in distant lands. Thanks to their governess, the children know how to appreciate a good story and were excellent listeners. But Lord Fredrick showed no interest whatsoever in the conversation and concentrated grimly on his food. His mother seemed too full of emotion to either speak or eat. Finally, she reached over and took her son by the hand.

"You must be angry at me for staying away so long,

my dear. I would not blame you if you were."

"Not at all, Mother. Everything's fine." He did not look up from his plate.

The widow withdrew her hand. "How suddenly our lives can change, and all because your father wanted to take a spa vacation! If only I had known the gruesome end that lay in wait for my Edward, I would never have agreed to the trip. Oh, the bloodcurdling horror of it all!"

"They say a spa can be very good for colds," Lady Constance announced. "Why, just today I had a terrible fit of sneezing–"

"Personally I shall never visit one again," said the widow. "No more spas. Never!"

"Nevermore!" said Cassiopeia. With relief, Penelope saw the boys resist the urge to toss their turnips in the air, as they were accustomed to doing with the peas.

The Widow Ashton adjusted her pince-nez and launched into her tale. "It was at the world-renowned spa at Gooden-Baden, near the Black Forest of Germany. From far and wide, people would come for the mineral springs, the eucalyptus saunas, the saltwater soaks, and the green mud baths, not to mention the Black Forest cake." She dabbed her eyes with the corner of her napkin. "It was Edward's idea to go. He thought he might find it rejuvenating, or so he said. His health had always been so delicate, you see."

Penelope remembered all too well the portrait of Edward Ashton she had once seen hanging in Lord Fredrick's study. He was a tall, portly man, hardly the type most people would call delicate.

"On our third day at Gooden-Baden, as I lay abed waiting for my morning tea tray to arrive, Edward went for a soak in the medicinal tar pits. He never came back. All they found was his Bavarian hunting hat, floating on the surface of the tar, with those jaunty feathers sticking up and a sweet little sprig of edelweiss pinned to the hatband. A sticky trail of bubbles and a ruined hat. That was what was left of my husband. The hat was new, too; he had only just purchased it in the gift shop. . . ."

The widow was overcome by emotion and had to pause. "Poor hat," said Beowulf with feeling, perhaps missing the deeper meaning of the widow's tears. Penelope also found the tale moving, but despite her sympathy she found herself wishing that the Widow Ashton had not chosen to tell such an unappetizing story at the dinner table. And why, oh why, did she have to mention edelweiss?

"I could not bear the thought of coming home to Ashton Place by myself," the widow went on. "And how could I leave Gooden-Baden? I knew my Edward was down in the tar pits somewhere, for the body was never recovered. I moved to a nearby convent to mourn. Years passed, and the Sisters of Perpetual Sobbing begged me to shed my mourning clothes and rejoin the world of the living. 'No,' I said. 'No! I will never!'"

This time all the Incorrigibles chimed in. "Nevermore!" they cried. Somehow a turnip found its way from Cassiopeia's plate to Alexander's. Penelope tried to kick a warning under the table, but her foot hit the admiral's cane instead and gave a nasty stub to her toe.

"Finally, the kind sisters threw me out. Perhaps my incessant wails of grief were getting on their nerves. Who knows? I rented a small chalet in a neighboring village and joined a croquet club. It was there that I met Admiral Faucet."

"Good gravy," the admiral remarked as he helped himself to the last of it. "Can't get food like this in the jungle, no sir!"

The widow smiled through her tears. "The admiral grew fond of me, and in time I came to enjoy his company as well. He made his honorable intentions known. Yet something was amiss. One night, unable to sleep, I took a long walk in the Black Forest."

"Cake!" the children yelled.

"After dinner," said Penelope quietly. "Finish your vegetables first." The children stared ruefully at their plates.

The widow closed her eyes, remembering. "Deep in thought among the towering pines, the answer came to me: I could not start a new life until I faced the past. I needed to come home and get Fredrick's blessing. And I wanted Fawsy dear to see Ashton Place and to understand who I once was, before the dreadful accident that took my Edward. . . ."

"I like it here," the admiral said, energetically slicing his meat. "After so many years exploring Parts Unknown, I'm ready to settle down. I have plans, big plans. There are fortunes to be made, with the right bird and a bit of capital to get things started."

"Surely you are not thinking of living here, at Ashton Place?" Lady Constance exclaimed. "The house is much too small."

"Don't be silly, dear, the house is enormous. A herd of elk could live inside and you'd scarcely notice them. Oh, Edward!" the widow cried suddenly, as if her husband had just walked into the room. "Everywhere I look I see memories, haunting the rooms like ghosts! How well I recall the medicines he used to take . . . the therapeutic ointments . . . the quack doctors and faith healers who would come by on a weekly basis. . . ." Her voice trailed off into a fresh series of tragic sobs.

Lady Constance put down her fork. "Fredrick, you never told me your father was sickly."

"Was he? Blast, I hardly recall."

The Widow Ashton removed her pince-nez to wipe the lenses, for they had grown foggy from all the moisture. "You wouldn't remember, Fredrick; it was before you were born. But I cannot forget: All that howling and barking and scratching, whenever the moon was full. *'Ahwoo,'* he would moan, the whole night long. *'Ahwoo*, Hortense! *Ahwoo!'*"

The children looked intrigued. *"Ahwoo?"* Alexander inquired politely.

"Yes, *ahwoo!* I could never get a good night's sleep at the full moon. It was not until the night Fredrick was born that my husband's ailments ceased. I thought it was a miracle: My husband had been cured, and we had a fine, strong child as well—the first of many, I hoped. Until a month went by . . . poor Fredrick . . ." She looked at her son and pity softened her features. "And how is your condition, Freddy dear?"

"Oh, I'm fit as a fiddle, more or less," he said, eyes darting this way and that.

"Have you been cured?" his mother exclaimed. "Surely that is cause for celebration!"

"Cured of what?" Lady Constance's trilling laughter was like the shattering of a window. "I hope you haven't been keeping secrets from me, Fredrick."

Fredrick drained his glass. "Now, Mother, I haven't troubled Constance with any of that nonsense. There's nothing to tell, really. Itchy rash. Coughing fits. A stiff brandy and a headache lozenge, and I'm good as new."

"Don't make light of your suffering, dear." The widow turned to Lady Constance. "Since the day he was born, every four weeks like clockwork, the episodes would come on. Scratching and howling and barking like a wild thing! The doctors were mystified. It was as if the condition had jumped from Edward to Fredrick without missing a moon. It's why I never had another child. I was terrified that it was something hereditary. It was very clever of you to take in wards, Fredrick. I dread to think how any natural-born children of yours would suffer from the same ailment." She beamed at the Incorrigibles. "And now you have these three delightful children to raise, just as if they were your own. Surely that will be enough."

"How odd that you never mentioned any of this to me before, Fredrick." Lady Constance turned her fake smile to her mother-in-law. "But what about Fredrick's grandfather? Surely *he* was a specimen of health."

"The Honorable Pax Ashton." The Widow Ashton's lip curled in distaste. "He was a judge. He died before Edward and I married, so I can't speak for his health, but he was said to be a most unpleasant person."

The admiral gestured for more wine. "I'd be unpleasant, too, if I were a judge. All those hangings! It'd wear on a man, I should think."

"Fredrick has a great friend who is a judge. Judge Quinzy," Lady Constance said proudly. "He is an older gentleman, very distinguished and charming, if I do say so. Perhaps your husband knew him? I expect they would have been about the same age."

Penelope's ears perked up, for she knew, as the Ashtons apparently did not, that the person who called himself Judge Quinzy was using a false name. This she had discovered while in London.

"Quinzy?" The widow frowned. "I do not know the name. He must not have been very important, if Edward didn't know him."

Penelope glanced at the grandfather clock and stifled a yawn. It was nearly ten, but all this talk of lethal tar pits and strange illnesses had kept the children riveted. And now hangings! She wondered if they would be able to sleep that night, and if so, what sort of dreams they might have. Personally, she had heard quite enough of these unsavory tales and longed for the sweeter pleasures of *Rainbow in Ribbons*, or *A Friend for Rainbow*, or even *No More Sugar Cubes for You, Rainbow*, which was a rather preachy tale about a trip to the veterinary dentist that lacked some of the charm of the other books in the series. Any of the Giddy-Yap, Rainbow! books would do nicely.

"Pax Ashton was known to be cruel and dishonest and was famous for taking bribes," said the widow. "Even so, no one deserves to die in the horrible and excruciatingly painful way he did. His end was not more gruesome than my Edward's, perhaps, but close. . . ."

"It was gruesome all right," Lord Fredrick agreed. "Pass the turnips, what?"

"And how exactly did your grandfather die, Fredrick? I don't believe you've ever told me," Lady Constance asked in a high, strained voice.

"Pecked to death by murderous pheasants," Fredrick mumbled, his mouth full of turnips.

"Peasants!" Lady Constance half bolted from her seat. "Why, the countryside is full of peasants! Who knew they could be so easily provoked? Surely we ought to get rid of them at once."

"Nonsense, dear. Without peasants, who would do all the work? Anyway, it wasn't peasants; it was pheasants. Murderous pheasants."

The children, who knew all about pheasants (or Phasianidae, as this family of birds was properly called), helpfully squawked to clarify the matter for Lady Constance.

"That's it." Lord Fredrick nodded and flapped his arms like wings. "*Caw! Caw!* Big, stupid birds they are. Tasty, too. Think I'll have some more."

Lady Constance watched in a daze as her husband speared another drumstick from the platter. "Surely you are joking. I have never heard of murderous pheasants."

"That's what the coroner said, too." Lord Fredrick bit into the bird with gusto. "Grandfather Pax and his pheasants, my father and his tar pits. All the men in my family meet gruesome ends, it seems. Wonder what mine will be?"

His mother's complexion turned white as the linen tablecloth. "Don't say such things, Fredrick."

Lady Constance tried to lighten the mood. "Silly Fredrick! You make it sound as if the Ashtons were cursed. Ha ha ha!"

Nobody laughed. A gust of wind blew open the

shuttered windows, and all the candles in the room went out.

In the darkness, there were only voices. Lord Fredrick cried, "Find some matches, what?" and "Blast!" The children yapped in alarm, the admiral shouted words of courage, the widow wailed, and Lady Constance shrieked.

It was difficult to tell in all that noise, but Penelope could swear she also heard a distant howl.

Nevahwoo!

Nevahwoo!

Nevahwooooooo!

The Fifth Chapter

A journey through Unmapped Territory, leading to Parts Unknown.

"Silence!" Admiral Faucet bellowed in the darkness. "Don't panic, men! Nor women and children, either."

He struck a match on the bottom of his boot and circled it 'round the room like a tiny searchlight, revealing each person in turn. The children crouched on their chairs, alert and ready to pounce. Penelope brandished a candlestick like a weapon. (At the Swanburne Academy, the girls had once put on a

Penelope brandished a candlestick like a weapon.

famous play that begins with the appearance of a ghost and ends with a dramatic duel involving a poison-tipped foil, a perfectly thrilling scene in which no fewer than four of the leading characters meet very gruesome ends indeed. Clearly, the experience had left its mark, as well as some residual skill at swordplay.) Lady Constance whimpered from beneath the dining-room table. And Lord Fredrick Ashton was hanging on to his mother, who did not seem to mind at all.

Nevahwoooooooooo!

Bang! Bang!

It was the wind, howling mournfully through the open windows while the shutters banged back and forth. Throwing down her candlestick, and for the second time that day, Penelope ran to the windows and wrestled them closed. "The latch seems to have snapped," she said. "But this will do until a locksmith can be summoned." Quick as a wink, she removed a hairpin and used it to secure the broken latch.

Once she was done, the admiral relit the candles. "Well done, governess. You'd be a useful person to have along on a safari. After all, an explorer must be resourceful! Why, once when I was in Africa, I sailed down the Nile in a raft made of nothing but lashed-together reeds and a sail woven out of palm leaves. What's for dessert?"

Oddly, the brief scare of the snuffed-out candles and howling wind seemed to break the spell of gloom cast by the Widow Ashton's gruesome tales. Or perhaps it was the prospect of dessert that lifted everyone's spirits; in any case, the entire party moved to the parlor for after-dinner sweets and drinks. A sticky bread pudding was brought in. There was warm honeyed milk for the children, and coffee and sweet Madeira wine for the adults.

After the pudding was served, and with only a tiny nudge from his governess, Beowulf stood up. "I have a gift for you, your gracious widowhood," he announced to the Widow Ashton. From behind his back he produced the picture he had drawn earlier, which had been carefully rolled up and concealed in Alexander's spyglass case until the right moment came to present it. The Widow Ashton fumbled for her pince-nez as the admiral took the drawing in both hands and gave an admiring whistle.

"That's my Bertha, all right. Did you do this yourself? Why, you're a regular Audubon."

"Audawho?" Beowulf asked, puzzled.

"John James Audubon drew birds that were dead

and stuffed. But I'd wager Bertha was moving at a fast clip when you spotted her, and even so, you caught her likeness very well. That makes you better than Audubon, laddybuck!"

Beowulf grinned from ear to ear and seemed to grow taller on the spot.

Lord Fredrick put down his coffee cup. "I'm feeling rather stuffed myself. What say we go to my study, Faucet? Let the ladies play whist, or stitch advice onto pillows, or whatever it is they do when we're not around."

"It's your house, Ashton; I'll do whatever you like. Say, lad–Beowulf, is it?–if it's birds you want to draw, come to your uncle Freddy's study. There's enough taxidermy in there to keep you scribbling for a year." Standing, the admiral turned to Alexander. "You come along, too, young man. You look old enough to try a cigar, eh?"

Penelope jumped to her feet so quickly she nearly spilled her pudding. "You are so kind to include them, sir, but it is long past the children's bedtime–and I fear the cigar smoke would upset their tummies after such a rich meal." In fact, cigar smoke was the least of Penelope's worries. The one time she and the children had wandered by accident into Lord Fredrick's study, the sight of his vast collection of taxidermy had upset more than just their tummies. All those dead animals, in lifelike poses, with their sightless, staring glass eyes—surely the boys would remember?

"I want to go," said Beowulf, slipping off his chair to the ground. "If Audubon draws stuffed birds, I draw stuffed birds."

"Me too, Admiral Laddybuck." Alexander jumped to his feet and assumed the wide, bow-legged stance of a sea captain that he often used when playing pirates.

Lord Fredrick shrugged from the doorway. "Bring 'em along, I don't care. As long as I get my port, what?"

The admiral turned and clicked his heels at the boys. "You heard your uncle Freddy. Follow me, men! Brave explorers are we, off to Parts Unknown! Hup, hup, hup, hup."

"But, Admiral—it is already past ten o'clock. . . ."

As a rule, brave explorers do not have worried governesses mouthing objections to their adventures in Parts Unknown. Alexander and Beowulf gave only the briefest apologetic parting glance at Penelope, who felt utterly helpless to stop them from going with the admiral and Lord Fredrick.

"But what about Cassiopeia?" she called after them,

for she knew the little girl would be hurt not to be included in the admiral's invitation, had she known about it. Luckily, she did not. The exhausted child was facedown in her pudding, fast asleep. In any case, the boys were already gone. Penelope returned to her chair as if in slow motion; when she folded her hands in her lap, her knuckles turned white.

"Well, now it is just us ladies, left to enjoy ourselves in peace. Isn't that nice?" Lady Constance did not sound nearly as cheerful as her words suggested; in fact, she sounded quite cross. "Dear Mother Ashton, shall I ring for a deck of cards, as Fredrick suggested?"

"No cards for me," said the Widow Ashton, rising. "The hour is late, and I have too much on my mind. Look at sweet Cassagurr! She is worn-out, poor thing, and needs a mother's tender care. I shall go to bed, too, and leave you to tuck her in."

"As I do every single night, without fail," Lady Constance declared. "And sing lullabies, too. La la laaaaa, la la laaaaa–"

"You might want to rinse her off first; she looks a bit sticky." The widow paused. "But I suppose even the stickiest pudding is better than a tar pit. Good night."

Once her mother-in-law was out of the room, Lady Constance would have nothing to do with the messy, sleepy child. It was up to Penelope to wash the pudding off Cassiopeia's face and hands with a napkin dipped in water, and carry her all the way upstairs to the nursery. There she changed the groggy girl into a nightgown and rolled her into her bed. "Nev*ahwoo*," Cassiopeia mumbled, drifting back to sleep.

Penelope was tired, too, and worried about the boys. She tried to calm herself with reading, but she could not concentrate on the story, and the words swam upon the page. When Albert suggested to Edith-Anne Pevington, "Let's be friends," Penelope read, "Gruesome ends." When Edith-Anne announced that Rainbow needed a "new bridle and bit," Penelope could have sworn it said "medicinal tar pit."

Frustrated, she shut the book. She wished—oh, what did she wish? She wished her friend Simon Harley-Dickinson were here to talk things over with. Simon was the perfectly nice young playwright whom Penelope had met in London. They had shared some memorable adventures, and the children had become quite fond of him as well. It was Simon who taught Alexander how to use the sextant and had even sent him his spare one as a gift. He had a knack for navigation, a loyal heart, and a keen interest in getting to the bottom of things. And there was something about his company that made Penelope feel a bit fluttery on the inside, as if a flock of warblers on the wing had taken a detour through her tummy.

It was just like how Edith-Anne Pevington felt about her new acquaintance Albert, except Albert was fictional, of course, and Simon, with his mop of wavy brown hair and that darling gleam of genius in his eyes, was wonderfully, winsomely real. But he was far away, too; too far to readily ask for advice.

"'The plot thickens'—that is what Simon would say," Penelope thought, chewing her lip. "A strange, wolflike illness that comes on the full moon; a family history of meeting gruesome ends . . . Madame Ionesco, the Gypsy fortune-teller we met in London, said something about the children being under a curse. Could the Ashtons be under a curse, too? It would be an unlikely coincidence if they were, but I suppose that for anyone to be under a curse is highly unlikely to begin with. I do wish I could speak to Simon! No doubt he would find it all very inspiring and get loads of plots out of it, enough for a whole trunk full of plays. I shall have to write him a letter tomorrow"—and here she yawned, for it was well past her bedtime as well—"asking him to interpret the widow's strange tales."

Cuckoo. Cuckoo. Cuckoo–

The clock struck the quarter hour. Penelope awoke with a start. She had nodded off in her chair; it was now fifteen minutes past eleven o'clock. Cassiopeia snored softly from her bed (it sounded as if the poor child might still have some pudding up her nose), but the boys' beds were empty.

The sight of those smooth, unrumpled blankets struck fear in Penelope's heart. "Agatha Swanburne would march to Lord Fredrick's study right now and insist on putting the boys straight to bed," she thought, and started for the door, but then she had second thoughts. "Or perhaps she would say something philosophical, like 'A watched clock never chimes,' and fix herself a cup of tea." Alexander and Beowulf were in their own house, after all, under the supervision of two adult gentlemen, one of whom was their legal guardian. What was she so worried about? The boys were probably having a rip-roaring time, and being welcomed into the company of men was surely good for them, even if it did leave Penelope sitting helplessly, waiting for their return.

She sat once more in her chair, closed her eyes, and tried to imagine Alexander and Beowulf as they might grow up as Lord Fredrick's wards, at home in the world of proper English gentlemen: a world of private clubs and taxidermy-filled studies, brandy snifters and expensive cigars, games of billiards and talk of the stock exchange. And, of course, hunting expeditions. She tried, but she could not do it. Such a future for the Incorrigible boys seemed entirely improbable in her eyes, but she did not know what other, different fate to picture for them, either.

"One thing is certain: They will not be boys forever," she thought, remembering Mrs. Clarke's comment about the too-short trousers. And Lord Fredrick Ashton was a wealthy and powerful man. If he began treating the Incorrigibles as if they were his own natural-born children, as his mother seemed to think he should, wouldn't that be lucky for them?

Perhaps it would, but whether it was gooden luck or baden remained to be seen. "And there is something peculiar about the Ashtons," Penelope thought as sleepiness descended upon her again like a fog, "with their howling fits and gruesome ends. I hope the day does not come when the children think they would have been better off"–she yawned–"living in the woods. . . ."

Cuckoo. Cuckoo. Cuckoo. Cuckoo–

"Hup, hup, hup, hup!"

"Shhhh!"

It was quarter past midnight when the boys finally marched back to the nursery. They were much too excited to stop talking but too giddy with exhaustion to make any sense.

"A-hunting we will go!"

"To Bertha we will go! Hup, hup, hup!"

Penelope roused at the sound of their "hup, hup, hup." Groggy with sleep, she struggled to understand what they were obviously eager to tell her.

"We are going hunting!"

"For Bertha!"

"We are in charge of tracking. No dogs. Dogs would bite."

"We are good at navigating and good at bird-watching. We can track and not bite. Hup, hup, hup!"

In bits and pieces, and all while shushing and reminding them to put on their nightshirts for bed and not wake their sister in the process, Penelope came to understand that the two boys planned to accompany Lord Fredrick and the admiral on an expedition into the woods of Ashton Place, with the goal of finding Bertha, catching her, and bringing her back to an ostrich-proof enclosure that the admiral had already designed and that would be constructed behind the barn over the next few days.

"Brave explorers are we!"

"Unmapped Territories! Parts Unknown!"

"This ostrich-gathering expedition sounds interesting, and perhaps even educational," Penelope whispered, picking up the trail of clothes the weary boys had left on the floor, "but you are not going anywhere until you get a good night's sleep. We shall discuss it further in the morning." She sniffed at the dirty clothes and made a face. Everything smelled like cigar smoke.

"No point catching Bertha if there's no place to put her. That's what the admiral says." Alexander climbed onto his bed and slipped under the light summer blankets. "She'd only run away again."

"Perhaps Bertha is not as excited about ostrich racing as the admiral is," Penelope replied, tucking him in. "Good night, Alexander. Good night, Beowulf."

"Nets, Alawoo," Beowulf mumbled to his brother. "We should bring nets."

"Must make list and pack," Alexander replied dreamily. "I'll bring my sextant."

"I'll bring pencils."

"And a tent."

"Ostrich treats to lure her home."

"And guns, too. Hup, hup, hup!"

Penelope was so startled she forgot to whisper. "Guns? Why would you need guns? I thought the plan was to catch Bertha, not shoot her."

"Berth*ahwoo*," Cassiopeia grumbled from her bed, turning over and burying herself deeper under the covers.

"Guns are not for Bertha." Alexander snuggled his head into his pillow and closed his eyes. "Guns only to shoot wild animals. Uncle Freddy says we must be careful in the forest."

"Yes," said Beowulf with a yawn. "There are dangerous animals in the woods. That's what Uncle Freddy says."

Ten seconds later, they were both asleep.

TIRED AS SHE WAS, THE bleary-eyed governess tossed and turned for the rest of the night, dreaming of spooky forests full of dangerous beasts and flocks of scowling, black-feathered ostriches who cried "Nevermore!" as they raced in circles 'round her, and dinner platters full of tasty-looking roast pheasants that suddenly came back to life and started to peck—and peck—and peck—

"That is quite enough of that," she resolved the third time she awoke from this same unsettling dream. As she rose and dressed, she racked her brain trying to figure out what sort of expedition the gentlemen really had in mind, and whether it was a good idea for the boys to go along, and if not, how she might prevent it.

"I am only the governess, after all." She stabbed the hairpins into her bun with a great deal more ferocity than usual. "Lord Fredrick is their guardian. How am I to overrule him, if it comes to that?"

And then, of course, there was this business with the guns. She sat in the small rocking chair by her bedside and rocked in time to the ticking clock. "The boys said the guns are for 'dangerous animals' only. But which are the dangerous animals, and which are the safe ones?" The question was impossible to answer, for even a warbler is dangerous to an earthworm, and (as Penelope had recently learned) a mild-mannered pheasant could be murderous if provoked. A studious child who could spell "circumnavigate" and had almost mastered long division might be deadly to a tasty-looking pigeon, if the child happened to have been raised by wolves and had gone too long without a snack.

And a pack of slavering, sharp-toothed wolves

might not prove dangerous at all to a trio of human cubs abandoned in the woods, if the wolf pack was willing to take them in and raise them as their own. For all Penelope knew, the Incorrigibles might not have survived without the care of those terrifying beasts.

Penelope's rocking slowed, then stopped altogether. She thought of how nearsighted Lord Fredrick was, how prone to shoot first and figure out what sort of prey he had bagged later. "The most dangerous animal in the woods might well prove to be 'Uncle Freddy,'" she thought with a shudder. "That settles it. If the admiral wants his ostrich back so badly, he is going to have to figure out how to catch it himself."

After the children were up and dressed and fed a breakfast that was halfway to being lunch (for the boys had slept quite a bit later than usual), Penelope set them to work writing poems that had to a) be about some sort of bird, and b) use the same rhyme scheme as Mr. Poe's "The Raven." The children took up the assignment with gusto. Once their pencils were scribbling away, Penelope went off in search of the admiral.

He was behind the barn, just as the boys had said he would be, supervising the construction of a large, high-walled corral made of wooden posts and slats interwoven with lengths of twisted wire. Penelope had to dodge piles of lumber and burly workmen holding jagged-edged saws, but it did not slow her approach. She sported the set jaw and formidably upright posture that every Swanburne graduate learned in a required class called A Swanburne Girl Knows How to Make Her Point.

"Admiral Faucet, good day. I am sorry to disturb you, but there is an urgent matter that we must discuss."

"Good day, governess." He turned and bowed to her. "Those students of yours are extraordinary. Hats off on a job well done. How do you like my POE?" He gestured at the elaborate construction going on around them.

Penelope paused. She had planned to be stern and unyielding in her demands, but the admiral's compliments caught her off guard, as did his reference to poetry. "Thank you, Admiral, that is kind of you to say. And I am a great admirer of Mr. Poe. The children are studying him right now, in fact. 'Quoth the raven, nevermore.' It has a jaunty sound to it, don't you agree?"

"Not Poe. POE." He waved a thick roll of blueprints around. "P. O. E. It stands for Permanent Ostrich Enclosure."

Penelope gave him a puzzled look. "Why not just lock Bertha in the barn?"

"Governess, you may be a fine educator, but I can see you have no head for business." The admiral twirled his cane, obviously in high spirits. "I plan to import the finest racing ostriches from Africa and sell them to the sorts of wealthy society people for whom racing Thoroughbred horses has become passé. Once they have an ostrich, they'll need ostrich feed, and ostrich harnesses, ostrich trainers, and all the rest. Now, from whom are they going to buy all of that? Given that I will be the sole importer of ostrich equipment in Europe?"

"From you, I suppose."

"Clever girl! I'll be lucky to break even on the birds. The profit is in what comes after. Now, think, governess. The ostrich needs a place to live. If I say to my customers, 'Just lock the bird in a barn,' as you ignorantly suggest, where's the profit in that? I can't sell barns; England is full of barns! But I can sell a Permanent Ostrich Enclosure, manufactured on-site to these unique and patented specifications." He smacked the blueprints against his leg with pride.

"Still, I am sure a barn would do in a pinch," Penelope replied curtly. "Admiral, I must speak to you about the children."

"Talented lads. Sorry Ashton and I kept them up so late. We were testing their tracking skills. Did you know those two boys can tell the difference between a badger print and a fox print at twenty paces? And they can do animal calls that sound just like the real thing." He cupped his hands to his mouth and demonstrated. "*Caw! Hoo! Ruff!* The little one—Beowulf, is it?—sketched maps of the forest that showed nooks and crannies Ashton himself had never heard of. Strange fellow, that Ashton. An odd duck. But he'll be my son-in-law if all goes well, so live and let live, I say."

Penelope frowned. The first rule of making one's point was "Stick to the subject at hand," but the admiral was already off on a tangent and she would have to steer the conversation back to port, so to speak. "The children are quite talented, I agree. Unfortunately, your proposed expedition will interfere with their schoolwork. I regret that they will not be able to join you—"

"Nonsense, governess. They have to come. I need them."

"Why?"

"To find Bertha, of course. Those lads can track, and they know the woods. And don't tell me to use Ashton's hunting dogs. I can't. They'll frighten Bertha into the hills and we'll never see her again." He leaned forward on his cane until his face was at the same level as Penelope's. "Let me make something clear, Miss Lumley—that bird represents an enormous investment on my part, and I intend to get her back. These Incorrigible children of yours are remarkable! I'm tempted to take them on safari with me. They're smarter than dogs, easy to train and transport. I need those boys to find my bird, and that's all there is to it."

"But Admiral—their lessons—"

He waved away her concerns. "Lessons, bah! Exploring is a highly educational business. Flora and fauna, latitude and longitude, points on the compass and all the rest. It builds character, too. Believe me, you don't know what you're made of until you're alone in a canoe and drop your paddle in piranha-infested waters." He made a fierce, rapid munching sound with his teeth that made Penelope shiver.

"No doubt it would be a grand adventure," she interjected, for she had no wish to dream about flesh-eating piranhas that night; the murderous pheasants had been bad enough. "To be blunt, I am worried for the children's safety. They told me Lord Ashton plans to bring his gun. As you may have noticed, his eyesight is less than keen." Slyly she added, "He might pose a danger to Bertha as well."

The admiral scowled. "At last you have made a valid point, governess. The boys are essential, but Ashton . . . Ashton is a problem. His mother is nearsighted, but the son is blind as a bat. He might very well shoot Bertha before we have a chance to catch her. Still, it's his house, and his land, and I want him to think well of me so I can marry his charmingly wealthy mother, so I can't just tell him to stay home, can I? Unless . . ." He pulled at his whiskers. "Is this full-moon business true? Does he actually turn loony once a month?"

"On occasion I have seen Lord Fredrick acting in a most peculiar way at the full moon," she said warily. She did not fully trust the admiral, and so did not mention that Lord Fredrick's most prized possession was an almanac with all the full-moon dates circled. Nor did she reveal that the master of Ashton Place had been known to disappear entirely on those nights, even if they coincided with important events, like a lavish holiday ball thrown by his wife, or the West End premiere of an eagerly anticipated new operetta about pirates. Nor did she say anything about the secret room in the attic of Ashton Place, from which a mysterious howling sound had, at least on one occasion, been heard, and that was during a full moon as well. But it did not matter, for the admiral had heard enough.

"That solves it, then. We'll go when the moon is full. With any luck, Ashton will be too indisposed to come along. It's a sneaky maneuver on my part, I know, but in the jungle, one must hunt or be hunted. You'd do well to remember that." The admiral checked his pocket watch, as if this conversation had just run over its allotted time. "Don't worry, governess. I'll bring the lads home safe and sound. Now if you'll excuse me, I need to inspect my POE."

The admiral's sense of adventure was as contagious as a bad pun, and Penelope was starting to feel the effects herself. And if Lord Fredrick stayed home, the danger of a wayward shot was all but eliminated . . . but this "hunt or be hunted" business made her deeply uneasy. She stepped in front of the admiral, blocking his way. "I must be clear, sir. Alexander and Beowulf are children, not hunting dogs. They cannot travel without an escort. If they are to accompany you into the woods, then I insist on going as well. And I shall have to bring Cassiopeia, as there would be no one to mind her in my absence." This was not entirely true, of course, since in theory Penelope could have left Cassiopeia in the care of Margaret or one of the other housemaids. But

Penelope knew Cassiopeia would never agree to stay behind when there was such a marvelous adventure to be had.

"Parts Unknown is no place for a young lady." The admiral gave her an appraising squint. "Or a wee child. But you seem to have pluck, governess, and the girl is as fierce as a hyena, as I recall. Does she track prey as well as her brothers do?"

"I do not know," Penelope confessed. "However, it is quite possible that she does."

"The little growler might come in useful, then. All right. Join us if you must. But there will be no allowances made for teatime and nose powdering and all that rubbish. We will be 'roughing it,' as befits a band of brave explorers in the wilderness. Can you manage that?"

Penelope considered the offer. She was not in the habit of powdering, and she thought she could do without teatime so long as she had eaten a proper lunch. And just think of the fascinating letters she could send Simon, once their expedition was finished and Bertha was locked safely in her Permanent Ostrich Enclosure! He could not fail to be impressed.

"Very well. I accept your terms, Admiral." She extended her hand to seal the bargain. The admiral shook it so vigorously it made her wince.

"Done!" he said. "We leave on the full moon. The hunt is on, governess. I hope neither of us comes to regret it."

The Sixth Chapter

Penelope leaves her native habitat, while the Incorrigibles prepare to enter theirs.

As should be clear by now, Miss Penelope Lumley was a highly curious and intelligent person with a wide range of interests and skills. She had a firm command of the multiplication tables (even those tricky sevens and eights), could conjugate Latin verbs with only the occasional reference to a dictionary, and knew the capital cities of a great many midsized European nations—but the truth is, she had no idea how one went about exploring in the woods.

Chalk it up to a lack of experience. The Swanburne Academy for Poor Bright Females was situated in a sleepy farm valley near the village of Heathcote. There was no dense and mysterious forest nearby, only bright orchards of fruit trees arranged in tidy rows, and the spires of Swanburne's chapel were visible for miles around. Unless you had been blindfolded and spun 'round and 'round until dizzy (as you might do if you were preparing to play pin the tail on the elk, for example), it would be nearly impossible to get lost, even if you had no knack for navigation at all.

The closest Penelope had ever come to losing her bearings was in the autumn a few years past, when a local farmer mowed his field into a hay maze and charged a ha'penny a head to enter. The girls from Swanburne had been taken there on an outing and set loose in the maze; they raced this way and that, amid much delighted squealing. Penelope adopted a more tactical approach; as a result, she was the first of her group to finish the maze and come face-to-face with a rather bored-looking cow that stood in the center, flicking gnats off its flanks with a long, ropy tail.

(If you already know the Greek myth of Theseus and the Minotaur, in which a brave Athenian hero finds his way through a deadly labyrinth and slays the

Minotaur within, you will notice intriguing similarities between Theseus's adventure and Penelope's. However, the Minotaur was a bloodthirsty monster that was half man, half bull, not a mild-mannered Hereford cow with droopy ears and a bell tied 'round its neck. Theseus found his way out of the labyrinth by trailing a thread behind him; to Penelope this seemed a waste of good embroidery floss. Instead, she brought a small kit of watercolors with her into the hay maze and painted arrows on the hay stalks at each right or left turn. It would not have been a good strategy for a rainy day, but thanks to fair weather, Penelope prevailed over both maze and cow.)

But apart from that one time in the hay maze, when it came to wandering out-of-doors (particularly in a dark forest, and most particularly at night), Parts Unknown was very far from being Penelope's native habitat. She had never hiked up a snow-capped mountain with a bedroll strapped to her back, or pitched a tent in a monsoon, or gathered wood for a campfire over which to prepare her morning tea. The whole prospect of "roughing it" outdoors (as the admiral put it) made her feel vaguely itchy, as if bloodthirsty mosquitoes were already buzzing about her with dinner napkins tied 'round their tiny insect necks.

"I must remember, 'New boots never fit as well as the old,'" she told herself, recalling the words of Agatha Swanburne. "By which I suppose she meant all new experiences are bound to pinch a bit, until you break them in. Luckily, there are three days before the next full moon. That should give me plenty of time to master the art of outdoor exploration. How hard could it be?"

How hard, indeed? It was in that can-do, Swanburnian, and possibly optoomuchstic spirit (which is to say, there may have been an extra spoonful of optimism ladled into the mix) that Penelope returned to the house and began making a list of items she deemed necessary to pack.

By the bottom of the seventh page, she knew she was in trouble. Nearly every object in the nursery seemed essential to bring along, and she had the children's comfort to consider as well as her own. She would need cool clothes for them to wear during the day and blankets to keep them warm at night, one large canteen for milk and another for water, a portable tin for biscuits and a kettle in which she could make tea, books to read (of course), and at least a small assortment of games and puzzles, for there would be long hours of nothing to do, she was quite sure, until Bertha was found.

"I *suppose* the abacus can stay," she said to herself, frowning, "for we can work our math problems with acorns for the time being, as Cassiopeia does with Nutsawoo." And what if it should rain? They would require boots, waterproof coats, a sheet of tarpaulin, rolls of mosquito netting, a ball of twine in case something needed to be tied up, or tied down, or lashed together, or suspended from a tree (twine seemed the sort of thing that was bound to come in useful, one way or another). . . . The list grew and grew until it seemed as if Penelope would simply have to bring the whole of Ashton Place along with her.

"This is impossible!" she exclaimed, much to the children's surprise. "If only we could move the woods indoors, into the nursery. That would make everything so much easier."

Alexander had given up on his Poe poem and was now adding latitude and longitude lines to a large hand-drawn map of the forest. His siblings had also become distracted from their schoolwork and were busy practicing animal calls. Cassiopeia had mastered the deep *rumm, rumm* of a bullfrog, and Beowulf could produce a perfectly lifelike rabbit noise. It was inaudible to Penelope, but his siblings clapped with approval each time he did it.

At Penelope's remark, Alexander stopped his map-making and peeked over her shoulder at the growing list. He shook his head. "Too much to carry, Lumawoo."

Penelope slumped in defeat. "I agree, but what choice do we have? Food, clothing, shelter, cultural diversions . . . it all seems quite necessary to me."

Alexander gently took the paper from her. He produced a pencil from behind his ear and began crossing items off the list.

"No blankets, Lumawoo. We sleep in leaves."

She began to object, then stopped. "All right, but leaves do not sound very comfortable, if I may say so."

He made another cross-out. "No tent. Cave."

"But what if there is no cave?" The itchy, anxious feeling had returned, and Penelope scratched at her arm without even realizing she was doing it.

"There is cave. We know where the cave is," Beowulf said, coming over to look.

"Rumm, rumm," said Cassiopeia, leapfrogging closer.

Alexander flipped the page. "No canteen," he said, striking it out. "Water from the stream."

"No books," suggested Beowulf. "Tell stories instead."

Alexander started to cross out "books," but Penelope

looked so tragically disappointed that he stopped.

"One book. All right, two. No biscuits. Berries and nuts."

"And mice and squirrels," Beowulf added.

"*Rumm!* No squirrels!" Cassiopeia's voice was firm. Beowulf shrugged but made no argument, for he too had grown fond of Nutsawoo.

"Mice are good, though," Cassiopeia conceded, rubbing her tummy. "Yum, yum!"

Alexander nodded. "And sandwiches."

"Sandwiches are a splendid idea," Penelope said, perking up. "What kind shall we bring? I can request that Cook prepare a picnic basket full of them. Of course, a basket will be awkward to carry, and we shall have to take turns, but the good news is, the more sandwiches we eat, the lighter the basket becomes. . . ."

For some reason the children found this funny. They nudged one another and chuckled among themselves.

"No picnic basket, Lumawoo," Cassiopeia finally said, before dissolving into giggles.

Confused, Penelope looked from one smiling face to the next. "How shall we carry the sandwiches, then?"

"No carry." Beowulf tried to explain. "Berries in the woods. Nuts in the woods. Stream in the woods. Cave in the woods. Sandwiches in the woods."

Penelope pressed the palm of her hand against her forehead; she wondered if she might have a fever coming on. "There are sandwiches in the woods?"

The children looked at her with pity. "Yes. In the cave," Alexander said, kindly and a bit slowly, as if talking to a dimwit. "Water in the stream. Nuts on the trees. Sandwiches in the cave."

The other Incorrigibles nodded. "Do you like my rabbit noise?" Beowulf scrunched his face in concentration and made the rabbit noise. Penelope heard nothing, but Alexander and Cassiopeia grinned and clapped him on the back. Then they all went back to preparing for the trip.

Sandwiches? Caves? Rabbit noises? Penelope did not know what to think. She closed her eyes and breathed in—*a Swanburne girl does not panic*—and out. In—*a Swanburne girl does not panic*—and out. . . .

Later on, Cassiopeia came over to have her hair brushed. When they were done, she grabbed the pencil. "Biscuits would be good, too," she whispered, scrawling the word onto the list.

She spelled it "biskit," but Penelope was still too muddled to correct her. "I suppose that means there are no biscuits in the cave?" she asked, hoping for some explanation.

Cassiopeia snorted as if her governess had made a hilarious joke. "No biscuits," she said. "Only sandwiches. And friends."

Penelope's breath came short again. "What kind of friends?"

Cassiopeia threw back her head and crooned a soft *"Ahwooooo."*

Penelope found it difficult to sleep that night. She tossed and turned and drifted in and out of strange, restless dreams about a guidebook. On the cover it read *Three Incorrigible Children, Thought to Be Raised by Wolves, As Seen Outdoors in the Deep, Dark Forest.* But when she opened the pages, she saw only wolves: three of them, snarling and yellow eyed, with blood dripping from crescent-shaped fangs. Even in her dream she recognized them as being the wolves from the painting that adorned the secret attic of Ashton Place. She and the children had found it quite by accident in the mayhem that ensued after Lady Constance's disastrous holiday ball. It was an Ominous Landscape, painted by the same second-rate artist whose portrait of Agatha Swanburne hung in a secret gallery at the British Museum . . . and both were signed with the letter A. . . .

"Who painted you?" she asked the wolves in her dream, but they would not answer.

The two nights that followed were no better. On the second night she dreamed she was riding on a train; either it was a very large train, or she was a very small Penelope, for her feet dangled off the edge of the seat and came nowhere near the floor. She climbed up onto her knees and pressed her nose against the glass, gazing at the mountains in the distance. The hat she wore was trimmed with long ribbons of yellow silk. She chewed upon the ends of the ribbons (for in the dream little Penny was anxious, although the older, dreaming Penelope could not tell why), and the frayed edges tickled the tip of her nose until finally the child sneezed.

"Gesundheit," said the man who accompanied her. Sleeping Penelope scratched her nose and pulled the covers over her head.

The third night she awoke from a dream so frightening she could not remember it at all, save for the sound of galloping hooves.

This time she could not get back to sleep. She swung her legs over the edge of the bed and looked at the clock. It was three hours past midnight, "what a poet might call 'the darkest hour,'" she thought, meaning it was the darkest time of night, just before the first rosy glow of dawn began to brighten the eastern sky.

In only a few hours' time, she and the children would line up outside the POE for inspection by the admiral, with their rucksacks strapped to their backs and pith helmets fastened beneath their chins. Penelope had spent the last three days reading up on outdoor survival skills. Now she knew how to use crampons and a pickax to scale a glacier, and was keenly aware of how cautious one must be around cannibals. But was this what she would need to know to survive in the forests of Ashton Place?

She found herself wishing Simon could come exploring with them (his navigational skills would have been a real asset, not to mention his twinkling eyes and finely formed features), but she knew it was out of the question. In any case, she had learned a handy tip about the way moss grew on trees that she felt would be invaluable should they get turned 'round in the woods, if she could only remember: Was it the east side of trees that grew the moss, or the west?

The moonlight played on the leaf-and-ivy pattern of the carpet and the floral print of the wallpaper. In the darkness of her cozy bedchamber, with her moss-green bedspread and the drawer pulls in the shape of mushrooms, she could almost pretend she was in the forest already.

Even so, Penelope could not shake her feeling of dread. She rose and stepped through the tall French windows that led to her private balcony. "The trees cannot hurt me," she whispered, clutching the rail. "The darkness cannot hurt me. Why, then, am I afraid of the woods at night?"

The cool air washed over her, fluttering her nightdress against bare legs. It was the hour before dawn, but the moon was high and bright, only one night short of being full. Surely it was enough to light the way of a person who might be in the mood for adventure.

"Miss Mortimer always encouraged the girls to go for walks when we were puzzling over a difficult assignment," Penelope thought. "'Walking is thinking,' she liked to say. And if I face my fears tonight, I will be all the braver tomorrow, in front of the children, and that is what matters most."

Barefoot and silent as a cat, Penelope padded downstairs. Throughout the sleeping house, the clocks were softly chiming three o'clock. "Hup, hup, hup, hup," she said under her breath to bolster her courage. "A brave explorer am I."

She made her way to the side door near the kitchen

"Why, then, am I afraid of the woods at night?"

that the servants used to go in and out. With a final deep, calming breath, Penelope stepped out into the moonlight and began to walk.

Terrified at first, but gaining courage with every step, Penelope had gone scarcely fifty feet from the house and was just beginning to relax and enjoy the feel of the dew-wet grass on her bare feet and the chirping predawn trills of the first songbirds of the day when she heard a strange (one could even say enigmatic) grunt.

"Who's there?" she said sharply, turning.

"They say the early bird gets the worm. But isn't it a bit too early for worms?"

It was Old Timothy, the coachman. He was a wizened fellow who seemed to always turn up at the most unexpected times. He had a habit of making grouchy, riddling remarks, but he had also shown himself to be a friend to Penelope and the children, at least when he chose to be. Even in the daylight he made Penelope nervous, though, and now—what was he doing here, in the dead of night? Had he followed her from the house?

"Timothy!" she exclaimed, and then lowered her voice. "You startled me. Why are you wandering the grounds at this hour?"

"The same might be asked of you, miss." He glanced down at her feet. "At least I had the sense to put my shoes on."

She was glad he could not see her blush; what had possessed her to leave the house in her nightdress? "I could not sleep," she explained, "and decided to walk outside on impulse. Even I do not quite know why."

"I think I do." He cocked his head to one side. "You're taking the wee ones into the woods tomorrow, aren't you? Looking for that giant turkey of the admiral's."

"Bertha is an ostrich." She hugged herself against the cool night air. "A flightless bird, native to Africa. Their brains are surprisingly small, but the eggs–"

"Ostrich, turkey; it's all the same to me. And you want to know if it's safe. So you came wandering out of doors to check." He gestured around them. "Any danger so far? See any pirates?"

She smiled then, for she remembered how bravely Timothy had helped them escape from those awful pirate thespians in London, with their sharp-edged swords and loud, intricately rhymed choral numbers. "To be frank, you are the most frightening thing I have encountered."

He snorted and grinned his crooked grin. "Sounds like you'll be all right, then."

Somehow his curt reassurance made all her fears come rushing back. "Do you truly think so? Are the woods safe?"

"Safe for who, miss?" He cocked his head to the other side, one eye open wide, one squinting. "It's safe for bears, unless a wolf's around. And it's safe for wolves, unless there's a hunter in the trees. The hunter feels safe with his gun in his hand, unless he should come upon . . ." He made a flapping gesture with his arms.

"Murderous pheasants," she replied, sounding grim. "I understand. One never knows where danger lurks."

"Aye." For a moment Penelope imagined his eyes switched places, but it was just that the open one now squinted and the squinty one had opened. "The woods are full of surprises. But so is the house, miss. So is the land, and so is the sea. Look in the mirror while you're at it. You'll find surprises there, too. Questions and answers, plain as the nose on your face and the hair on your head! Mysteries and mouseteries, that's what you'll find. . . ."

His eyes were switching places again, and his wild talk made Penelope's head hurt. "Timothy, I believe you mean well, but please do not speak in riddles. A simple answer is best."

"Then ask me a simple question." He leaned close.

"What is it you really want to know? Is it safe in the woods for three children who howl at the moon? Safe for a scared governess who doesn't know a warbler from a nuthatch?" He folded his hands and pleaded in a little girl's voice: "'Old Timothy, please, look in your crystal ball and tell me: How will it all turn out?' Well, I'm no Gypsy fortune-teller, miss. You want to know if it's safe to go into the woods tomorrow? You won't find out eating crumpets on the settee. Go into the woods. You'll get your answer there."

A cloud passed over the moon. The darkness was sudden and so complete it made Penelope gasp; it was as if someone had thrown a bag over her head.

"One way or another, you'll find out." Old Timothy's voice swam through the pitch black. All up and down Penelope's arms, her skin turned to goose bumps. A breeze rustled the leaves, and she shivered.

When the cloud passed and the moonlight returned, the coachman was gone.

"BLAST! WHERE'S MY ALMANAC?"

The morning of the day of their excursion dawned warm and hazy; a person could almost (but not quite) convince herself that the enigmatic talk of the cool moonlit hours had never happened. The household had a drowsy summertime feel about it, and everyone seemed to be moving in slow motion—all except for Lord Fredrick Ashton, who was twitchy and agitated and once again seemed to have misplaced his prized possession.

"Have you seen it, Mrs. Clarke? No? Look a bit harder then, would you?" He loped up and down the stairs with Mrs. Clarke in hot pursuit, batting himself rapidly behind one ear with a cupped, pawlike hand, as a dog might do if it was trying to rid itself of fleas. "Feeling a bit of a cough coming on—*bark! Woof!* Pardon me—don't tell me I've got my dates mixed up again. . . ."

"It'll turn up, m'lord," Mrs. Clarke assured him. She was scarcely out of breath, even after all that running up and down stairs. "In the very last place you look, mark my words!" But Lord Fredrick was too busy scratching to concentrate, and his condition seemed to grow worse by the minute. He demanded an ice pack and a headache lozenge and retired to his study, and Mrs. Clarke set the servants to searching each room in turn. They all knew what the almanac looked like; their miserably uncomfortable master seemed to mislay it with every full moon.

Admiral Faucet, on the other hand, was in superb

spirits. The Permanent Ostrich Enclosure had been finished (to Penelope it looked like a fenced yard with an oversized chicken coop at one end, but the hand-painted sign that read POE was a thing of beauty), a hearty pre-expedition breakfast had been eaten, and Lord Fredrick's withdrawal from the trip seemed imminent. "It's all going according to plan," the admiral whispered to Penelope as she and the children gathered near the entrance to the POE. "Better for all of us if Ashton stays home, what?"

Penelope could not disagree, but she felt uneasy; Lord Fredrick was her employer, after all. Was it dishonest to have planned this trip precisely in such a way that he could not come along? Could a governess be fired for failing to report such a ruse? Penelope often had to remind herself that her role in the lives of the Incorrigible children was based on her being an employee of the Ashtons. The children were not her wards, after all; they were Lord Fredrick's. "If I am ever to lose my position, he could send them off to boarding school, or to an orphanage, or anywhere he pleased, really," she fretted as the children eagerly presented themselves for inspection. "And who would care for them properly then?"

It all seemed so risky and ill-advised. Yet the

thought of Lord Fredrick galumphing blindly through the woods with a hunting rifle at his side was even worse. "Sometimes there is no right thing to do," she concluded. "There are merely a number of wrong things, and one must choose the least wrong among them." (Those of you who have ever taken a multiple-choice quiz and found yourself searching in vain for "none of the above" will no doubt understand exactly what she meant.)

The admiral showed no sign of such misgivings; he marched back and forth and twirled his cane with glee. "Line up, troops!" he barked. "Size order, men! And, uh, little growling girl."

Giggling, the children obliged. In the preceding days, Mrs. Clarke had somehow managed to secure explorer outfits for all of them, and for Penelope as well, and they stood straight and tall in their safari jackets, boots, and cunning little pith helmets.

Stern and officious, the admiral scowled down at each Incorrigible. "You've signed up for this mission, pups, and there's no turning back. The ostrich is loose, and the ostrich must be found."

"The ostrich must be found, sir!" the children chanted in reply.

"The forest is deep and dark, and full of danger.

There will be danger and discomfort at every turn."

"You said 'danger' twice," Beowulf interjected.

The admiral threw him a sidelong glance. "That's because there's a lot of it, lad! You will use all of your skills, your sniffing and tracking–"

"Sniffing and tracking, sir!"

"Rumm, rumm," Cassiopeia added, puffing up her cheeks like a bullfrog.

"And your croaking, if called for. And we shall not rest until Bertha is found and securely leashed, for her safe return to this very POE. Understood?"

"Aye, aye, Captain Admiral, sir!" To the children it was all great fun. Penelope's scalp was already sweaty beneath her pith helmet, and she found herself shooing away imaginary gnats.

"Aye, aye, yes, that's the spirit," the admiral muttered, glancing at his pocket watch. "Ashton's late. No surprise there. We'll give him sixty more seconds, and then hup, hup, hup! Off to Parts Unknown!"

The children started to hup, hup, hup and march in place. At approximately the forty-second mark, Lady Constance Ashton appeared on the drive, making a beeline toward the POE. She was nearly skipping and seemed to be in a happy, even festive mood. At some distance behind followed the Widow Ashton, accompanied by Margaret, who held a sunshade over the older woman's head.

Lady Constance carried her own parasol trimmed all 'round with ruffles, in the Parisian style, and wore a frightfully flouncy frock. "What a glorious, glorious, glorious day," she trilled. "How are my three Incorrigible children today, hmm? How is my Cassawoofy-woofy-woo? Ready to go off into the woods?"

She reached into her reticule and drew out a folded letter. "Admiral Faucet, I regret to inform you that my husband is indisposed. He has sent a note for me to give you expressing his sincere regrets. Here it is."

The admiral unfolded the note and read aloud. "'Sorry, old chap. Can't make it. Sick as a dog. Good luck with the bird. Still think you ought to shoot it, what? I'll form a hunting party and catch up with you tomorrow. Remember, if my hounds find it before the wolf children do, it gets shot and stuffed and goes in my study with all the rest. Finders keepers, what? Yours, Ashton.'"

A shadow moved over the admiral's face like a cloud passing over the moon. By now the widow and Margaret had arrived, in time to hear Lord Fredrick's note. "I am sure he doesn't mean that, Fawsy dear," the Widow Ashton said. "He was always a joker, my

Fredrick. Why, did I ever tell you about the time he smeared honey and pepper all over one of the kitchen cats, just to see if he could make it sneeze?"

"Fredrick never jokes when it comes to his hunting parties," chirped Lady Constance. "And speaking of parties, I must go, for I have a luncheon engagement at a charming French café in town. *Bonne chance* on your expedition, little foster children!" She reached down and tweaked Alexander on the cheek.

"Ow!" he yelped.

Lady Constance clasped her hands over her heart. "*Au revoir*, Incorrigibles! While you trudge through the underbrush and pitch your tents in the mud, I shall pass the long hours by wearing pretty clothes and going to tea with my lady friends." She dabbed away a tear. "And shopping, too. I will miss my maternal responsibilities during your absence, of course, but I shall endure it somehow."

"So come with us?" Cassiopeia sweetly suggested.

Lady Constance almost dropped her parasol. "Oh, no, no, no no no! You must have all the fun. Out there." She gestured vaguely toward the forest. "In the wilderness, with the bugs and the badgers and those hungry, hungry wolves!"

Since the widow was watching, she then proceeded

to give each Incorrigible a hug, although she did so by putting her arms in a wide circle and placing them 'round each child like a hoop, so that she did not actually come into contact with any of them.

"This trip feels dangerous to me. Be careful, my darlings." The Widow Ashton was already starting to sniffle. "After all I have suffered, how could I bear losing you three in some gruesome accident out there in the woods?"

"How could she 'bear' it; did you hear that?" The admiral nudged Alexander with an elbow and chuckled. He turned to the widow. "Don't be dramatic, dear. Think of it as a nature hike. Bertha is fast but none too bright; it shouldn't take us long to catch her. With any luck we'll be back by supper. Wouldn't want to trouble that trigger-happy son of yours to come find us, eh?"

The Widow Ashton nodded and draped herself around Lady Constance. "With Fawsy gone, and the children too, and Fredrick indisposed—why, Ashton Place will be empty as a tomb! You, Constance, will be my rock. Cancel your plans; we must spend every moment together. Not shopping and lunching and gadding about like silly things, but here at home, quietly, reading to each other and sewing and praying for the safe return of our loved ones. You will be like a daughter to me—the daughter I never had." Her voice caught, and she buried her weeping face in the delicate silk shoulder of Lady Constance's white dress.

After a long, frozen pause, Lady Constance stiffly patted her mother-in-law on the back. "Mother Ashton, I am afraid sewing would be much too dangerous. The needles are exceedingly sharp." She disentangled herself from the sobbing widow, and the little pink circles of her cheeks turned pale as she examined the ruined shoulder of her dress. "Margaret, cancel my lunch with Lady Guilford. It seems I will be staying at home today. Have a headache lozenge and a box of chocolates sent to my private parlor, at once!"

Without waiting for a reply, Lady Constance wheeled 'round and marched back to the house, her small, pale hands clenched into fists. The Widow Ashton followed, walking backward the whole way, blowing kiss after tearful kiss until she and Margaret disappeared from view. Just before they did, Margaret gave a little secret wave to Penelope and the children, and mouthed the words "Good luck."

"Soft-hearted women," the admiral grumbled. "Any more soggy good-byes and we'll be standing here until Christmas. Off we go, troops!" He adjusted his pith helmet, and the children followed suit.

"Hup, hup, hup, hup!" he chanted, to set a marching rhythm. The children swung their arms in time, and Penelope gave a final backward glance at the house.

"Mysteries and mouseteries, eh?" Like a jack-in-the-box, Old Timothy had popped up from nowhere. Penelope gasped at the sight of him; where on earth had he come from? Had he been hiding inside the POE? But there was no time for questions.

"Timothy, you must help us." She spoke in a low voice, for she did not want the children to hear. "Lord Ashton has threatened to follow after us tomorrow, with a hunting party. I know he often takes you with him when he goes hunting–can you make sure that he does not shoot at Bertha?" Or at anyone else, she was about to add, but Old Timothy cut her off.

"Musn't dilly-dally, miss. Remember, 'A trip worth taking is a trip worth beginning,'" which made Penelope startle again, for she was quite certain that Agatha Swanburne had once said the very same thing.

She was about to ask him if he was familiar with the wise sayings of Agatha Swanburne, and if so, how, but as if in a promise of annoyances yet to come, a pesky mosquito chose that moment to land on the tip of Penelope's nose. Cross-eyed, she batted it off, but it left behind an itchy tickle that could not be scratched away.

"Ah-choo," Penelope sneezed.

"Gesundheit," the enigmatic coachman answered under his breath. The admiral began to march, and the children fell in behind. Penelope scurried to catch up, and when she looked behind her, Old Timothy was gone.

"Hup, hup, hup, hup!" the admiral said, and the expedition was under way.

The Seventh Chapter

Luckily, there are no cannibals in the woods—or are there?

Was Penelope both deeply excited and more than a little afraid to begin this rough-and-tumble excursion into Parts Unknown?

Do bears live in the woods?

(Note that in this case, the rhetorical question about bears is meant to mean: absolutely, positively yes. Bears do live in the woods, and Penelope was both excited and fearful, and about either fact there can be no doubt. "Is the pope Catholic?" is another popular version of this type of question, but new ones are invented all the time. Is a Swanburne girl plucky? Does an ostrich have long legs? And so on.)

Although in the end she had packed lightly, according to the children's instructions, Penelope had insisted on tucking two books into the large pockets of her rugged twill safari skirt. One was her favorite book of melancholy German poetry in translation, which she always carried with her when she felt in need of reassurance. The other was a fictional tale of danger and exploration that she had found in Lord Fredrick's library while doing research into wilderness survival techniques. It was about a man who had been shipwrecked on a remote Tahitian island and managed to survive by means of his determination, his skill at building shelters and canoes, and his fortunate knack for avoiding being eaten by cannibals.

Penelope found the tale unsettling, frankly, but as much as she would have preferred to bring *Rainbow in Ribbons*, she thought this shipwreck saga might be of practical use should she and the children get separated from the admiral and have to survive on their own for, say, eight-and-twenty years. This was the length of time the poor sailor in the book was stranded on the island, which, understandably, he came to call the Island of Despair.

But before we continue any further with the adventures of Miss Penelope Lumley and the three Incorrigible children as they venture into the forest in pursuit of a runaway ostrich, let us look away for a moment (for they will have to do quite a lot of hup, hup, hupping before they get far enough into the woods for things to become interesting) and consider some matters of linguistic significance, starting with three letters: namely, P, O, and E.

When the admiral first said POE, Miss Lumley thought he meant Poe, as in Edgar Allan Poe. This is because POE and Poe are homonyms, which means they are two different words that are pronounced the same way.

POE is also an acronym, which is a word made out of the first letters of other words. To the admiral it stood for Permanent Ostrich Enclosure, although POE could just as easily stand for something else: Pie Over Everything, for example, a tasty, if filling, notion. Or Ponder On Elks, which, as you already know, is nearly impossible to avoid doing once you have been told (and told, and told yet again, in the strictest possible terms) not to ponder on elks.

Some acronyms prove so catchy that they become words in their own right. Marine explorers know that "scuba" is an acronym for Self-Contained Underwater Breathing Apparatus. Those of you who enjoy shooting laser beams at your friends for sport can bamboozle your opponents by crying out, "Here comes my Light Amplification by Stimulated Emission of Radiation!" just before you fire.

If you now think that you would rather confront a herd of Profoundly Outraged Elephants in a Perilously Oscillating Elevator than hear another word about homonyms, acronyms, or any other kind of nyms—well, think again. There is power in words used accurately and well, and tragedy and missed train connections in words used carelessly. Consider how disappointed you would feel if, after booking an expensive spa vacation, you found yourself on holiday with the Society of Professional Accountants instead. (Note: A word that no one has heard of is called a whatsthatonym, since the listener is bound to say "What's that?" in response. A word that no one cares about is a sowhatonym. Alas, there is presently no word in English that means a word that does not exist, but perhaps the clever among you can invent one.)

"Please, Lumawoo. No more lessons," Cassiopeia whined. For Penelope, too, had been using the occasion of their long march into the woods to review some of the finer points of the English language.

"We may be marching into Parts Unknown in search of a missing ostrich, but that is no excuse to neglect your education." Penelope sounded more stern than usual, for her new hiking boots were beginning to pinch, and the trail had been going uphill for some time now. "But if you insist, let us move on to a more cheerful topic. Synonyms!" The children groaned, but Penelope paid them no mind. "Synonyms are two different words that mean more or less the same thing."

"Dull and boring," remarked Beowulf, poking his brother.

"Very good," Penelope replied, choosing not to get the joke. "Dull and boring are fine examples of synonyms."

"Tedious and uninteresting," Alexander offered, concealing a smirk.

"Don't care and cinnamins," Cassiopeia said firmly. "Can I have biscuit?" Penelope sighed and offered her one. The pack she carried on her back was heavy enough, but even so, she wished she had not been so quick to leave the globe and abacus back at the nursery. Giving lessons "on the hoof," as it were, was proving to be a mighty challenge.

"Pish posh, governess. A day or so away from the

schoolroom won't do the cubs any harm." The admiral paused to wipe his brow, for the sun was now high overhead. They were somewhat sheltered by the forest's canopy of leaves, but the day grew warmer by the quarter hour. "And they're studying all the wrong things, anyway. How to tell tomorrow's weather from the color of the evening sky. How to start a fire with wet wood and no matches. How to catch your evening's meal and cook it over a spit. How to suck the venom out of a snakebite before it stops your heart dead—*aargh!*" To the children's delight, the admiral faked a gruesome death by snakebite, clutching his chest and staggering to the ground while his tongue waggled out the side of his mouth. After a moment, and to polite applause, he recovered. "Those are the things a person needs to know to survive, governess. Not thisonyms and thatonyms."

Penelope did not bother to explain that the Incorrigibles were more than capable of catching their own meals and would probably prefer to eat them uncooked, rather than roasted on a spit. But the admiral did have a point about snakebites.

"Very well," she conceded. "Synonyms can wait. But I shall read to the children this evening at bedtime, regardless; it is our custom. You need not listen if you find the tale dull. Or boring. Or tedious, or uninteresting," she added, straight-faced. The children giggled at the way their clever governess had snuck the lesson in nevertheless.

"Stories at bedtime, eh?" The admiral checked his watch. "With any luck I'll be back at the house long before then, smoking Ashton's cigars, with Bertha safely locked up in the POE. 'Finders keepers,' he says. What nerve! The spoiled young lordship needs to be taught a lesson, if you ask me." He pounded his cane into the mossy ground. "But never mind that. Ostriches are long of leg and short on brains. Bertha can't have gone far. Cubs, fall in! Sniffing formation, hup! Now, any whiff of the bird?"

The children passed around Cassiopeia's plume and sniffed deeply. At Alexander's signal, they started tracking, moving in zigzags and ever-widening circles with their noses first to the ground, and then lifted high in the air. Soon they had disappeared into the surrounding woods. For five endless minutes the children were out of sight. They reappeared shortly, with muddy hands and knees, breathless and excited to be sure, but empty-handed.

"No bird to the north," Alexander announced, checking the sextant.

"No bird that way, either," Beowulf said, pointing southward.

"And no egg, nowhere. Nevahwoo!" Cassiopeia added.

"Blast," said the admiral. "Well, it's a big forest. We'll just have to keep going." With a grunt, he resumed the march.

Penelope limped along after him; her right heel was blistering inside those stiff new boots, and the bedroll strapped to her back dug painfully into her shoulders. She was desperate to sit down, remove her hot, itchy helmet for a few minutes, and fix herself a cup of tea. After a few painful strides, she caught up and tugged on the admiral's sleeve. "We have been walking for three hours, at least. The children will need lunch soon, and a nap."

"Naps!" He snorted contemptuously. "Nature is red in tooth and claw, governess. Tooth and claw! You don't want to let it catch you napping." He consulted his pocket watch once more. "Another hour and we'll stop for grub. Hup, hup, hup!"

It turned out that by "stopping for grub," the admiral meant pausing to distribute pieces of some sort of dried salted beef and a handful of nuts to each person, which

"Another hour and we'll stop for grub. Hup, hup, hup!"

they were then expected to eat on the march. "Can't lose our momentum now," he said cheerily, tearing off a bite. The children seemed to like the leathery strips, especially Beowulf, who never met an object upon which he would not happily gnaw, but Penelope felt as if she were trying to eat the sole of a shoe. She nibbled on the nuts instead and was grateful for a swallow of warm, metallic-tasting water from her canteen.

Midday turned to afternoon, and early afternoon to late. With blisters on her feet, gnats buzzing all around (real ones now, and hungry for blood), sweat trickling down her back, and an empty tummy that went from grumbling to growling to grumbling again, Penelope found it hard to believe that she had ever felt optimistic about anything. Surely it was the admiral's problem if his ostrich was so ill-mannered that it ran away without so much as a by-your-leave? "Yet if we do not find her, Lord Fredrick might—and that will never do," Penelope thought, wincing with every step.

"Boring. Tedious. Uninteresting. Don't care," the Incorrigibles chanted dully as they marched, deeper and deeper into the woods. Soon they became too tired to say even that much, and BTUD (Boring Tedious Uninteresting Dontcare) did not hold much promise as an acronym, even if the children had thought of making it into one. Gradually they fell out of formation; instead of marching in a crisp line with lifted knees and swinging arms, they bounded along, sniffing and leaping and tumbling over one another. This seemed to lift their spirits considerably.

In fact, the farther they marched, the more obvious it became that the children felt thoroughly at home here in the forest. Alexander's stiff-backed schoolboy posture gradually altered into a light-footed loping stride. Every twenty paces or so, Beowulf would shinny up the trunk of a tree and leap from branch to branch, making quicker progress through the treetops than the rest of the party made on the ground. Soon Cassiopeia forgot herself completely and began to run on all fours. Penelope had to tug at the back of her dress to remind the girl to walk on two feet so as not to ruin her stockings.

The admiral noticed the change as well. The shadows that crept along the forest floor grew long and melted into the dusk. Finally, as they reached a small clearing, he ordered, "Halt! At ease," and they stopped to make camp for the night before it was too dark to see. He set the children to gather kindling wood for the campfire. While they were busy at their task, he approached Penelope, a greedy, conspiratorial look in his eye.

"Governess, I have a business proposition to discuss with you."

Penelope was trying her best to erect a shelter for herself and the children; at the moment she was puzzling over which side of the tarpaulin was the top, and making no progress whatsoever. She ached from head to toe; she wanted a hot bath and a bright fire to read by and was in no mood for the admiral's bluster. "My business is giving lessons, Admiral. Is that what you mean? As you recall, I only know the sorts of things you consider to be useless: thisonyms and thatonyms."

"You can keep your whatonyms and whatnots. My business is profit, and when I see an opportunity to make some, I act upon it." He leaned forward on his cane. "Exotic creatures are my specialty, governess. I've traveled the globe in search of the rare, the fascinating, the one of a kind. Or, in this case, three of a kind."

The tarp slipped from Penelope's hands. "Exotic creatures? What on earth do you mean?"

His voice was low and excited. "I've plundered the pyramids in Egypt, swum with sharks in the coral reefs of Botany Bay, and scaled the slippery summit of Mount Crisco, but never in all my travels have I come across three specimens like these Incorrigible wolf children of yours. Think of the exhibitions we could give!"

Penelope turned so abruptly that her pith helmet slid forward over her face. She pushed it back and looked the admiral in the eye.

"Are you suggesting that you would put the children on display? Like animals in a zoo?"

"They'd be wasted in a zoo, governess. It's their abilities that amaze. I'd put them in a special habitat, where their talent for tracking could be fully appreciated. A Permanent Incorrigible Enclosure."

The thought of Alexander, Beowulf, and Cassiopeia being put in a PIE was more than Penelope could stomach. "As their governess, the only ability of theirs that concerns me is their ability to make accurate use of the apostrophe," she retorted. "And may I remind you, Admiral, they are doing you a service by helping you find Bertha. Surely you would not repay them by baking them in a PIE?"

Of course, she meant to say "locking" rather than "baking," but this is precisely what is so tricky about acronyms and homonyms. Penelope knew the admiral meant a fenced-in enclosure designed to house the Incorrigibles, but in her mind's eye all she could see was a rolled-out pastry crust with the children's three auburn-haired heads sticking out one side and their feet wriggling out the other, just like the four-and-twenty blackbirds in the famous nursery rhyme:

Sing a song of sixpence, a pocket full of rye,
Four-and-twenty blackbirds baked in a pie.
When the pie was opened, the birds began to sing;
Oh, wasn't that a dainty dish to set before
the king?

The admiral drew himself up to his full height and peered down at Penelope as if she were nothing more than a zoo specimen herself. "It takes a person of vision to appreciate a golden opportunity when it arrives. I thought you might be such a person, governess. It seems I was wrong." Cunningly he added, "Anyway, it would be for the children's own safety. When Ashton gets tired of them, what do you think he'll do? He's not the sentimental sort, from what I can tell. They'll end up in an orphanage. Or worse. Now if they could earn their keep by doing a few simple, enjoyable demonstrations for an adoring and well-paying public, all while living in a snug, homey PIE of their own, you wouldn't have to worry about Ashton's whims." His tone grew ominous. "Or his eyesight."

"Are you trying to frighten me, Admiral?"

"Not at all, governess. Merely discussing business."

But the discussion was over. He strode across the clearing to the woodpile where the children were stacking the kindling and asked, "What say you, pups? Any scent of Bertha?"

Penelope tried once more to fashion the tarpaulin into a tent. The admiral's proposal was absurd—imagine, putting the children in a PIE!—but it raised another, deeper anxiety, one that had been growing within her all day as she watched her pupils gradually revert, bit by bit, to their animal-like habits: What was the risk that the three Incorrigible children would be overcome by the lure of their woodsy, wolfy origins and, like Bertha, run off altogether?

She watched as they carried the last of the kindling to the woodpile, bounding on all fours with sticks in their mouths and looking for all the world like a trio of joyful puppies playing a game of fetch.

What if they decided they much preferred the muffled sounds of the forest, the soft, springy moss beneath their feet, the scent of a tasty field mouse on the breeze—the howl of the wild, if you will—to the world of books and poetry and socially useful phrases that Penelope had so painstakingly and lovingly introduced them to?

What if they never wanted to go back to Ashton Place at all?

The morning had been bright, but now that nightfall was upon them, strange winds were kicking up. One did not have to be a sailor to tell that a storm was brewing. Spending a night or two outdoors in a securely pitched tent was a tolerable idea, but thunder? Lightning? Penelope was fully prepared to fend off a bear with a stick, carve a canoe out of a fallen tree trunk, and teach long division with acorns, but if there should be a violent storm during the night, she did not think she would be able to manage without hiding under the covers of her bedroll, and what would the children think of that?

The Incorrigibles seemed untroubled by the rapidly changing weather. The campfire was ablaze, a hearty dinner had been cooked and eaten (fashioned from the provisions they had packed and a few fat squab the children had wordlessly produced, although their proud faces and the tiny feathers stuck to their clothes said as much as needed to be said). Alexander had even filled a small, portable tin kettle with water from a nearby stream so Penelope could put it on to boil for tea.

Despite her worries, she had to admit it was rather pleasant to finally take off her boots and relax with a full tummy in the flickering light, listening to the pop and crackle of the fire. The admiral was in his tent, reviewing the maps of the forest the children had drawn for him so he might plot a course for the morning. And it was not raining yet; perhaps the storm would pass over them without shedding a drop.

Penelope felt a glimmer of her old optimism coming back. "Who would like a bedtime book?" she asked, and when the children responded with enthusiasm, she smiled. "Very well. Let us tidy up our campsite first, and then I shall read to you. Be quick about your chores, for I have chosen a particularly thrilling tale for the occasion, written by Mr. Daniel Defoe."

After the dinner plates had been rinsed, the tea poured, and everything made ready for the morrow, Penelope settled onto a large, flat rock that was somewhat shaped like a stool and close enough to the fire to have light to read by. She waited until the Incorrigibles were gathered 'round attentively, took out her book, turned to the first page, and began: "*The Life and Strange Surprizing Adventures of Robinson Crusoe, of York, Mariner: Who lived Eight and Twenty Years, all alone in an un-inhabited Island on the Coast of*

America, near the Mouth of the Great River of Oroonoque; Having been cast on Shore by Shipwreck, wherein all the Men perished but himself. With An Account how he was at last as strangely deliver'd by Pyrates."

"Pirates! I'll cut them to ribbons, *woof*!" Cassiopeia slashed back and forth with an imaginary sword.

"Is that the whole book?" Beowulf asked dubiously. "Not much happens."

Penelope squirmed; sitting on a rock was not nearly as comfortable as her cozy armchair in the nursery would be. "No, that is just the title. And look here: Underneath all that it says, 'Written by himself.' That is to say, we are meant to believe that Robinson Crusoe himself wrote the book."

Alexander looked confused. "Crusoe? No Defoe?"

Penelope frowned and tried to explain. "The book is fiction; that is to say, a made-up story written by Mr. Defoe, but he wants us to imagine it as a true account, as if it were written down by Robinson Crusoe himself. Who was actually a character made up by Mr. Defoe."

"Too complicated." Beowulf rose and peered out into the darkness. "Listen!"

They all listened. There was a noise, not too far off. A slow *crunch . . . crunch . . . crunch*, like the approach of footsteps. As if someone were trying, and failing, to walk quietly on the twigs and leaves of the forest floor.

Cassiopeia jabbed at the shadows with her stick. "Nevermore, pirates!" Before Penelope could stop her, she bounded over to the admiral's small tent and shouted within:

"Admiral, wake up wake up wake up*ahwoo*! Pirates off the starboard bow, wow, *woof*!"

There was a loud snore from within the tent. At Cassiopeia's cry, the snore turned to a sputter, the sputter to a crash and then a bellowed "Blast!" The tent shook on its pegs. After a moment the admiral batted his way through the flap.

"Who's there, what?" he cried. "Are we under attack?"

Penelope kept her voice calm. "We heard something, in the woods. Footsteps, possibly."

"Footsteps? It might be Bertha. Good news. I'll go round her up." He went back into the tent, still talking as he rummaged. "Hmm. I'll need my Always Waterproof Fashion Ostrich Leash. And my Savory Pickled Ostrich Treats; those will help lure her, if she's feeling skittish."

Crunch . . . crunch . . . crunch.

The sound grew closer. The children sniffed.

Alexander closed his eyes in concentration.

"Not a bird. Not a train," he concluded after a moment.

"Not Mrs. Clarke, either," Beowulf added.

"And not Bertha," said Cassiopeia. All three of them nodded.

"Got my SPOTs!" The admiral emerged from the tent and began to walk into the woods, calling, "Here, Bertha old girl. Come to Fawsy. I have wittle ostrich tweats for you!"

Penelope blocked his way. "Admiral, wait. The children do not think it is Bertha."

"Nonsense. Who else could it be?"

"Pirates!" Cassiopeia yelled, slashing away with her stick.

"Bears, perhaps–" Penelope began, but he cut her off.

"Bears don't frighten me. And if it is Bertha, I have no intention of letting her get away again. I'll go investigate. You and the children stay here." At her look of dismay, he added, "You'll be safe, as long as you don't wander off. Keep near the fire. Wild animals are afraid of fire." He narrowed his eyes at the children. "Most of 'em are, anyway."

"Good luck, Captain Admiral, sir." Alexander

saluted, and Beowulf followed suit.

"Get those pirates!" Cassiopeia handed him the stick she had been using as a sword.

"Aren't you a silly cub? Pirates don't live in the woods." He snapped the stick over his knee and dropped the pieces into the fire. Armed only with his AWFOL, and with his pockets crammed full of SPOTs, the admiral marched off.

As anyone who has ever taken a camping trip knows, nighttime out-of-doors is far from silent. The crickets and cicadas make a ceaseless, deafening buzz, coyotes cry mournfully in the distance, songbirds cheep and squawk at the first hint of dawn. And then there is the sound of one's own frightened heart, beating much too loudly as one begins to think one has made a dreadful mistake to ever leave the comforts of home.

The four of them sat there, listening, waiting. After a few minutes, the admiral's footsteps could no longer be heard.

"Ostriches," said Alexander after some more time had passed, "are not nocturnal."

"What an interesting bird-related fact; you must add it to the guidebook when we get home," Penelope said with false cheer. Much as she distrusted the admiral, his absence made her feel panicky. Why was it taking him so long to come back? The children were restless, too, and their noses twitched in hopes of catching another whiff of whoever their unseen visitor had been.

Penelope summoned her last reserves of pluck and returned to her stony seat by the fire. "Let us continue the tale of Robinson Crusoe. I will skip the title this time, since you heard it already. . . . In fact, I will skip the whole beginning. Nothing terribly interesting is likely to happen before the shipwreck, don't you agree?"

"Hespawoo," Cassiopeia agreed, for the poem "The Wreck of the Hesperus," which also centered on a shipwreck, was a particular favorite of the children's.

"Shipwreck . . . shipwreck . . . let me see." Penelope flipped the pages, looking for some passage that both she and the children might find sufficiently distracting to make them forget that the admiral had not yet returned. "Ah! This part seems rather exciting. Robinson Crusoe, having managed to survive on the Island of Despair for some years, one day finds a human footprint in the dirt, and fears there might be cannibals nearby."

"What are cannibals?" Beowulf asked.

"Cannibals are people who hunt other people, in order to eat them," she replied. "Now, about this footprint . . ."

All three children made faces of disgust.

"Pardon me, Lumawoo: If Defoe is real, and Crusoe is pretend, are cannibals real or pretend?" There was a tremor in Alexander's voice as he asked.

Penelope realized her error, but it was too late. "Cannibals are real," she replied cautiously, "but there are no cannibals in England. Cannibals live in faraway places."

"So do ostriches," Beowulf observed gravely. "But one is here, anyway."

"You do have a point, Beowulf." Now uneasy, Penelope snapped the book shut and slipped it back into her pocket. "Perhaps we ought to read something else. I know. Would any of you like to share your poem written in the style of POE? By which I mean, Poe?"

Alexander began at once.

"Once upon a forest creepy, I was feeling sore and sleepy,
Walking, walking, walking, walking. Still we had so far to go."

Then Beowulf chimed in.

"I took out my pen for drawing. Suddenly there came a clawing
As if someone started gnawing, gnawing at my pinkie toe.
"'Tis a cannibal,' I muttered, 'sawing at my pinkie toe.'"

With a swashbuckling gesture, Cassiopeia boldly finished:

"Take that, Edgar Allan Poe! Woof!"

"That—that was very good, children," Penelope said weakly. How she wished she had brought *Rainbow in Ribbons* instead of Poe and Defoe! All of this doom and gloom was just making things worse.

Cassiopeia held up a hand. "Listen."

Crunch . . . crunch . . . crunch . . .

"Stay calm, everyone. If it is a wild animal, it will not bother us if we stay near the fire." Penelope did not actually know if this were true, but the admiral had said it was—although it was also true that Miss Charlotte Mortimer kept a lazy calico cat named Shantaloo who would lie so close to the fire her tail would get singed and give off a nasty smell of burning fur—

"Are cannibals afraid of fire?" Beowulf asked.

"I do not know. I am not well acquainted with the habits of cannibals; perhaps there is some reference in the Robinson Crusoe book. . . ." Frantically she thumbed through the pages. "Dear me, an index would have come in useful here . . . cannibals, cannibals . . . I see there are quite a few mentions, but nothing particularly about fire. . . ."

As she said the word "fire," there was an earsplitting *crack.* Her first panicked thought was that Lord Fredrick was out hunting in the middle of the night with his rifle and had somehow found them. But another booming crack followed, and then a bright streak of lighting. The rain came down in sheets.

The campfire sputtered; then it was out. The extinguishing of the light made Penelope cry out in alarm. Within moments she and the children were drenched.

Alexander wiped the water from his eyes. He sniffed, and growled, and uttered a few words in the low, guttural language that he and his siblings sometimes used among themselves. "Lumawoo," he said after the children had done conferring. "Time to go to the cave."

"In this weather?" she cried, although even she realized how silly a remark it was, since they were already out-of-doors.

"Is not far," Beowulf added reassuringly.

Penelope weighed the options: They could stay here, sodden and cold, and wait for the admiral to return. Or they could wander off in search of a cave, in the dark of night, in a wild, soaking storm.

Lightning flashed again, revealing the soggy pile of ash that was all that remained of the campfire. The tarpaulin she had worked so hard to put up had collapsed into a puddled heap with the first strong gust. Behind every tree Penelope imagined she saw the eyes of bloodthirsty cannibals, glinting hungrily in the dark.

"The cave it is, then," she said, trying to sound as if she were still in charge. "But we must all three hold hands and not let go. I do not want us to get separated in this dark wood." Penelope had taken any number of excursions with the children in which she had warned them not wander off, but this time she knew that she was the one most likely to get lost.

The children seemed to understand. Beowulf took her by one hand, and Cassiopeia took the other.

Alexander paused for a moment and carefully put

away his sextant; it was of no use without a star to navigate by, and the sky was so thick with storm clouds that not even the light of the full moon could penetrate. But the children knew the way.

"To the cave," Alexander said, pointing–at least Penelope thought he pointed; she could scarcely see two feet in front of her. Feeling as helpless and lost as if she had just been named It in a game of pin the tail on the elk, had a kerchief tied across her eyes, and been spun 'round and 'round so she could not tell right from left, Penelope allowed the Incorrigible children to lead her blindly into the dark.

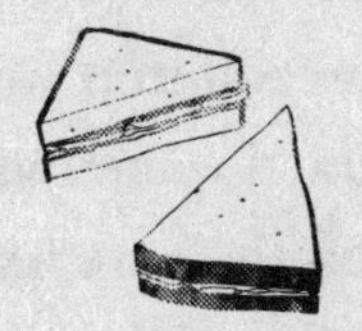

The Eighth Chapter

The cave holds many surprises.

As has already been firmly established, bears certainly do live in the woods. However, human children do not, generally speaking. The question of how the Incorrigibles survived during their early years out-of-doors was one that Penelope had been keen to answer since the day she became their governess. Sandwiches, it seemed, may have played a role. Wolves, too.

But at the moment it was dark, and the wind was whipping about, and the rain came down in torrents, and all Penelope could think about was clinging tightly to the hands of Beowulf and Cassiopeia as they dragged her through the forest, with Alexander leading the way. The children were not frightened at all; in fact, they seemed quite merry, and by the time the foursome reached the cave, the Incorrigibles were howling and growling a little marching song of their own:

"Hup, grrr, woof, ahwoo!
Hup, grrr, woof, ahwoo!"

Penelope tried to chime in at one point, to keep her spirits up, but it made the Incorrigibles laugh so hard that she stopped. Instead, she turned her full concentration to not slipping on the wet moss of the forest floor and falling into the mud.

"Here we are. Come inside, Lumawoo," Alexander finally announced, after what had seemed like many hours but must have been a much shorter interval than that since there was still no hint of dawn in the sky.

"Well done, children." Penelope felt in front of her with her outstretched hands, for she could see nothing in this pitch darkness. "How you managed to navigate through the woods in the middle of a moonless night is a mystery to me; I know Mr. Harley-Dickinson will be very impressed when I write him a letter all about it. So this is the cave, then? How does one go in? Is there–whoops, sorry! I hope I did not poke you in the eye, Beowulf–a door of some kind?"

"This way," Alexander said, and disappeared into a sliver of shadow that somehow seemed darker than the rest. Beowulf did the same. Cassiopeia tugged gently on her governess's fingers.

"Is nice cave," the girl said. "No rain inside. Come."

Penelope squeezed Cassiopeia's hand and stepped into the shadow. The soggy ground beneath her feet turned to cold stone. Somewhere in the distance and deep belowground, water trickled and plunked onto ancient rock. The darkness enveloped her like a veil of ink.

Step by step, Cassiopeia led her onward, until Penelope could stand it no longer. "Are we in the cave?" she asked. An echo answered in the affirmative: *cave cave cave cave . . .*

"Be right back, Lumawoo." Cassiopeia let go of her hand, and Penelope did her best not to panic. (Luckily, Swanburne girls were well trained in not panicking, but even so, Penelope had to use every technique she had been taught: taking deep breaths, thinking about cake, whistling happy tunes, and so on.) There was some scrambling about, and the sound of creaking, like a rusty hinge, followed by delighted yelps from the Incorrigibles. Helpless, Penelope stood like a statue, not daring to take a step lest she tumble off some unseen precipice.

The children, whose nighttime vision was evidently far keener than her own, seemed to be busy arranging something at her feet. "Bedtime now," Cassiopeia said, guiding Penelope to the ground. But instead of stone, she found herself lying on a thick, soft quilt. Someone—was it Alexander?—tucked a pillow beneath her head.

"Good night, Lumawoo," he said. "Time to sleep."

"No." She struggled to rise. "I will stand guard while you sleep. It may not be safe here."

"Is very safe. Friends are watching." This time it was Beowulf who answered.

"Friends? Which friends?"

"Ahwoo," the boys replied, but precisely what this meant Penelope could not tell. Cassiopeia snuggled next to her and yawned. "Sandwiches for breakfast, maybe," she said. "Yum, yum!" Then she fell asleep.

What else could Penelope do? She and the children were safe and out of the rain; there was a fluffy pillow beneath her head, and the promise, or at least the possibility, of a tasty meal when she awoke. So she let herself sleep, too, and dreamed only of happy things: chirping songbirds and Black Forest cake, and sweet-tempered ponies with long red ribbons braided through their silky manes.

"Giddy-yap," she mumbled, dreaming. "Giddy-yap, Rainbow!"

Plunk—plunk—plunk—

Penelope slept deeply and much later than her usual hour, for there was no sunlight streaming in the windows to let her know that morning had arrived. She might have slept longer, after the exhausting hike of the previous day, but that *plunk—plunk—plunk*ing sound was as insistent as a blacksmith's hammer.

"The roof of Ashton Place seems to have sprung a leak," she thought, still in a deep doze. "I hear water dripping. I shall have to notify Mrs. Clarke at once, so she can arrange repairs." Then she opened her eyes. Instead of a carved wooden bureau and a set of French doors leading to a balcony, she saw walls of rough stone. The only light came from the sunbeams that angled in at the cave's arched mouth, some twenty feet away.

She stared, fascinated, at the strange rock formations that furnished this stony room. "Why, those are stalactites and stalagmites," she thought. "I recognize them from my Fundamentals of Geology class at Swanburne. They come in pairs: One grows up from the ground like a spire; the other hangs from the roof like an icicle." But which was which? She could not for the life of her remember, for she had taken the class some years ago, and this was the first time the subject had come up since.

She rolled onto her back and stretched out luxuriously on the soft quilt that had been her bedding for the night. "What a marvelous opportunity this would be for a lesson on cave geology! If only I had an encyclopedia handy to check a few important facts—but of course, one would be unlikely to find an encyclopedia in a cave . . . what? Wait!"

Penelope bolted upright, eyes wide. For, as unlikely as it would be to find an encyclopedia in a cave, surely there ought not to be soft quilts either, or feather pillows, or dry kindling, or beeswax candles and matches to light them with, or any number of civilization's comforts and conveniences. And yet, somehow, here all those things were, and more: The Incorrigibles were up and preparing breakfast, having already neatly made their beds (for there seemed to have been enough quilts and pillows for everyone).

They had started a campfire just outside the cave's entrance, and someone had put a box of matches and a short but perfectly usable candle stub in a holder not two feet from Penelope's pillow.

"Good morning, Lumawoo," Cassiopeia sang out happily from near the cave's entrance. She poured water from a jug into a small kettle and set it on the fire. "Making tea for you!"

"Thank you, Cassiopeia. That is very thoughtful." Penelope stood up warily and looked around in wonder. "This is a cave, to be sure, but a well-stocked and comfortable one. Look, there is even artwork on the walls." She lit one of the candles so that she might examine the pictures more closely. "What extraordinary drawings," she marveled. "They are childlike, yet graceful, depicting animals on the run. Perhaps these antelopes are fleeing a hunter. Why, this could well be a significant archeological discovery! These paintings may have been made here long ago, by primitive peoples, long before there even was an England. . . ."

"Made by Beowulf, actually," Alexander said, pushing his brother forward. The bashful boy hung his head.

(Note that the idea of caves whose walls were

covered with paintings created by the primitive peoples of antiquity was a perfectly sound one, although Penelope was somewhat ahead of herself in thinking of it. In fact, it would not be until a few decades later that such caves would be discovered in Europe. The artwork within them was tens of thousands of years old and included animals that had long been extinct. The purpose of these pictures has been much debated by scientists; however, it is quite possible that those early cave dwellers, like Beowulf, simply liked to draw.)

"I was little." Beowulf shrugged. "Not my best work."

"Oh." Penelope tried to conceal her disappointment. "Well, they are still quite good. And there are so many of them! It must have taken you a long time to do all of these." Beowulf nodded. "Which would mean that you had some art supplies at hand, I suppose?"

"Just chalk," he said. "Some paints, too."

"And where did you get the chalk and the paints?"

He pointed. "From the trunk."

She turned and held the candle forward so that she might see into the dark recesses of the cave. There, hidden by shadows, was a large, battered trunk, of the sort that people brought on long sea voyages.

Shielding her candle with one hand so that it would

not go out, she stepped closer, into the gloom. The trunk was large and rectangular, made of wood and trimmed in brass-studded leather, with a curved lid in the shape of a dome. The lid hung open. Its interior was covered with stickers depicting all the places its owner had been, and the trunk itself was lined with old newspapers.

Penelope swiftly catalogued its contents: blankets and sheets. Candles. Matches. Boxes of chalk, some well used. A ball of twine and an ample supply of dry kindling, neatly cut to length. There were even rudimentary first-aid supplies: bandages, iodine, and so forth.

The three Incorrigibles gathered around her. Cassiopeia handed her a small tin mug of tea. "No milk," she said apologetically.

"Thank you." Penelope took the mug and continued to stare in amazement at the contents of the trunk. There was no milk, perhaps, but there were cups, spoons, a tin of black tea, even some sugar. The labels plastered across the inside of the trunk's lid included many midsized European nations, as well as places with names such as Tiki-Tiki, Maui-Maui, Ahwoo-Ahwoo, and other exotic destinations she had never heard of before.

Penelope walked slowly back toward the entrance of the cave and put the candle down on a flat stone. She sat on a rock and drank her tea, thinking all the while. When she was finished she put down her tea, sat up straight, and folded her hands, just as she did when beginning the morning's lessons back at the nursery. All three Incorrigibles immediately scampered over and lined up at attention. They gazed at her expectantly.

"Children, thank you for building a fire and making tea," she said. "And for fashioning such cozy beds on short notice. That was very resourceful of you. Agatha Swanburne would be proud. 'Whatever will do in a pinch, will do,' as she liked to say."

The children beamed at the praise, although the boys began giggling and pinching each other as soon as they heard the word "pinch." Penelope stopped them with a glance and went on. "Now, if you will forgive my curiosity, I would like to ask you some questions about this lovely cave you have brought us to."

"You mean a quiz?" Alexander asked eagerly, for he was the sort of student who enjoyed puzzles and tests of all kinds. "Like spelling words?"

Penelope could not help smiling at the notion. "Yes, like a quiz. But any one of you can reply to any question, and if the answer is satisfactory, you will all receive credit. Now. I take it this is the cave you lived in before you came to live at Ashton Place." Realizing she had not put it in the form of a question, she quickly added, "True or false?"

"True!" Beowulf called out. The other children murmured in agreement. Cassiopeia took a step to the right so she could scratch her back against one of the stalagmites (or was it a stalactite?). "We like our cave," she said appreciatively as she scratched.

"It is very comfortable, to be sure, thanks to the contents of that trunk." Penelope glanced back at the mysterious luggage, hidden in the shadows. "Next question: Has the trunk always been in the cave?"

The children nodded. "Easy questions," Beowulf whispered to his brother. "I will get A."

"I will get A plus," Alexander bragged back.

"A plus plus plus for me," Cassiopeia crowed.

"You will all get very high marks, never fear." Penelope smiled reassuringly, but inside she was aflutter with curiosity. "Here is a more difficult question for you: Who, exactly, put all these useful items in the trunk?"

The children fell silent. Beowulf shrugged.

"None of the above?" Cassiopeia guessed.

Penelope shook her head. "The candles, the

kindling, the blankets, the chalk . . . someone must have put them inside, surely?"

"They are just there," Alexander explained.

"Like the sandwiches." From behind his back Beowulf produced a sandwich; a large bite had already been taken out.

Penelope was so surprised she nearly slipped off her rock. "Sandwiches! Beowulf, where did you get that?"

He pointed. Growing near the mouth of a cave was a type of fern known as a wicker fern, named so because its fronds had the densely woven appearance of wicker. This made it an ideal place to conceal a wicker picnic hamper with a lid, which, upon closer inspection, turned out to be exactly what was hidden there.

Penelope opened the hamper and looked inside. "By Jove—there *are* sandwiches in the cave," she exclaimed. There were ham sandwiches on crusty brown bread, and cucumber and cream cheese sandwiches on white bread with the crusts trimmed off. There were even a few of Penelope's exact favorite type of sandwich: cheddar cheese with thinly sliced apple and a dab of mustard. Each was wrapped in a clean linen napkin. Mrs. Clarke herself could not have packed them up more neatly.

"Do we get A's?" Beowulf asked with difficulty, as

he was in the midst of chewing.

"Yes, of course. A pluses for everyone." Penelope lowered the lid and looked around, flummoxed. There was the picnic hamper of sandwiches, the trunk full of supplies, the cave walls full of Beowulf's childish scrawls. "This is all quite curious," she said finally. "For the three of you to survive as you did, caring for yourselves in the wild, has always seemed miraculous—but it appears as if someone was well aware of your presence here in the forest. Someone who went to great trouble to make sure you were warm, and fed, and had the tools you would need to survive. But who was it?"

"Mama Woof?" Cassiopeia suggested.

Mama Woof? Penelope could barely contain her excitement—was it possible that the Incorrigibles' mother was living someplace nearby? "I would like to meet this Mama Woof person," she said. "Where might I find her?"

"We will call," Alexander replied. The three children climbed upon some nearby rocks and cupped their hands to their mouths.

"Ahwoooooo!"

"Ahwoooooo!"

"Ahwoooooo!"

From distant hilltops came the answering howls:

"Ahwoooooo!"

"Ahwoooooo!"

"Ahwoooooo!"

With a rapidly sinking heart, Penelope realized her mistake. "Cassiopeia, when you said 'Mama Woof'—did you by any chance mean Mama Wolf?"

"What I said. Mama Woof," the girl repeated. She bared her teeth and howled once more, face to the sky. "Mam*ahwoooooooo*!"

"Oh dear." Penelope's voice rose until it squeaked, much as the housemaid Margaret's might have done. "Oh my, oh dear! Perhaps—perhaps I was too hasty in asking to meet Mama Woof. Perhaps another day would be more convenient. Come, children. Let us go hide in the cave—that is to say, get out of this sun before we break out all over in freckles." Shooing the Incorrigibles before her, she stood as tall and narrow as she could and positioned herself behind a stalagmite (or it might have been a stalactite), as if somehow the thin spire of rock could hide her from the eyes, and nose, and teeth, and claws, of their soon-to-arrive visitor—

Sudden as a snuffed candle, a shadow fell across the mouth of the cave. Someone—or something—had blocked all the light. Which meant that this something—or someone—must be exceedingly large, indeed.

The children yapped with joy and ran outside to greet their guest.

"Wait," Penelope cried, forgetting her fear and chasing after them. For no matter how adept they were with wild creatures, the Incorrigibles had been living among humans for nearly a year. There was no guarantee that the animals of the forest would remember them—or still consider them friendly, if they did.

Breathless, Penelope pushed ahead of her three pupils and skidded to a stop at the mouth of the cave. Before her stood the largest, most terrifying wolf she had ever seen (and you may rest assured, the fact that Penelope had never seen a real live wolf before in no way minimizes just how large and terrifying the beast was). It was nearly the size of a pony, although there was little about it to suggest that it might someday become the beloved, beribboned best friend of some wolf-loving fictional heroine. Its snout was long and tapered. Its fur-covered ears were sharply pointed and tilted forward, toward Penelope and the children. Its mouth hung open, dripping slimy trails of saliva. Its breath came in hard pants, and its staring, close-set eyes were yellow as two tiny bowls of lemon custard.

Despite her shaking knees Penelope managed a curtsy, for she knew that good manners always went a long way toward easing a tense situation. "Mama Woof," she squeaked, "I am so pleased to make your acquaintance."

The wolf's gaze lingered on Penelope for a long moment. Then it threw back its head.

"Ahwooooooooooo!"

As YOU DOUBTLESS KNOW BY now, Miss Penelope Lumley was a great fan of books. Countless were the times she had read of people caught in frightening circumstances; when things seemed at their most dire, inevitably these unlucky people would be described as having "a shiver run down their spines." Until now Penelope had assumed this was merely a neat turn of phrase that authors used to show that someone was well and truly panicked. Apparently there was more to it than that, for the wolf's mournful cry sent an actual cold shiver trickling from the base of her neck downward, as if some mischief maker had slipped a shaving of ice down the back of her dress at a picnic.

What should she do? Should she run, or fight, or cower helplessly in the hope that the wolf would take pity and leave them alone? The beast could easily outrun, outleap, and outclimb them; that much was clear. Nor did they stand a chance in a fight, for the wolf was protected by its rough, impenetrable fur and armed with fangs and claws, while she and the children were sheathed in soft human flesh, with only their weak fists and a dog-eared hardcover book of poetry as weapons. The verse was exceedingly melancholy, to be sure, and certain passages never failed to reduce Penelope to a state of misty-eyed reverie, but even the saddest German poems (in translation) were unlikely to be a match for a wolf.

Penelope's mind whirled in desperation. What would Agatha Swanburne do? What would Edith-Anne Pevington do? What would Simon do? What would sweet, brave Rainbow do? At least Rainbow had hooves to kick with, but Rainbow would always rather make friends than fight.

There was no time to think. "Nice wolfy," she cooed. "Nice, pretty, wolfy-wolfy-woo. What a fine, furry coat you have." Then, just to be clear about her intentions, she extended her two hands, palms up, and added, "We come in peace."

"Grrrrrrr."

The answering growl was like a deep rumble of thunder, or the roar of a steam engine approaching the station, or the sound of a snowy avalanche on some distant alpine peak. However you might choose to describe it, it was not a friendly sound.

"Alexander. Beowulf. Cassiopeia. Stay behind me, please," Penelope whispered hoarsely. "Move slowly. Be. Very. Quiet."

The three Incorrigibles had other ideas, though. They had already put down their mugs of tea and half-eaten sandwiches. Now they sank down onto their haunches. One by one, each child yowled a greeting.

"Ahwoooooooo!"

"Ahwoooooooo!"

"Ahwoooooooo!"

The wolf pulled its black-rimmed lips back into a horrid grin that bared every one of its wet, razor-sharp teeth. Then it pounced.

In a useless, frantic gesture, Penelope threw her arms wide to protect the children.

"Stay back, wild creature!" she called. "Stay back, I say! For these children are my pupils, and you shall not harm them—*oof!*"

The bounding wolf flew past her and knocked her flat on her back, with a *whoosh* of hot wolf breath and dank fur smell. Scrambling to her feet, Penelope saw:

The wolf, crouched over Alexander, growling and snarling not six inches from his face.

Alexander, pinned beneath the enormous beast,

grinning, growling, and snarling right back.

Beowulf, straddled upon the wolf's back as if it were, in fact, a pony.

And Cassiopeia, with a look of deepest contentment on her sweet little girl's face, wrapped 'round the creature's neck like a fox fur stole.

"Lumawooo!" she called gaily. "Meet Mama Woof!"

The wolf lifted its head and turned to Penelope. It blinked its cold, custard-yellow eyes.

Not knowing what else to do, Penelope threw back her head. *"Ahwooooo?"* she said, in a tremulous voice.

The wolf reared onto its hind legs. Penelope shrieked.

"Giddy-yap, giddy-yap!" Beowulf yelled, clutching the thick gray fur. Upright, the wolf was a good deal taller than Penelope. She could feel its hot, panting breath and see the scarlet roof of its toothy mouth. Cassiopeia swung from its neck in bliss.

The wolf placed its huge, hairy paws on Penelope's shoulders. It lowered its head until it was eye to eye with the petrified governess.

"Woof," said the wolf. Then, with a mighty slurp, it licked its long, wet tongue along the full length of Penelope's face.

"Lumawooo!" she called gaily. "Meet Mama Woof!"

The cave already had cozy quilts, beeswax candles, and an art collection. And now it had a sofa, too—a warm, furry, and occasionally growling sofa. For the wolf was so large that when she lay on her side, curved neatly against one wall of the cave, all three Incorrigibles could nestle cozily against her.

There would have been room for Penelope, too, but she politely declined. It had taken all of her willpower not to wipe the wolf slime from her face until she was sure Mama Woof was not watching. Even now she longed for a washcloth, a basin of hot water, and some strong soap, so she could give herself a proper scrubbing.

While the children enjoyed this strange but happy reunion with Mama Woof, Penelope fetched the picnic hamper and offered more sandwiches all around, for it seemed prudent to make sure their guest was not hungry. The wolf did not care for the cucumbers, but she did enjoy the bits of cheddar cheese Penelope offered, once the mustard had been carefully wiped off, of course.

Afterward the children played happily with their old friend, tugging on her fur and pulling her by the ears while she gently nipped and rolled them around between her massive paws. "Raised by wolves, indeed,"

Penelope thought, amazed. "But not only wolves. Someone knew all along–and still knows, judging by the freshness of the sandwiches–that there were three children living in the forest."

Mama Woof seemed to feel the children were in need of baths, for she proceeded to thoroughly wash their hands, faces, and even their ears with her tongue. Penelope found this revolting, frankly, but it kept the children happily occupied and thus provided an opportunity for her to exercise her powers of deduction. "If only we could determine who had been caring for you in the woods," she mused aloud. "For that person may know something of your origins, as well."

"Mama Woof cares for us," Alexander said as he turned 'round to let her do the opposite ear.

"Yap," said the wolf.

"Mama Woof is obviously an excellent nanny, but I doubt she would have a ready source of fresh candles and fluffy pillows. Nor would she be able to prepare these delectable sandwiches. Her paws are too"– Penelope almost said "too clumsy," but thought better of it–"too large and powerful to slice bread so neatly. No offense, Madame Woof."

The congenial thumping of the wolf's tail against the stone floor echoed in hidden caverns far below.

"Whoever this someone was, he or she had the means to provide blankets, art supplies, and now and then a meal that did not have to be caught and devoured raw," she thought. She recalled how the Incorrigibles still preferred their meat cooked quite rare and doused with ketchup; perhaps the sandwiches had only been an occasional treat during their formative years. "And yet this same someone did not bother to rescue the children, but left them here to live in the woods, among wild animals. Until the day they were found by Lord Fredrick, and Old Timothy, of course."

She helped herself to another cucumber sandwich, as Mama Woof had made short work of the cheddar. "Who could this mysterious person be?" she wondered. "If this person were a friend to the Incorrigibles, surely he or she would have rescued them and brought them indoors. But if a foe, why bother helping the children survive at all?"

It was a conundrum, to be sure, but a good night's sleep and a tasty breakfast had restored Penelope's supply of pluck, and she felt more than ready for the challenge. Why, in the past twenty-four hours alone, she had traversed a forest on foot in uncomfortable boots, spent the night in a cave, and befriended a terrifying wolf. Getting to the bottom of this business about the trunk and the sandwiches and the children's upbringing could scarcely be more difficult than that.

"As Agatha Swanburne once remarked, 'Patience can untangle the knottiest shoelace, but so can a pair of scissors,'" she announced. Briskly, she refolded all the napkins and put them back in the wicker basket. "With so many intriguing clues to consider, I am quite sure that with an afternoon's careful deducing, the mystery of your parentage will be well on its way to being solved. But we shall have to return to that task later, for we have a busy day ahead of us. Admiral Faucet must be wondering where we have gone off to—that is, if he ever made it back to our campsite during that dreadful storm. And then, of course, there is Bertha. . . ."

From many directions at once, a great howling arose in the forest.

Mama Woof's ears pricked up. The children leaped to their feet.

"Grrrr," said Mama Woof, trotting to the cave's entrance. The children and Penelope followed.

"Is a warning song," Alexander explained. "It means Uncle Freddy is getting ready."

Beowulf nodded. "With his horses. And his friends. And his dogs."

"Uncle Freddy's dogs bite," Cassiopeia said gravely.

"Not sweet woofy-woofs like Mama Woof." She kissed the wolf on her great, wet snout, but Mama Woof ignored the embrace. She was all alertness; her ears swiveled, searching for sounds, and her nose twitched as it picked up fresh scents on every current of air.

"It is the hunting party." Penelope spoke with a heavy heart. "If we do not find Bertha before Lord Fredrick does, she will end up stuffed in his study."

Cassiopeia plucked the plume from her hair and held it out to the wolf. "Mama Woof will help, won't you?" Mama Woof sniffed at the feather. She looked puzzled for a moment—no doubt she had never sniffed an ostrich before—and licked her chops with enthusiasm.

The girl tapped the wolf reprovingly on the nose. "No, Mama Woof. Not a bird for eating. A bird for catching."

The wolf sniffed the plume again and gave a short, low bark of assent.

"It is too dangerous," Penelope objected. "If Lord Fredrick sees a wolf, he will shoot."

"Uncle Freddy can't see much," Alexander said, and the children giggled, as if from long experience evading the blurry-eyed master of Ashton Place. Before Penelope could argue her objection further, three more wolves appeared at the mouth of the cave. All were gray furred and yellow eyed, and nearly as large as Mama Woof. At the sight of the children, the three newcomers wagged their tails, but there was no time for a happy reunion.

The wolves exchanged yelps and growls among them, and each had a turn smelling the plume. Cassiopeia grabbed Penelope's hand. "Hurry, Lumawoo. Woofs will take us to Bertha right now."

Penelope looked at the quartet of panting, salivating beasts; the icy feeling at the back of her neck returned. "And how are the woofs going to take us to Bertha, pray tell?"

Cassiopeia grinned. "Giddy-yap, woof-woof!"

The Ninth Chapter

The hunt for the runaway ostrich is on.

In Miss Penelope Lumley's day, the Epsom Derby was considered the greatest horse race in the world. This opinion continues to be held by many, for the race is still run once a year without fail, and attracts the world's most fleet-footed Thoroughbred horses and their fearless jockeys, not to mention the many thousands of enthusiastic spectators who come to cheer on their favorites. If someone were to give you a nickel for every cry of "Giddy-yap, giddy-yap!" heard on Derby Day at Epsom, you would have a great many nickels indeed.

(The piggy-bank owning among you should take note: At present, there is no plan to distribute nickels at the Epsom Derby. It is what is called a "hypothetical situation." Just as a rhetorical question is one that is asked with no expectation of being answered, a hypothetical situation is one that is described with no expectation of it actually happening. Unless there is a change in policy at Epsom, you will have to continue earning your nickels through good, old-fashioned, honest labor: rummaging through the sofa cushions, emptying trouser pockets on wash day, and so forth.)

And speaking of what things are called: It is called the *Epsom* Derby because it is held in a place called Epsom Downs; it is called the Epsom *Derby* because it was named in honor of the Earl of Derby. In some places "derby" is pronounced *dah-bee*, in others, *derr-bee*, but as a poet once said, a rose is a rose is a rose, and the same goes for derbies. Nowadays you may hear of races called the Kentucky Derr-bee, the Irish Dah-bee, and even the Roller Derby, but all of these are named after the original contest at Epsom.

Fortunately, the rules of horse racing are much simpler than the rules of English pronunciation. The horse that gets to the finish line first is the winner, and that is all there is to it. And although there were no actual horses involved, the Incorrigibles' mad race to find Bertha before Lord Fredrick had the bird stuffed full of sawdust and mounted in his study could be considered a derby of sorts. Call it the Bertha Derby, if you like, for poor Bertha was the one who stood to lose the most, should Lord Fredrick end up in the winner's circle.

Penelope might have come up with the name Bertha Derby herself had she had time to think about it, but at the moment her full attention was elsewhere. She clung desperately to Mama Woof's back as they galloped through the forest of Ashton Place, sniffing and searching for the runaway bird. The four wolves and their passengers raced through dense thickets; they bounded over rushing streams and leaped over fallen trees. There were no reins to hold on to, and the coarse, gray fur kept slipping from her grasp, so she wrapped her arms tightly around Mama Woof's neck, closed her eyes, and imagined trusty Rainbow beneath her. She thought of how nervous Edith-Anne Pevington had been when she and Rainbow were learning to jump over fences, as was so movingly described in *Jump, Rainbow, Jump*, and yet how happily everything had turned out in that book (and in every other Giddy-Yap, Rainbow! book, too, come to think of it).

To calm herself even further, Penelope kept up a steady stream of chatter under her breath. "And, it's neck and neck, neck and neck–Grayfur, ahead by a length–Yelloweyes is coming up on the rear! It's Grayfur! Yelloweyes! Grayfur! Yelloweyes! They're coming around the final turn. Yelloweyes is pulling ahead! Grayfur turns on some extra steam–and it's Grayfur by a snout!"

"Silly Lumawoo," Cassiopeia yelled. Her trusty wolf steed was galloping just to the right of Mama Woof.

Penelope blushed, for she had not intended to be heard. "Someday we shall have to go to the Epsom Derby," she shouted over the rushing wind. "I am sure it would be very educational–whoa!"

The wolves had stopped short. The sudden halt was enough to knock Penelope off the back of Mama Woof. The Incorrigible children slid more gracefully off their mounts and began to sniff at the air, while the three smaller wolves ran in tight circles, whimpering and skimming their muzzles along the ground. Mama Woof held perfectly still, head raised, nose twitching. After a moment she tensed and let out a low bark.

"Look," said Beowulf. "Bertha!"

On the other side of the trees was a grassy clearing. The ostrich stood in the center, nibbling upon a low shrub. Her long neck stretched down to eat; then she lifted her head high and scanned her surroundings with large, wide-set eyes. The moment she saw these new arrivals, she flapped her wings in warning and took a jump backward. The wolves panted and showed their teeth. The one that Cassiopeia had been riding dropped into a crouch and shifted its weight onto its hindquarters, as if to pounce.

Cassiopeia grabbed the beast sternly by one ear and bonked it hard on the nose with her tiny fist. "Remember, woofs! Bertha is friend bird. Not dinner bird."

Four sets of yellow eyes blinked, as if trying to understand. Could such a message get through to their meat-mad wolf brains? The beasts sniffed and whined, but one by one, they lay down flat on their bellies. If one flinched or looked in any way eager to leap at the giant bird, Mama Woof warned it back into position with a cuff from her massive paw.

Penelope was deeply impressed; straightaway she wanted to reward the wolves for their superb self-control. She patted her pockets, but alas, there were no biscuits left. "It would have been clever to bring wolf treats with us," she thought, "or at least some bits of cheddar sandwich, which Mama Woof seemed to enjoy. Curious; I found no mention of the use of treats to manage the native wildlife in *Robinson Crusoe.* Of course, in his case, cannibal treats would have been what was required. . . ." Precisely what cannibal treats would be made of was a disturbing question, and one that Penelope had no opportunity to consider at present, for Bertha looked ready to bolt. Her comical, flat-beaked head swiveled nervously this way and that. As if preparing herself to depart, she raised one clawed, two-toed foot.

Penelope thought quickly. "Alexander, during your work on the bird guidebook, did you happen to learn any ostrich calls?"

The boy nodded and took a step forward. Tucking his chin low on his chest, he hooted a low-pitched *foo, foo, foooooo.*

At the sound, Bertha spread her flightless wings into a threatening arch and emitted a long, furious hiss.

"Oops." Alexander turned to Penelope and whispered, "That was mistake. *Foo, foo, fooooo* is war call. I think I just challenged her to a fight."

Bertha hissed again. She began prancing boldly and pecked at the air like a boxer taking punches at an imaginary foe. The wolves, still on the ground, let out low growls and inched forward on their bellies. This time Mama Woof did not stop them. Saliva dripped from every sharp-toothed mouth.

"Think, children! Surely there was something in your research about peaceful communication between ostriches. Oh, if only we had some of the admiral's Savory Pickled Ostrich Treats as an offering of friendship!" Alas, the supply of SPOTs had been left at their campsite during the storm.

"Let me try." Beowulf moved slowly, so as not to provoke Bertha any further. He cupped his hands to his mouth and took a deep breath.

Penelope heard nothing. "Is he doing it?" she whispered to Cassiopeia.

"Shh! Listen," Cassiopeia said.

Penelope tried, but the friendly ostrich call was even less audible than Beowulf's rabbit call, if possible. Bertha, however, had a different reaction. First she looked puzzled. Then she lowered her wings and smoothed her feathers into a more relaxed position. She cocked her head to one side, as if curious about what sort of ostriches these odd-looking, mismatched creatures might be. Then, lifting one spindly leg at a time, she took a tentative step toward them.

Penelope readied the Temporary Ostrich Tether she had fashioned out of the twine that had been left in the trunk, back at the cave. "Do it once more, Beowulf.

I need her to come close enough that I can toss this TOT over her head," she whispered. Beowulf obliged. At the sound of his seemingly noiseless call, Bertha hopped forward. Her tail gave a friendly little shimmy.

"And oopsie, whoopsie, here comes the TOT," Penelope sang, swinging the loop of twine 'round and 'round above herself like a lasso. It sailed through the air and slipped past Bertha's beak and down her long, flexible neck so gently that the bird did nothing but blink.

Penelope could not have been more pleased with herself had she roped a wild mustang pony, the way those marvelous American cowboys did (and as Edith-Anne Pevington would learn to do in an as-yet-unwritten volume titled *Rainbow Out West*, in which she and her trusty pony pal take a trip to the western part of America so that her father, Mr. Pevington, might pursue business opportunities during something called the "Gold Rush." This volume of the Giddy-Yap, Rainbow! books would be penned and published many years later, when Penelope was quite grown up. But, unlike a real girl, Edith-Anne Pevington never seemed to get any older; it is one of the advantages of being fictional, or one of the disadvantages, if you prefer to see it that way).

"A job well done, everyone," Penelope said, "thanks to the superb noses of our trusty wolf steeds, and some fine bird calls by Beowulf–and Alexander," she added, not wanting to leave him out; after all, he had demonstrated a perfectly effective ostrich call, even if it had not been the exact one needed at the time. "Now, all we need to do is lead Bertha back to Ashton Place and put her in the POE. If the woofs–pardon me, wolves–can help us locate Admiral Faucet along the way, so much the better."

Penelope was justifiably proud of her success as an outdoorswoman, but the notion that she and the children would be back at Ashton Place in time for a proper dinner, hot baths, and a bedtime book that was not about cannibals made her positively giddy with delight. As was her habit when overexcited, she began to make plans. "The moment we get back to the house, I shall visit Lord Fredrick's library to look up some facts about cave geology. I propose a brief lesson after dinner; we have much to discuss regarding the difference between stalagmites and stalactites, caverns and grottos, troglobites and . . ." She vaguely recalled that troglobites had something to do with caves, although for the life of her she could not recall what they were. "Well, other sorts of bites."

(In fact, troglobites are creatures that live only within caves and nowhere else; they include insects, fish, spiders, and salamanders. Most of us would find their lives dismal and peculiar, but no doubt they would think us quite mad for living out in the blinding sun and the fresh, ever-changing air, with its wobbly breezes.)

The children were intrigued by Penelope's remarks and began a lively debate about all the different sorts of bites they could think of: chomping bites, nibbling bites, gnawing bites, and vicious, flesh-tearing bites, among others. Even the wolves found this conversation interesting, as you might well imagine, but the discussion was cut short by a hooting, unnatural sound, coming from a far distance. Those that had ears that could perk up and swivel did so; the rest turned their heads to listen.

"Uh-oh," Cassiopeia said with a frown.

"Oh no." Beowulf, too, looked unhappy, and began to chew on the strap of his pith helmet.

Again the sound echoed through the trees. It seemed to come from the direction of Ashton Place.

"Time to go," Alexander agreed. "Tallyho."

Tallyho! Now Penelope understood: The call came from Lord Fredrick's hunting horn, and its hooting, leaping cry was the sound that signaled the start of the hunt.

Penelope clutched the end of Bertha's TOT in one hand and seized Mama Woof's thick fur with the other. "Lord Fredrick is on his way," she said, hauling herself onto the wolf's back. "Which means we must be on our way to the POE, and quickly."

"Poe! Poe! *Nevahwoo!*" the children shouted, leaping onto their trusty wolf steeds. Mama Woof gave a stern series of yelps, and the other wolves took up the cry.

"Ahwoooo!"

"Ahwoooo!"

"Ahwoooo!"

"Nevahwoo!" Penelope howled in spite of herself. She waited a moment, to see if she felt silly making such a racket, but she found it rather bracing, frankly. Just to be sure, she did it again. "*Nevahwoooooo!* Now, everyone! To the POE!"

The maximum speed of an ostrich on land is sixty miles per hour. A wolf can run only half that quickly, and a Thoroughbred racehorse (of the type that would run in the Epsom Derby, say) is only somewhat faster than a wolf, with a top speed of forty to forty-five miles per hour. Humans are considerably slower, by comparison. Even if

Mrs. Clarke trained and practiced until she was among the fastest sprinters in the world (a purely hypothetical situation, of course, as the dear lady was much too busy with her housekeeping duties to undertake such a grueling training regimen), she would still only be able to run twenty-five miles per hour at the most, and that would be limited to a short distance.

Without question, then, in a race between an ostrich, a wolf, a racehorse, and a middle-aged housekeeper in tip-top shape, the smart money would be on the ostrich. And with Bertha now setting the pace, and the threat posed by Lord Fredrick's hunting party urging them ever onward, it is fair to say that the wolves of Ashton Place, despite being weighed down by their passengers, ran faster than any wolf had ever run before.

Their mission was urgent, but even so, Penelope found herself enjoying the adventure. The sadness and worry about her parents that had been plaguing her for weeks, the gloomy refrain of "elk, elk, elk"—all of it had been drowned out by the constant surprises and discoveries of this excursion into the woods: the unexpectedly cozy cave, for example, and the unseen visitor who left useful items in the trunk. And, of course, there was the mystery of the sandwiches—who could have known that cheddar and apple was her favorite?

It was a great deal to ponder, but "A busy mind is a cheerful mind," she thought, recalling one of Agatha Swanburne's more popular sayings (that is to say, it had been stitched onto more pillows than any other; this may have been because it was one of the wise lady's shorter sayings as well). "It is not that I have forgotten about my parents, of course not! But I have been so busy with my own adventures, and we have been in more or less constant danger, which is highly distracting. It makes one forget about even very important things. . . . Why, perhaps that explains it!" she realized. "Perhaps my parents have not really forgotten me, either–perhaps they are simply busy having adventures. Oh my! Perhaps they are in danger, too! That would be dreadful–stop!" she cried, for she had spotted a curious object lying on the earth.

What could it be? It was black in color, curved on top like a dome, and about the size of–well, a human head, to put it plainly. As you know, the idea of cannibals had recently been introduced to Penelope's mind; her first horrified guess at what this head-sized object might be is far too gruesome to repeat here. However, despite her misgivings, she felt certain they ought to investigate.

The wolves and Bertha obeyed her order to halt, and

Mama Woof helpfully circled 'round so Penelope could get a better view. The head-shaped whatsit floated on the surface of a large puddle of uncertain depth, which no doubt had been left by the strong rains of the previous night. "It is a man's hat," she concluded with relief. "But whose? It looks a bit like one of those new derby hats that have lately become all the rage."

(Unbelievably, the word "derby" is also a nickname for a type of snug-fitting, dome-shaped men's hat invented by a Mr. Bowler, which was just becoming fashionable in Miss Lumley's day. The bowler hat soon became such a common sight at the Epsom Derby that people began calling it a derby hat. But this is the way it goes with words: Hats turn into horse races and horse races into hats, dah-bees into derr-bees and derr-bees into dah-bees, until no one knows exactly what is meant by what is being said.)

Alexander slid off his wolf and stepped delicately through the murky puddle. He picked up the hat and examined it.

"Not hat. Helmet. Very dirty." He rubbed the object with his sleeve and held it up to show Penelope. The dark color that she had mistaken for the stiff black felt of a bowler hat was merely a thick coating of mud.

"A pith helmet! Why, that must belong to Admiral

Faucet. But where could he be?" Penelope looked around but saw only moss, trees, and some lovely specimens of the common but ruggedly attractive swashbuckler fern, with its long, swordlike fronds and thick stems that were sturdy as peg legs.

Alexander wiggled his feet around in the muck. "Sunk in tar pit," he declared, gingerly backing out of the puddle.

"No more hup, hup, hup," Beowulf said mournfully. He and his sister were still astride their wolves, and the beasts whimpered in sympathy.

"Gruesome," Cassiopeia agreed. "Oh, well." She did not sound terribly sad, for she had still not forgiven the admiral for trying to take away her plume.

"Blast!" came a voice. "I'm up here!"

They looked up. The admiral hung upside down, suspended from a high branch of the tree. Both of his ankles were tangled in some sort of rope. His face was beet red and, judging from his tone of voice, he was in a foul mood, but otherwise he seemed unharmed.

"Blast that Ashton!" he said. "I'm caught in one of his hunting snares!"

"Tallyho," warned Alexander. "Uncle Freddy is on his way."

"Poor Admiral. Soon you will be stuffed." Cassiopeia

sounded rather cheerful at the prospect. "Don't be sad. I will visit you in Uncle Freddy's study."

"You will be easy to draw," Beowulf added. "I will draw you very nicely."

The admiral wiggled and kicked, which made him swing wildly, like a piñata in the midst of being beaten. "Cut me down at once! I have no intention of being stuffed, or drawn, or any of it. Say–looks like you caught my Bertha after all. Nicely done, cubs. Bad Bertha, running away! I ought to give you a whipping for all the trouble you've caused. But don't worry; soon you'll be locked up in the POE, safe and sound."

Bertha hissed. Penelope was strongly tempted to leave the admiral where he dangled and let Lord Fredrick and the hounds deal with him, but as usual, her kinder nature prevailed. "Perhaps the admiral will agree to sit still for a portrait, Beowulf. In the meantime, we had best cut him down and continue on our way. Lord Fredrick's party will be here any minute."

Beowulf shinnied up the tree in which the snare was set and quickly cut the admiral down by gnawing through the rope with his teeth. Admiral Faucet fell to the ground and landed in the puddle with a mighty, messy splash. Splattered with mud from head to toe, he sat up and rubbed his head. Alexander handed him his helmet.

"Ow," said Beowulf sympathetically.

"Ow, bow wow, woof!" his wolf steed agreed. It was only now that he was right side up that Admiral Faucet noticed the presence of the wolves. His eyes grew wide, and then wider still at the sight of Beowulf sitting astride his wolf as naturally as a child riding a hobbyhorse. "By Jove, will you look at that?" he exclaimed in wonder. "What sort of creatures are those?"

"Woofs," Cassiopeia explained, patting hers between the ears.

The admiral snorted. "Nonsense. If they were real wolves, they would have eaten you."

"They are real but unusual wolves." Penelope could not help boasting a little. "And fast ones, too. We are riding them back to Ashton Place."

"Fast wolves? Riding wolves?" He climbed to his feet, and his eyes narrowed with greed. "Racing wolves, you mean! What a capital idea!"

The day's adventures had made Penelope feel rather bold, and she spoke in her sternest and most Swanburnian tone. "I hope you have not forgotten, Admiral, we still have Bertha's safety to consider.

The longer we stand here, the closer Lord Fredrick's hunting party comes. Luckily our mounts are better suited to the dense forest than a group of men on horseback." Penelope slid off Mama Woof and gestured for the admiral to get on. "Admiral, you ride Mama Woof. She is the largest and strongest, and will be able to carry you with ease."

The admiral hemmed and hawed as the giant beast approached. Mama Woof smiled in her fashion, which is to say she pulled her carnivorous lips back over those razor-sharp teeth. She wagged her tail so hard that it whacked the admiral repeatedly on the side of his leg.

"See? She likes you," Beowulf said, but the admiral seemed unconvinced. His teeth began to chatter in fear.

"But who will carry Lumawoo?" Cassiopeia asked, turning to her governess. "You cannot run like Mrs. Clarke."

Penelope smiled. "That is true, although with a bit of practice I should hope I would be able to at least keep up with the dear lady." She glanced at Bertha, who had fixed the admiral with a menacing stare (and to be stared at by an ostrich is no laughing matter, for their eyes are the size of billiard balls; it is why there is so little room left in their heads for brains).

"I shall ride Bertha, if she will allow me the privilege. Beowulf, will you call her closer?" He did. Penelope gave a gentle downward tug on the TOT, and the bird knelt low enough for her to climb aboard.

Penelope was pleased with the change. The soft, feathered back of the ostrich was far more comfortable to sit upon than the coarse fur of the wolf had been, and she still held the leash ends of the TOT, which she could easily pretend were pony reins. "Imagine what I shall write to Simon about this!" she thought. "We have gone from watching warblers through a window to barebacked-ostrich riding, all in the course of week. He will surely be impressed–"

"Bow wow wow wow!"

"Bow wow wow wow!"

It was the baying of the hounds, now close enough to hear.

"Bow wow wow wow!"

"Bow wow wow wow!"

Boom!

Alexander gazed up at the blue sky that peeked through the leaves of the trees. "Thunder?" he asked dubiously.

"It sounds like your uncle Freddy has gotten off a shot." The threat of gunfire was enough to make

"Imagine what I shall write to Simon about this!"

Admiral Faucet clamber onto Mama Woof's back at last. "The man's blind as a newborn rat. Whoever taught him to shoot ought to be brought before a judge."

His remark made Penelope think of Judge Quinzy, the unsettling friend of Lord Fredrick's whom she had reason to believe was not a judge at all. But now was not the time to think of that.

"Follow me," Penelope cried. For effect, she gave a little shake on the leash ends of the TOT, just as if they were a set of reins attached to a pony's bridle.

Of course, the children could not resist yelling: "Giddy-yap, Bertha!" to get things started. Penelope did not mind this one bit. Nor did Bertha, who took off in a blaze of speed, while behind them the admiral shouted: "Run! Run like the wind, you bloodthirsty beast! *Awhoo-hoo*, this is capital! Better than the Epsom Derby. Governess—we must talk!"

The Tenth Chapter

The wolves confront the hounds, while the admiral keeps Lord Fredrick at bay.

Except in the book-fueled realm of her imagination, Penelope had never ridden a pony at full gallop. However, she did have a distant recollection of being given a piggyback ride by Dr. Westminster, the Swanburne veterinarian, when she was still a very small girl. Exactly how small she could not remember, but small enough to be given piggyback rides, in any case.

Like Dr. Westminster, Bertha ran on two legs, as opposed to galloping on four. No doubt it was the similarity of their gaits that prompted Penelope's memory, but the two had little else in common: For example, Dr. Westminster was extremely clever and Bertha was not clever at all. Bertha was taller and much speedier than Dr. Westminster, and Dr. Westminster was rarely covered with feathers. (One cannot truthfully say he was never covered with feathers, because there was one time when he spent the night in a chicken coop caring for some fledgling chicks that had, unfortunately, caught the people pox and were very itchy indeed. The night was cool, and he wore a boiled-wool coat of the type that fur and feathers tend to stick to. By morning he looked as if he were in a man-sized chicken costume. When he emerged from the coop, the girls screamed with delight and begged him to keep the coat as it was, but he thought he might frighten the cows if he made his rounds in the guise of a giant chicken. Practical as ever, the girls proceeded to pluck the coat and use the feathers to make pillows upon which to embroider the sayings of Agatha Swanburne. Sewing such pillows was a favorite pastime of Swanburne girls; they were often exchanged as gifts and occasionally used in pillow fights, and all the window seats at school were made cozy with them.)

"Bow wow wow wow!"

"Bow wow wow wow!"

Penelope had been right when she said the wolves and Bertha could stay well ahead of Lord Fredrick's hunting party; in the forest they hurdled over fallen trees and leaped through narrow crevices that a group of men on horseback would have to go around. However, Lord Fredrick's pack of hounds did not have these limitations, and from the sound of it, the dogs were getting closer by the minute. Too late Penelope realized that the pack had circled 'round the edge of the wood, ready to cut them off before they reached the POE.

"We are heading toward the dogs—we must change course!" she yelled, but Admiral Faucet was now well into the spirit of the chase and was whooping and hollering so much she could not make herself heard. Moments later they emerged from the forest. All that lay between them and the safety of the POE were the rolling meadows of parkland that surrounded Ashton Place, dotted here and there by a towering, wide-canopied tree and beribboned with the winding paths upon which Mrs. Clarke liked to take her morning jog.

The baying of the hounds grew louder, and the wolves ran faster still, panting hard to keep up with the swift and long-legged bird. It was not until the stately house called Ashton Place came into view that Penelope thought of how terrified the household staff would be to see a pack of wolves bounding across the property, so near the house and the livestock. Would the wolves be in danger? Or had all the men with rifles gone out with Lord Fredrick and his party?

"Bow wow wow wow!"

"Bow wow wow wow!"

The hounds tore around the edge of the trees, and the wolves came sharply to a stop. Bertha squawked and hissed, and the two breathless groups of canines stood nose to nose, staring and growling. Penelope signaled to the children to dismount and stand clear. The wolves were larger and stronger, but the beagles had them outnumbered five to one (that is to say, there were five beagles for every one wolf; as you already know how many wolves there were, the exact number of beagles can easily be figured with the use of an abacus). A dreadful fight seemed imminent.

The admiral slipped off Mama Woof's back and began waving his cane at the dogs. "Scat, you silly dogs," he shouted. "Off with you, now–and stay away from my ostrich." But being scolded only made the hounds more agitated. They bayed in chorus and tried to inch closer to Bertha.

"Bow wow wow wow!"

"Bow wow wow wow!"

"Woof." Mama Woof's deep, wolfy voice echoed over the hills. The *bow-wow-wow*ing turned to whimpers and whines.

"Woof," repeated Mama Woof, more sternly this time. The pack of hounds fell silent. Twenty tails drooped down between four times as many legs.

"Yap?" the lead beagle asked nervously.

"WOOF," insisted Mama Woof. The dogs fell to the ground and rolled on their backs, paws trembling in the air (you may work it out for yourselves exactly how many paws; however, it is safe to assume there was one paw per leg). Mama Woof and the other wolves took turns growling in the dogs' faces. Penelope had to restrain the Incorrigible children from doing the same; reluctantly they obeyed, but they added their own growls and snarls from a distance.

After that the dogs and wolves were on more friendly terms, with the wolves firmly in charge. Any hound that got snappy with Bertha was promptly corrected, and the pack of yowling beagles provided a noisy but festive escort back to the POE. The admiral rode proudly on Mama Woof, crowing and singing like a victorious general returning from battle, but

Penelope kept looking over her shoulder. "The wolves have been our protectors while we were in their native habitat," she thought, "but if they are seen in ours, it will not be so easy for us to protect them." Nature was "red in tooth and claw," according to the admiral, yet Penelope feared it was here, among the landscaped grounds and formal gardens, in sight of the peaceful, smoke-plumed chimneys and the thoroughly civilized neoclassical facade of Ashton Place, that blood might, at last, be shed.

Before long, Bertha had been set loose in her Permanent Ostrich Enclosure and was being fed SPOTs by the children. As you no doubt recall, these were the Savory Pickled Ostrich Treats the admiral had invented, and Bertha did seem to like them very much. Armed with the treats, the children could not resist trying to teach Bertha some tricks, but the small-brained bird was not a terribly good student. Cassiopeia tried to show her some basic facts of multiplication, but Bertha proved even less adept at math than Nutsawoo, who could at least comprehend that three acorns made a more filling snack than two.

Meanwhile, Admiral Faucet excused himself to a small shed off the main POE that he called the POE

Home Office, or POEHO for short. There, he said, he planned to "draft a new letter to my potential investors. Racing wolves! Half-human child jockeys! It's one brilliant moneymaking scheme after another!"

The exhausted wolves lapped water from a trough (contrary to popular belief, ostriches do drink water if it is available, although they can manage without it for long stretches of time as well). Penelope's fear for the wolves' safety was well founded, for moments after they had arrived at the POE, two workmen who were patching the roof of the barn saw them from above and raised a cry: "Wolves, wolves! Lock up your sheep! Wolves, wolves! Close the doors!" It was only a matter of time before an angry mob arrived.

Reluctantly, Penelope approached Mama Woof. Water dripped from the beast's whiskered muzzle, and her yellow eyes were dim with fatigue. "I know you have run a long way and would like to rest," Penelope said softly, "but for your own sake, you and the other wolves must go back to the forest at once."

Mama Woof threw back her head and howled, soft and sad. With a full heart, Penelope called the Incorrigibles over. "Alexander, Beowulf, Cassiopeia, it is time to say good-bye."

The three children threw down their SPOTs and

ran to embrace Mama Woof and the others. This was the moment Penelope had dreaded. Would the children wish to return to the forest with their animal friends? They had seemed so happy in the woods, and so at home in that surprisingly cozy cave—who was Penelope to say that life at Ashton Place was better? True, there was plumbing, and cooked meals, and knickknacks that were dusted daily, and banisters to slide down when none of the household staff was looking, but could these compare to the burbling streams that ran through the woods, the pinecones and hazelnuts one could freely gather from the mossy floor, the trees one could climb and the vines one could swing from?

The more Penelope turned it over in her mind, the more convinced she became that the children might actually be better off in the forest. "Think how marvelous it would be to live among so many fascinating ferns, growing in their native habitats," she thought with quivering lip. "And the children will still have one another, and the wolves, too. . . I am the one who will be left, all alone, once more. . . ." Elk, elk, elk—now that the distraction of the chase was done, there it was; like so many other matters about which one is tempted to put one's head in the sand, the problem of the long-lost Lumleys was no closer to solving itself than it had been before.

The four wolves and three children exchanged many hugs and licks, friendly barks and gentle nips. Penelope's feelings spun in such rapid succession she could not even name them; it was like a pinwheel of emotions whirling inside her, faster and faster, until each blended into the next.

"So long," said Cassiopeia, kissing one wolf on the nose.

"Farewell," said Beowulf as he let his face be washed once more.

"Auf Wiedersehen," said Alexander. He clicked his heels and bowed to the wolves.

"Good-bye, Mama Woof," Penelope whispered. "I hope we meet again quite soon." When or where that meeting might take place, she did not dare imagine. The wolves would not be welcome in the nursery; that much was certain.

The four wolves sat and offered their paws for a final shake. The beagles bayed a mournful parting song. Even Bertha raised a wing in salute. Then the wolves of Ashton Place were off, slipping like four shadows through the meadow grass and over the rolling fields until they disappeared beyond the tree line into the mysterious woods beyond.

Penelope scarcely dared look at the Incorrigibles. Six shining eyes gazed longingly at the forest; at least, that is what she imagined the children felt. "Surely they should be allowed to choose," she thought, bravely blinking away her tears. "If not, then I am no better than the admiral, to keep living creatures locked up in places where they would rather not be." The nursery at Ashton Place was a pleasant room, well stocked with books and toys, not to mention a fond and dedicated governess, but Penelope had no intention of turning it into a PIE—a Permanent Incorrigible Enclosure from which there was no chance of escape.

"Children, you do not *have* to stay," she tried to say, but scarcely any sound came out, for her voice was choked with feeling.

The Incorrigibles looked at her with an expression of joyful surprise. "Lumawoo, you have learned how to make rabbit call!" Beowulf said in admiration, but the thunder of approaching hooves prevented Penelope from correcting him. It was Lord Fredrick and his party, arriving at last. The men and their horses looked winded and unhappy. Lord Fredrick seemed particularly unwell; his eyes were bleary and red, and there were dark, puffy circles beneath them, as if he had been up all night.

Six shining eyes gazed longingly at the forest . . .

He was snappily dressed, at least, like all the other men. They were clothed for the hunt in scarlet coats, white trousers, and neat black caps. Penelope saw familiar faces among them: the Earl of Maytag was there, and Baron Hoover, both friends of Lord Fredrick from his gentlemen's club. She scanned the rest of the party to see if the man who called himself Judge Quinzy was also present. As far as she could see, he was not.

"Ostrich chase! More like a wild goose chase, that's what this was!" Lord Fredrick was in the midst of vigorously scolding some unfortunate person; his voice was hoarse and froggy, and now and then he made an odd, sneezy, barky sort of sound. "I may not be able to see much, *yap*! But I should think a pack of experienced bird hounds would be able to sniff out the one and only ostrich in England. *Woof!* Instead they lead us to geese, ducks, warblers, nuthatches–I've never known the dogs to have such trouble telling one bird from another. Next time, bring a guidebook, what? Ah-*whoo*!" he sneezed as they approached the POE. "And then the blasted beagles run off and disappear altogether, *yap*! *Yap, yap!*"

"Very sorry, my lord. Not sure what went amiss with the hounds today. I promise it won't happen again."

The speaker dismounted with a thud. It was Old Timothy! He wore the green waistcoat that marked him as the master of hounds. The hunting horn was slung at his hip.

Penelope thought quickly. If Old Timothy had served as master of hounds for the day, that meant it was Old Timothy who had blown the horn that warned her and the children that Lord Fredrick was coming. And it was Old Timothy who had apparently directed the dogs to lead this well-dressed hunting party everywhere but where Bertha might be found.

Penelope suppressed the urge to go throw her arms around the neck of this enigmatic fellow and give him a hug of thanks. Surely it all meant that the strange coachman truly was a friend to her and the Incorrigibles, in spite of his gruff manner and puzzling remarks. "On second thought, an embrace would be unseemly," she concluded, "but perhaps I could invite him to tea, as a way of saying thank you." Yet somehow she doubted he would accept such a friendly gesture. Still, she resolved to express her gratitude in some fashion.

"Ah-*whoo!* Blast this head cold, *yap*!" Lord Fredrick scratched frantically at one ear. "As far as I'm concerned, the day's been a total loss. Hardly worth dragging myself out of my sickbed—why, what's this?" Lord Fredrick squinted in the direction of the POE. "It's not a bird, what? Too big to be a swan, eh? The pigs haven't begun to grow wings, have they? Har har!"

"I'm no expert, of course, but I believe it may be the ostrich." Baron Hoover guided his horse near Lord Fredrick's. "Looks like the hounds have sniffed her out after all. Always find it in the last place you look, eh, Freddy? Ha!"

The Earl of Maytag slid off his mount and walked right up to the edge of the POE. Before Bertha could evade him, he reached over the fence and plucked a plume from her tail, which made her hiss mightily.

"Hoover's right, Freddy. See for yourself." He handed the long, arched feather to Lord Fredrick. "An exotic creature, to be sure. Once she's stuffed she'll make a handsome addition to your study. You can put her next to the elephant's-foot umbrella stand."

Lord Fredrick held the feather close in front of his eyes, trying to focus. "Hmm," he muttered. "I was expecting something bigger—*woof*!"

"Stand back from my bird, if you please!" The bellow came from Admiral Faucet, who emerged from the POEHO and strode angrily toward the assembled hunting party. "The hounds did not find Bertha. I did—with a bit of help from the wolf children. So the ostrich is still mine, Ashton. Finders keepers, that's what you said." Faucet awkwardly petted the bird on the neck, which made her kick forward (for ostriches can only kick forward, due to the way their knees are built) and snap at him with her beak. He smiled through gritted teeth. "As you can see, she's all out of sorts from being away from me, poor creature. I'll thank everyone to leave her alone."

Lord Fredrick shrugged and scratched under his hunting cap. "Keep your blasted bird, Faucet. If I'd known the hunt would be such a bore, I'd have stayed in bed. Take my horse, Timothy; I'm done for the day. I need my headache lozenges, and a nap. And—*woof!*—keep Constance away from me, would you? She's been bombarding me with questions ever since Mother told her all that nonsense about full moons, *yap*! Pardon me." He glanced up at the sky with nervous, darting eyes. "Blasted head colds. They never last more than a day or so. . . ."

After Lord Fredrick left, the hunting party broke up. There was talk of a lavish dinner to be served later that evening, followed by cigars and brandy, card games and billiards. None of the men paid any mind to

Penelope or the children, although Baron Hoover did tip his hat in her direction as he turned to ride off. She acknowledged his greeting with the merest nod. They had met twice before: once at the disastrous holiday ball at Ashton Place, and once at a gentlemen's club in London, where Penelope and the children had been sent to deliver Lord Fredrick's misplaced almanac and where she had hoped to get some helpful advice from Judge Quinzy—this was before she learned that he was no judge, of course.

Penelope did not like or trust any of Lord Fredrick's society friends, but Baron Hoover seemed not quite as awful as the Earl of Maytag. However, his wife, the Baroness Hoover, was monstrous, rude, and condescending, and like the Earl of Maytag, she scarcely considered the Incorrigibles to be human. Penelope hoped that the presence of her husband did not mean the baroness was now being entertained at the house as well. Even Lady Constance, who seemed to naturally prefer phony, ill-mannered people over gentle, true-hearted ones, found the baroness to be unpleasant company.

And speaking of hearts, true and not so true, Admiral Faucet's lie about being the one to find Bertha did not sit well with Penelope. On the other hand, the bird was clearly better off with the admiral than with Lord Fredrick, so she had let it pass. Life in a POE was far from ideal, but it was better than being stuffed full of sawdust. At least, Penelope hoped Bertha would see it that way.

"Next to the elephant's-foot umbrella stand, he says. Why, the cheek!" the admiral fumed. "These men of the aristocracy have no vision—no heads for business! Life's been too cushy for them; that's the trouble. Once I come into possession of my start-up capital, and Faucet's Ostrich Extravaganza is up and running, they'll be falling over each other for tickets. Let's see who has the upper hand then. And don't forget, governess—ostrich racing is only the beginning." Mumbling his grand schemes, the admiral strode back toward the house. Penelope could swear she saw Bertha sigh with relief as he went.

" 'An apple with no worms is best, but the apple with one worm tastes better than the apple with two,' " she said to the bird, quoting the wisdom of Agatha Swanburne, although she had little hope that Bertha would understand. "And perhaps, someday, there will be a way to return you to your native habitat. Although Africa is certainly a long distance away."

"Come, dogs, come, dogs." Old Timothy summoned

the hounds with a low whistle. Until now they had been nosing around the POE, gobbling up dropped bits of SPOTs, and scampering between Bertha's legs as if she were one of them, only taller and two legged and not nearly as smart. At the sound of his whistle, the dogs ran to Old Timothy's feet and sat in four neat rows, tongues out, their droopy ears lifted, waiting for his next command.

"You do have a knack with animals, Timothy," Penelope said approvingly. "Dr. Westminster would be impressed with your training techniques. . . ." But then her voice trailed off.

"Westminster, eh? Sounds like a fine gent. Penny for your thoughts, miss?" The remark startled Penelope out of her reverie, for "Penny" is what Miss Mortimer always called her, and no one else ever did. In this case, of course, Old Timothy meant "penny" as in a small amount of money; "Penny for your thoughts" was his way of asking what Penelope was thinking about.

In fact, she was thinking how unfortunate it was that poor Bertha had ended up so far from her original home and family, and how the bird might perhaps be worried that she would never see them again. "Just like me, and like the Incorrigible children as well," she thought with a wave of sadness. Of course she had no idea if ostriches cared about that sort of thing; perhaps there was some advantage to having a skull full of eyeballs instead of brains. But to Old Timothy, she merely said, "I was thinking that the children have been working on a guidebook about birds. You may borrow it if you like."

"And why would I want to do that?" he said with a sneer.

Penelope smiled through misty eyes. She could see through his gruffness now, or thought she could. "I heard Lord Fredrick say that all of these perfectly trained dogs could hardly tell one bird from another today." She touched Timothy's arm and gave him a knowing look. "Now, why do you suppose that was?"

The enigmatic coachman tilted his head to one side. "Couldn't say, miss. But even a bloodhound from Scotland Yard gets a head cold now and then. Say, looks like you've got a spot of mustard there on your skirt. Best ask Margaret to get that out for you, before the stain sets."

With another short, low whistle and the crook of a finger, he bade the dogs follow him. Then he wheeled and walked off without so much as a good-bye, but with two orderly columns of beagles marching in step behind him. Even their tails wagged in unison: hup, hup, hup, hup.

It was not until much later, after Penelope and the children had removed their pith helmets and lined them up on the nursery shelf, taken off their stained and rumpled safari outfits, bathed and changed into fresh, clean clothes, eaten a hot, home-cooked supper in the nursery, and settled in for a bedtime read-aloud (Penelope put *Robinson Crusoe* away for the time being, and instead chose to read from her book of German poetry in translation, in particular the poem called "Wanderlust," which was fast becoming the children's favorite, as well as her own)–it was only then, after the poem had been read and the children tucked into bed, and Penelope had returned to the comforts of her own charming room to brush her dark, drab hair one hundred strokes before bedtime, that it occurred to her to wonder: "How did Old Timothy know it was mustard?"

The Eleventh Chapter

A request for help of a supernatural kind is sent, by post.

When Admiral Faucet claimed that nature is "red in tooth and claw," he was actually quoting a Mr. Thomas Hobbes, who lived in England quite a long time before Miss Penelope Lumley's day. To give you an idea of just how long, imagine Agatha Swanburne herself as a laughing, red-cheeked girl being given piggyback rides by the family gardener. On that distant, sunny summer afternoon, Mr. Hobbes had already been dead for nearly a century.

No doubt some of you find it strange to picture little Agatha as a child, after hearing her described so many times as the wise old founder of the Swanburne Academy for Poor Bright Females, but it is a scientific fact: Everyone who is old was young once. Even the very last dodo on earth started out as a baby dodo, full of hope and promise. Of course, this raises the question: If Baby Last Dodo had known that he or she would be the final specimen of the dodo kind, would BLD have taken more precautions about avoiding head colds and looking both ways at street crossings and so forth? Alas, we shall never know, and it is too late to go back and change things now, but pondering such deep and unanswerable questions is the job of philosophers—which brings us back to Mr. Hobbes.

For Mr. Thomas Hobbes was, in fact, a philosopher. When he claimed that nature was "red in tooth and claw," he meant that in a true state of nature, without laws and governments to keep things orderly, without strict rules of good manners, firm bedtimes, fines for overdue library books, and so on, that all human beings would simply do anything and everything they wished, for there would be nothing to stop them. The strong would bully the weak, the hungry would devour the tasty, library books would never be returned, and general mayhem would surely ensue. As he phrased it in Latin, *bellum omnium contra omnes*, which is to say, everyone would be at war with everyone else.

It sounds like a most unpleasant way to live, and one wonders what sort of dinner companion Mr. Hobbes would have made. Did he steal the last roll from the bread basket simply because he thought he could get away with it, or sneak out without paying his share of the check? Luckily, other philosophers had a more optimistic (no doubt Hobbes would say optoomuchstic) view of human nature. For example, Monsieur Jean-Jacques Rousseau believed that people were basically generous and kind, and that disagreeable behavior was caused by a poor upbringing and the corrupting influence of civilization. He was born in Switzerland, and we can only guess how he felt about edelweiss and alpine scenery, but about one thing we can be certain: Monsieur Rousseau had never met Admiral Faucet.

For one thing, they lived in different centuries. For another, the admiral was something straight out of Hobbes: Personal gain was his only motive, and the well-being of others did not figure into his thinking at all. This was made clear the day after Penelope and the children returned from their adventure in the forest, when Penelope overheard the admiral regaling Lady Constance and the Widow Ashton about his business plans, now that Bertha was back in his possession.

She did not mean to eavesdrop, of course. She was merely on her way back from a visit to Lord Fredrick's library. There she had assembled an ambitious stack of books about stalactites, stalagmites, troglobites, and other cave-oriented topics, and one slim volume about cannibals, too. This last book was for her own edification and not the children's. Even so, she promised herself that she would not read so much as a paragraph within an hour of her bedtime, for it seemed the kind of tale that was likely to cause bad dreams.

"And truly, there is nothing to fret about," she told herself as she made her way down the hall, arms laden with books. Now that she and the children were back among the comforts of civilization, with its well-stocked libraries, soft featherbeds, and endless cups of tea (served hot, in pretty china cups with matching saucers), Penelope felt quite pleased with how their adventure in the forest had turned out.

For one thing, Bertha was safe from Lord Fredrick's grasp. "It was a pity she was snatched away from her native habitat to begin with, but things could be far worse. Bertha can compete in a few races and then retire to a pleasant farm somewhere, just as the Derby horses do." The books were stacked so high in front of her that she could barely see over them, but Penelope would know the way from the library to the nursery blindfolded, and she was lost in thought in any case. "The life of a professional athlete is a difficult one, but it has its rewards. The thrill of victory among them, of course! And she seemed to enjoy those SPOTs a great deal."

Penelope felt so cheerful she began to lift her knees higher, as if marching, hup, hup, hup. "The admiral ought to be satisfied now as well. I fear his interest in the widow is more mercenary than romantic, but even between the two of them, things might turn out better than they look on the surface." As you see, her optimism was already running away with her. This is what comes of getting a proper sleep and a hot breakfast after surviving a difficult adventure in the wilderness. "But that is their business, not mine. What matters is that now he will be fully occupied with his ostrich-racing business and forget all those unsettling things he said about the children."

Best of all, now that they were home, Penelope could resume teaching properly, with all the necessary equipment close at hand. Cave geology! Extinct flightless birds! The relative speeds of land animals! She had so many ideas for lessons she could scarcely wait to get back to the nursery and begin. "And if the children are less than eager to resume their studies, it is no matter," she told herself, as she hup, hup, hupped down the hallway. "For today I must write Simon a letter describing our adventures, and that will take some time, for so very much has happened. Wait until I tell him about the surprisingly cozy cave! And the mysteriously appearing sandwiches! And Mama Woof, and the others. Luckily, it has all ended happily. Tra la!"

That was when she found herself outside the parlor in which Admiral Faucet, Lady Constance, and the Widow Ashton were taking coffee. The admiral's voice boomed like cannon fire.

"The brain of an ostrich is tiny. No bigger than the brain of a squirrel. It has room for three ideas: running, eating, and laying eggs. Notice running comes first. They're all legs! You can ask the governess; she's lurking in the doorway there. She had a wild ride on the back of one—didn't you, governess?"

"I was not lurking, but merely passing by on my way back from the library." Penelope hefted the stack of books in her arms as evidence and managed a small curtsy to the ladies. "Good afternoon. And an ostrich is not all legs. There is a comfortable layer of feathers on top."

The admiral waved away her comment. "Feathered or not, the ostrich is nature's perfect racing machine. The meat is awfully tasty, too."

The heavy stack of books in Penelope's arms slipped to the floor. "I beg your pardon, Admiral. When you say tasty, surely you do not mean . . . ?"

"When I say tasty, I mean tasty! Yum, yum! Delicious cooked on an open flame, with a nice onion sauce. No sense keeping an athlete in harness once she's past her prime. I'll race the birds and breed the champions, of course, to improve the stock. And then to Faucet's Ostrich Premium Steakhouse they go. I'll introduce the savory tenderness of ostrich meat to English society. Imagine how much people will pay to eat a juicy grilled slab of last year's derby champion! I can sell stakes in the steaks while they're still racing. Stakes in the steaks, har har!"

Lady Constance sipped her coffee and tittered politely, although she showed no other sign of having been listening; in fact she seemed half asleep. The Widow Ashton wore yet another gloomy yet fashionable head covering from her extensive wardrobe of mourning caps; the veil covered her face so that her reaction could not be seen.

Penelope hastily gathered up her books. She thought of the dreaded figure of Mr. Alpo, from the Giddy-Yap, Rainbow! tales, who disposed of unwanted ponies by taking them to the slaughterhouse. Bertha was nowhere near as cute as a pony. But what did cuteness have to do with it? Surely they had not saved her from the taxidermic fate Lord Fredrick planned for her, only to have her end her days as the chef's special at an ostrich steakhouse? Make no mistake: Penelope had eaten her share of tasty meat dishes, but the thought of eating a Bertha burger, after all they had been through together, made her feel like . . . like . . .

"Like a cannibal," she thought, staring down at the slim book on the top of the pile. *An Encounter with the Man-Eating Savages of Ahwoo-Ahwoo, as Told by the Cabin Boy and Sole Survivor of a Gruesomely Failed Seafaring Expedition Through Parts Unknown: Absolutely Not to Be Read by Children Under Any Circumstances, and That Means You,* it was called.

"And those wolf children wards that your son took in. They're another stroke of genius! My genius, of course, not his. Picture it: the Wolf Derby of Ashton Place. Real racing wolves, ridden by half-human, half-cub jockeys. It will be a sensation."

The widow's veil puffed at intervals as she spoke, like a tiny black lace curtain caught in a gusty breeze. "It sounds rather dangerous, dear. Are you sure the children will enjoy it?"

"I wouldn't call them children, dearest. You should have seen them as I saw them, out in nature. Wild beasts, they are. Savage, drooling, clawing things. Barking and howling at every turn. They're the ones who are dangerous. But the fiercer, the better. It'll sell more tickets that way." The admiral leaned forward in his chair. "Speaking of tickets, we'll need massive amounts of publicity to get started. Posters, handbills, advertisements in all the newspapers. I'll build the finest racetracks in England for the ostriches and the wolf children, with a POE and a PIE installed at each one. . . . All the restaurant equipment will be imported from France. . . . I'll need snappy uniforms designed for the staff. . . ."

The admiral's voice droned on until it was like the buzzing of those pesky gnats that had given Penelope no peace in the forest. But this time she could not simply swat the truth away. How could she have failed to see it? They might have postponed Bertha's fate, but they had not altered it. And in helping Bertha, the children had caught the admiral's eye, and now they, too, had become part of his cold-blooded moneymaking schemes. "He must be stopped," she thought, feeling desperate. "But how?"

"It all sounds very promising, of course." The veil billowed and danced in front of the widow's mouth. "But racetracks, restaurants . . . there are so many things to build. How much of my money do you think you will need?"

"Not your money, darling. Our money." The admiral reached over and took her hand, and his voice turned sweet and gooey as pancake syrup. "If there's one thing I've learned being a brave and famous explorer, it's this: Life is short, and full of peril. We are not children, Hortense. Let us grab what happiness we can, while we can." At this, the admiral lumbered out of his armchair and got down on one knee. "Answer me now, Hortense. Will you consent to be my bride?"

"A wedding!" Lady Constance snapped out of her daze and clapped her hands. "How marvelous! I will need many new dresses for all the parties we will have! Say yes, Mother Ashton, and I will summon my dressmaker at once."

The Widow Ashton lifted her head and pushed back her veil. "Fawsy, dear, your devotion moves me, truly it does. And no one knows better than I do that life is full of peril, tragic loss, unforeseen catastrophe, gruesome ends, and the like. My head tells me I ought to give you the answer you seek, and yet . . . my heart sings a different song. . . ." Her long, tragic sigh was like the final wheezing note played on the last accordion in all the world, moments before accordions became extinct. "If I could only know what my dear dead Edward would want me to do! But no one can speak to those who have passed Beyond the Veil."

Once more Penelope dropped her books, for the solution had just hit her like a thunderbolt. "The Veil" she cried, unable to conceal her excitement. "The Veil!"

"I think it should be an *enormous* veil!" Lady Constance exclaimed. "Miles of tulle, everywhere! Pish posh on all those who say second weddings should be quiet affairs. I vote for a lavish dress, a veil and train, and as many parties as we can fit in. Try not to be so clumsy, Miss Lumley; that is the second time you have dropped your books. I try never to carry books myself, as they are much too weighty to be lifted in a ladylike fashion. So many words!"

The widow stood. "I shall have to make up my own mind, it seems. Give me an hour, Fawsy dear. I need to spend time in quiet contemplation, as the good Sisters of Perpetual Sobbing taught me to do when my heart was troubled. You shall hear my answer upon my return."

The admiral leaped to his feet and kissed both her hands. "There is only one answer possible, dear. You could not dare refuse me—for to do so would be to break my heart," he added, with a warning glance at Penelope. "One hour, no more. In the meantime, I will arrange for champagne to be served, so that we might toast our engagement at once."

"How well I know the pain of a broken heart," the widow murmured, extricating her hands from the admiral's. She nodded a good-bye and left the room.

There was a satisfied spring in the admiral's step as he bounded off to arrange the toast. Penelope wrapped her arms securely around the books and readied herself to follow. "I must speak to the widow at once," she thought. "But I will wait a count of three, so it does not appear I am chasing after her, and then I will excuse myself . . . one . . . two . . . three—"

"Put down those silly books, if you please, Miss Lumley, and fetch some paper and ink." The possibility of some new clothes had woken Lady Constance up handily. "I need to send a letter to my dressmaker, at once, and I am much too excited to hold a pen. A wedding! Think of all the parties we must have! Oh, how I love parties. Life is so dull and boring, tedious and uninteresting without them!"

LADY CONSTANCE KEPT PENELOPE IMPRISONED in the parlor for precisely three quarters of an hour as she dictated a series of letters to her dressmaker, hatmaker, shoemaker, and glovemaker. By this time the young governess was chomping at the bit, as is often said about racehorses. In other words, she was so desperate to leave and go in search of the Widow Ashton that she felt ready to burst out of her skin, and the *tick-tock, tick-tock, tick-tock* of the grandfather clock in the corner was only making things worse.

"It is like something out of Edgar Allan Poe," she thought with gritted teeth. "*Tick-tock, tick-tock*, says the clock–time is running out, and yet I am trapped here, while the widow is who knows where. It is enough to drive one mad! I must"–*tick-tock*–"I must"–*tick-tock*–"I must speak to her before she gives the admiral her answer!"

"Next we shall write to my favorite maker of petticoats, in Paris. You might want to take a moment to refill your inkpot, Miss Lumley, for I have a *great* deal to say on the subject of petticoats."

"Aaah!" Penelope cried in despair.

Lady Constance frowned. "Pardon me, Miss Lumley. Are you suffering from indigestion? If so, please keep your discomfort to yourself."

"Apologies, my lady, but I saw—a mouse!" Penelope pointed at Lady Constance's feet. "A wee mousie! Scampering there—yes, right underneath your chair!"

"*Eek!* More rodents! What has become of this house?" Lady Constance climbed on top of the end table and began squealing like a piggy; as you will recall, it was the second time that week.

"Never fear, Lady Constance. I shall get help," Penelope declared, as she ran to the door of the parlor. Lady Constance was now fully occupied with her squealing, and Penelope uttered a silent prayer of thanks as she finally made her escape, although she had to leave her pile of books behind.

"Never mind. I shall return for the books later, and Lady Constance is unlikely to bother with them in any case. Now: the race to find the widow begins. Full speed ahead! But where can she have gone?" She knew the Widow Ashton would be in quiet contemplation somewhere, for she had said so herself. And it had to be somewhere close by, for the widow had sworn she would give her answer in precisely an hour, which was not enough time to go far.

"Where would a person go for an hour of quiet contemplation?" Penelope ran to the most likely spots she could think of, but the widow was not in the chapel, or the gardens, or even hidden in a low branch of the enormous plane tree that stood about a hundred yards from the drive. (Penelope knew that the widow was unlikely to be up a tree, but it was where she herself might go if she wanted to think quietly for a bit, and therefore she felt it was worth a look.)

She ran back to the house and nearly collapsed in the foyer, where the entry clock provided unwelcome news. "*Tick-tock . . . tick-tock*–five minutes left!" Penelope thought, panting with exertion. "I know I shall find her in the last place I look, but what place ought that to be? *Tick-tock*–last place–*tick-tock*–last place–where would be the last place I would look?" Penelope spun in circles. "What did the Widow Ashton say? 'If only Edward could speak.' Edward Ashton! Eureka!"

She sprinted down the main hall, bounded up one flight of stairs and down another (two at a time), and then galloped down another long hall, until she arrived, red faced and winded, at the door of Lord Fredrick Ashton's study. How Penelope hated this room, with its display of dead animals and smell of stale cigar smoke!

The glass eyes of Lord Fredrick's taxidermy collection stared at her accusingly: the bear, the moose, the stags, the foxes, the many varieties of birds, and, of course, the elk. Their lifeless gazes seemed to follow her everywhere she moved.

But there among them, glassy-eyed with tears, perhaps, but still very much alive, was the Widow Ashton. She sat on a footstool with folded hands before the oversized portrait of her late husband, Lord Edward Ashton, which hung in a row with all the other ancestral portraits that lined the wall. The widow was bareheaded; her veiled mourning cap had been removed and was now perched on the corner of Lord Fredrick's elephant's-foot umbrella stand.

"My lady!" Penelope still struggled to catch her breath, but she had much to say and little time in which to say it. "Forgive me for intruding. I could not help overhearing your conversation with the admiral earlier, in the parlor. I had no wish to eavesdrop, believe me, but since I was there in the same room, it was impossible not to—in any case, I have something of great urgency to tell you."

The widow's eyes never moved from the portrait. "I cannot speak to you now, Miss Lumley. I have a grave decision to make. It is not easy to know what to do."

"Yes, I know. It is regarding the admiral's marriage proposal."

"Indeed. Now, please, leave me be. I have but a few moments left to think before my time is up. Then I must give my answer."

"That painting is of your husband, Edward," Penelope blurted. "You wish to speak to him."

"I do," the widow replied sadly. "Oh, how I do! But no one can speak to those who have passed to the Realm Beyond."

"I know someone who can!" Boldly, Penelope stepped between the widow and the portrait. "That is what I have come to tell you. There is a fortune-teller I met in London, a woman of spooky reputation. She has the power to see Beyond the Veil. If you so command, I will have her brought to Ashton Place." Penelope thought of Madame Ionesco: her short stature, the poor condition of her teeth, her collection of voluminous scarves, and her excellent recipe for Gypsy cakes, of which the children had grown quite fond. Would she come, if summoned? Could she even be found?

The Widow Ashton's pale cheeks went two shades paler still. She stood up and clasped Penelope by the arm. "If she truly has the gift you describe . . . do you think she could contact my Edward? Could she help me discover his wishes?"

Once more Penelope felt an icy shiver trickle along her spine. For when she and the children were in London, the semitoothless soothsayer had told Penelope some remarkable things—for example, that there was a curse upon the Incorrigible children. "Wolf babies," she had called them, and had added a warning, too: "The hunt is on!"

"If anyone can, she can," replied Penelope, and that, she believed, was nothing but the truth.

The widow closed her eyes for a moment. When she reopened them, she seemed filled with fresh purpose. She turned away from the portrait, picked up her mourning cap, and pinned it back on her head. With a gentle tug, she lowered the dark veil back over her face. "Please, send for your Gypsy, Miss Lumley. The admiral will have to wait a little longer for his answer, for I will decide nothing until she arrives—and until Edward has spoken."

Penelope nodded, scarcely able to hide her relief. Side by side, she and the widow turned and regarded the portrait of Edward Ashton. He was a big man, with a cold and penetrating stare. "He had such beautiful eyes," the widow murmured. "So dark and mysterious. How I loved to look into them."

". . . do you think she could contact my Edward? Could she help me discover his wishes?"

She turned her veiled gaze to Penelope. For a moment, Penelope could swear that Edward Ashton's painted eyes were now fixed on her as well. "I have been sitting here for nearly an hour, asking Edward for a clue, a hint, a sign," the Widow Ashton declared. "And it seems, Miss Lumley, that you are the answer he sent me."

THE INVISIBLE BEYOND! THE GREAT What's to Come! The Ineffable Realm of Unknowables! Penelope was so excited she could barely keep from galloping; with great willpower she held herself to a fast trot. First she went back to the parlor, from which a strained, piggylike squealing sound continued to emanate at regular intervals. Lady Constance was atop the table with her hands covering both eyes, since (in her view) mice that could not be seen would therefore be less likely to exist. Two anxious servants armed with feather dusters were already on their third inspection of every nook and cranny of the room.

However, as these were imaginary mice to begin with, getting rid of them was not nearly so complicated as all that. "All clear of mice," Penelope loudly announced as she whizzed into the parlor, gathered up the library books that she had left there, and whizzed out again. Even with her arms full, she fairly flew up the stairs to the nursery. There Mrs. Clarke sat cross-legged on the floor with Alexander, who was teaching her to play chess. Cassiopeia was adding more lines to her Poe poem, while Beowulf helpfully drew page after page of spooky ravens to inspire her.

"This rook's a handsome fellow, isn't he?" the housekeeper said as she moved the chess piece across the board. "A bit single-minded, though. He only goes in straight lines. That's bound to get dull, boring, tedious, and uninteresting after a bit."

"Cinnamins," Cassiopeia commented absently.

"Certainly, dear. After we're done here you can come to the kitchen with me and we'll ask Cook to make some sticky cinnamon buns, how's that?" Of course Cassiopeia actually meant synonyms, but it was all lost on Mrs. Clarke. However, the confusion about words prompted its own lesson, for the boys began discussing whether rooks and ravens were different names for the same kind of bird, or easily confused names for two different but similar kinds of birds, and how crows fit into the scheme of things, and whether all three sorts of birds (that is to say, rooks, ravens, and crows) could talk, or if none of them could, in which case Mr. Poe was obviously using his poetic license in having the particular raven in his poem shout "Nevermore!" whenever the rhyme scheme called for it.

"Eureka, I've got it!" Penelope exclaimed as she burst into the room and threw the library books in a heap in the corner.

"Got what, Miss Lumley? I hope it's not the chicken pox." Mrs. Clarke chuckled.

"No, not the chicken pox," Penelope cried, although just saying the words made her want to scratch. "When I say, 'Eureka, I've got it,' I mean, 'Eureka! I have figured out how to stop the admiral from'—well, from doing several unpleasant things that he ought not to do. And I feel sure I am performing the Widow Ashton a great service as well. But I need help. Quick, children, fetch me some paper suitable for urgent correspondence! Bring fresh ink and a quill. Mrs. Clarke, I am sorry to interrupt your chess game, but could you summon Jasper and have him at the ready to run a letter to the post, posthaste?"

"Jasper's got the day off today on account of his sister having a new baby and needing some extra help around the farm." Mrs. Clarke sprang lightly to her feet. "But don't you fear, Miss Lumley. If it's that important, I'll run the letter into town myself."

"It *is* that important," Penelope replied, but with

the three children gazing up at her, wide-eyed with curiosity, she had no intention of explaining just how mouthwatering the admiral's plans for Bertha were. Nor did she intend to tell them how he wanted to take possession of the Incorrigibles themselves and make them world famous as the Bloodthirsty Wolf Children of Ashton Place.

"You will do very well as our fleet-footed messenger, Mrs. Clarke. First, I must write the letter; I shall meet you downstairs in five minutes' time" was her answer. From the corner of her eye, she saw that the good-hearted housekeeper was only two moves away from being checkmated by Alexander, so it was just as well that she had offered to run to the post herself.

Penelope sat at the writing desk and smoothed the paper before her. How eagerly she had looked forward to writing Simon Harley-Dickinson about all their adventures in the forest! The storm, the cave, the sandwiches, the wolves, and, of course, the many fascinating varieties of ferns! But there was no time for all that now. She stuck to what was essential.

Dear Simon,

I write to you in urgent need of help. Please bring Madame Ionesco here to Ashton Place at once. I enclose money for train tickets and to cover Madame's fee, for her soothsaying services will be required upon her arrival.

With deepest thanks, from your friend,
Miss Penelope Lumley

Excusing herself briefly from the nursery, she ran to her bedchamber and stuffed the envelope with all the money that she had saved since taking the job as governess. She sealed the envelope with wax, using the seal that had been a graduation gift from Miss Mortimer. It was the Swanburne Academy emblem, a florid capital A entwined with a swirling letter S.

Downstairs she went to meet Mrs. Clarke, who waited for her at the servants' entrance on the first floor. The housekeeper had changed out of her usual buckled shoes and voluminous floral-print dress, and into a pair of sturdy boots and a borrowed shirt and trousers from one of the farmhands. Her hair was tied up, and she gave each leg a quick stretch. She was an odd sight, perhaps, but perfectly dressed for the occasion.

Penelope handed her the sealed letter. "Run quickly, Mrs. Clarke. The sooner this letter reaches its destination, the better."

"Will do, Miss Lumley. I've been picking up my pace of late. A jaunt like this is just what the doctor ordered."

A blink later, Mrs. Clarke was off and running. She was not as fast as an ostrich, or even a Derby-winning Thoroughbred, but still, when it came to being true hearted, Penelope knew she could not have chosen anyone better for the job.

Would Madame Ionesco prove as true? Would Simon? As Agatha Swanburne once said, "Sometimes there's nothing more to be done but have a cup of tea and sit and wait for the post." Which–after providing the children with a brief introduction to cave geology and making sure to hide the slim volume about cannibals between the covers of one of her Giddy-Yap, Rainbow! books, so she could locate it again later, privately, when the children were not looking–is precisely what Penelope did.

The Twelfth Chapter

A reunion is held, in secret.

"A séance! How perfectly entertaining! Why, they are all the rage. Just last month Lady Furbisher hosted a spiritualist at one of her notorious dinner parties—or do I mean legendary? I always get those two mixed up. In any case, it was a sensation! Everyone's fortune was told in secret. They say one of Lady Furbisher's daughters fainted when she heard what the fortune-teller had to say. Hmm, I think I like this one." Lady Constance tipped her head from one side to the other in front of her dressing-room mirror, the better to admire the elaborate chapeau that she had just placed upon her upswept curls. It was pale green silk, with an arrangement of peacock feathers extending upward from the brim. "But green is such a sickly shade. It makes my eyes look the color of seawater. Never mind, it is awful! Hand me another, please, Margaret."

"Aren't you afraid of ghosts, my lady?" Patient as ever, Margaret stood with an armload of hats for her mistress to try on and find fault with, one after another after another. "I surely am. I don't much like being around a dead animal, never mind a dead person. Just thinking about it makes my skin feel creepy-crawly all over."

"Creepy-crawly—wherever do you learn these expressions, Margaret? At least dead animals stay where you put them. They don't go skittering around beneath your chair and frightening you half to death!" Lady Constance peered into the mirror. "This one casts strange shadows across my nose. Most unattractive. Next, please."

"The butlers searched all over the house, ma'am. They swore they didn't see any mice."

"Just because one does not see something, that does not mean it isn't there," the lady replied, in an accidental moment of insight. "Why, for all we know there are unseen ghosts hovering about us in this very room, eavesdropping on every word we say. Halloo, ghosties! Look, Margaret, I think I see one waving back at us, there, in the mirror!"

This remark made Margaret squeak in terror. Lady Constance laughed at the poor girl's fright, which was really not a very nice thing to do. "Silly Margaret, I am only teasing you. Would you like to be mesmerized? I would! They say that once the mesmerist has you in a trance, you can be made to do anything, and you don't remember a scrap about it afterward. It sounds like wonderful fun. Look, there in the mirror! Another ghost! Boo! Oh, how ridiculous you sound when you shriek!" It went on that way for some time, with Lady Constance trying on one outlandish hat after another and making poor Margaret scream by pretending to see ghosts. Finally, Mrs. Clarke put an end to it by taking over the hat-holding duty herself and sending Margaret down to the kitchen to recover.

Clearly, Lady Constance was in high spirits. That the possible marriage of the Widow Ashton and Admiral Faucet had provided an excuse to shop for new outfits was one reason for her merry mood. The other was her belief (which was really more of a wish) that, once remarried, her mother-in-law would take a long honeymoon and then set up her household somewhere far away with her new husband. "After all, Admiral Faucet is a fearless explorer of Parts Unknown," Lady Constance gaily confided to Mrs. Clarke, after poor Margaret had been sent away. "They might decide to live anywhere. The North Pole, for instance; explorers seem drawn to it for some reason. Or even Canada."

"I hope they don't move that far away, my lady," said Mrs. Clarke. "It's a great comfort to have family close by, and Lord Ashton has hardly seen his mother for many years as it is."

Lady Constance was done with the hats and had now moved on to gloves, which she tugged on and off in rapid succession. "Let us be frank, Mrs. Clarke. The woman makes Fredrick anxious. Personally I find her conversation unwholesome. All those horrible tales of death and tar pits! It is enough to curl anyone's hair, even in dry weather. Why some people persist in talking about unpleasant topics I shall never know. Thank goodness Fredrick is not like that. He hardly says a word, and when he does I rarely understand what he means. But at least he does not bore me into a stupor with talk of strange moonsicknesses and 'nothing left but his precious hat.'" She lowered her voice to the sort of loud, gossipy whisper that fairly begs to be overheard. "I know the Widow Ashton is

Fredrick's mother, but truthfully, I am not sure what the admiral sees in her. Except her fortune, of course! Ha ha!"

But this was no joke, as Penelope well knew: It *was* the Widow Ashton's fortune that the admiral craved. The widow apologized to the admiral for the delay, but her position was clear: She would neither accept nor decline his offer of marriage until after the séance. "It will be better for both of us if I can entertain your proposal knowing that I have Edward's blessing," she explained. "For a half-hearted marriage is no marriage at all. Surely you agree, Fawsy dear?"

According to Mrs. Clarke, who reported on the whole situation to Penelope, the admiral grumbled and said, "I'll wait if I must, but time is money, dear. I need to have more ostriches shipped from Africa as soon as possible, before the bad weather sets in. Wouldn't want our future champions to be shipwrecked on some unmapped island somewhere and get eaten by cannibals!"

Of course, if the residents of this hypothetical island ate ostriches, they would not, strictly speaking, be cannibals (unless they themselves were ostriches, that is). But Penelope was too distracted by her own concerns to point this out to Mrs. Clarke. The fleet-footed housekeeper had made the previous day's post with time to spare, but still, it would take a day for Penelope's letter to get to London, and a day for Simon's reply to come back, assuming he answered her at once. Had she been foolish to promise something to the widow that she could not yet guarantee would happen? Perhaps, but she had faith in Simon. At the very least, her suggestion that Madame Ionesco conduct a séance to speak to the spirit of Edward Ashton had bought Bertha and the Incorrigible children some time.

As for Lord Fredrick, who had miraculously recovered from his brief spell of barking and scratching (which happened to coincide exactly with the full moon)—well, it all seemed a bit too much for him to take in, according to Mrs. Clarke. "Mother getting married? Some quack fortune-teller raising the dead, in my own home? Not sure how I feel about any of it, frankly. If anyone is looking for me, I'll be at my club."

SIMON'S REPLY CAME IN THE evening post on the second day. "Will do," it read in his own dear, sweet, familiar cursive, with its poetic loops and flourishes. "Expect us on the morning train. Don't trouble yourself to meet us; sounds like your hands are full enough with plot twists already. We'll hire a carriage at the station. Yours, SHD."

Penelope was giddy with gratitude. That night, after

the children were tucked in and she was near bedtime herself, she could not concentrate on her own book, but instead found herself conjuring up an assortment of flattering definitions for the acronym SHD, which, of course, stood for Simon Harley-Dickinson, "but in Simon's case might just as easily mean Steadfast, Humane, and Dependable," she thought. "Or Sensible, High-minded, and Decent. Or Stalwart, Handsome, and Deserving." She felt a twinge of embarrassment about the "handsome," but she had run out of H's and, frankly, she did find Simon pleasing to look at. "It must be the neoclassical symmetry of his eyebrows," she murmured, and pretended to sketch those very eyebrows in the margin of her book with a fingertip. "They are perfectly arranged, see: One over each eye–and, oh my!–he will be here, at Ashton Place, tomorrow!"

She placed the book on her bedside table. It was the cannibal adventure she had found in Lord Fredrick's library. Despite her vow to avoid this disturbing tale before bedtime, she had been unable to resist taking a peek. Unfortunately (or perhaps fortunately), she found the text difficult to understand, as it was all handwritten in blotchy ink that looked as if it had weathered many a storm at sea. Not only that, but the whole gruesome tale was set in rhyming verse of a most eccentric nature.

Penelope enjoyed poetry as a rule, but this volume was too peculiar to easily make sense of. If she were not already in her nightgown and under the covers, she would have gladly traded it in for lighter fare, such as *All the Pretty Ponies*, in which Edith-Anne decides to get a second pony to keep Rainbow company (but who could have known that Rainbow would be so jealous?), or even the plodding and preachy *Rainbow Goes to Work*, in which Rainbow spends an unhappy summer as a pony for hire, while Edith-Anne is sent off to stay with her sick aunt in Norfolk.

"But who can concentrate on books at a time like this?" the perplexed young governess thought, which just goes to show what an unusual state of mind she was in. "Simon will be here tomorrow morning–and he says 'Expect *us*,' which must mean he has persuaded Madame Ionesco to come as well. I shall have to intercept them before they arrive at the house, so I can fill them in on the details of our scheme . . . but however shall I manage it?"

With that, she put her book down and blew out the bedside candle. She was tired, to be sure, but there was still a great deal of plotting and planning to do regarding this séance, and scant time in which to do it. She even had a fleeting worry about what she ought to wear for Simon's arrival.

"Unimportant," she thought, yawning. "Immaterial. Doesn't matter. Perhaps my brown worsted . . ."

"When in doubt, sleep on it." So said Agatha Swanburne, according to a great many hand-stitched pillows at Penelope's alma mater. As usual, the wise lady was correct. Within minutes of waking, the tangle of problems that had flummoxed Penelope so thoroughly the previous evening had somehow sorted themselves into neat skeins of wool, as it were.

Armed with a clear head, fresh purpose, and a quick but nourishing breakfast, Penelope flew out of the house an hour past dawn, found Old Timothy polishing the doors of the brougham, and asked the enigmatic coachman if he could take her halfway to the train station and then wait on the road so she might flag down a carriage. To his credit, he did not ask any questions but simply nodded and put a horse in harness.

Penelope sat in the backseat and chewed her lip the whole way. It was not only that she half wished she had chosen the navy-blue dress rather than the brown, although that did cross her mind. It was because her plan about the séance, which had seemed so simple and foolproof when she first thought of it, now appeared to have more holes in it than a mole-infested garden. "Truly," she thought, "it is not easy to make plans that involve the supernatural, for who can predict the behavior of the dearly departed?"

The very thought made her shiver, for as much as Penelope liked to think of herself as scientifically minded, with finely honed powers of deduction and a sensible Swanburne-trained head on her shoulders, in fact she was just as superstitious as the next person. This should come as no surprise, for in Miss Lumley's day, séances, Ouija boards, hypnotic healings, and the like were very much in fashion. In fact, they were nearly as popular as ferns (and ferns were wildly popular in Miss Lumley's day, and may well be ripe for a comeback, as they are both attractive and easy to grow). It was only now, on her way to explain her plan to the soothsayer herself, that Penelope began to consider just what kind of haunted bucket of worms she might be opening up by proposing that Madame Ionesco attempt to communicate with the dead.

"Penny for your thoughts, miss?"

There, he had said it again. Just hearing the word "penny" made her think of Miss Mortimer, who no doubt would be full of excellent and pithy advice right now. With no reason to lie, she answered, "I am thinking about the séance that the Widow Ashton plans to have."

"A dangerous business, that. Some holes are better left undug. Unless you already know what's buried, a' course."

Something about his remark made Penelope sit up straight. "What do you mean by that?"

"I mean, some presents are better left unopened. Unless you already know what's in 'em, a' course."

Penelope felt certain he was trying to make a point, and one that might prove useful to her, but what was it? "I am sorry, Timothy, but I still cannot quite understand what you mean. Perhaps if you say it slowly?"

The old coachman grunted in annoyance and spoke at a snail's pace. "What I mean is, some questions are best left unasked. Unless you already know the answer–"

"A' course!" Penelope exclaimed, for the answer she was seeking had just come to her. "And eureka," she added, but softly, for now she had that much more to think about.

They rode in silence for the better part of an hour, until Timothy brought the brougham to a stop just before the crest of a hill, near the forest's edge. From there they would see any oncoming travelers long before they could be seen themselves. Soon the rhythmic thud of hoofbeats on earth alerted them that another carriage approached.

"That's them, I'll wager," said Old Timothy, peering into the distance. "I recognize the coach; that driver often takes fares from the station." With a few clucks and some skillful handling of the reins, he urged the horse to pull their carriage sideways, blocking the way.

With a fluttering heart, Penelope climbed out and stood in the middle of the road, waving her arms. The oncoming carriage came closer and closer still. Finally it stopped, and the driver began to scold.

"Have you lost your mind, miss? This is a carriage road; it's no place to be doing your morning calisthenics. Move along, now."

"Simon!" she called, jumping up and down, for she was sure she had spotted him inside.

"Simon says, jumping jacks, I don't care what you call it! Now step aside and let me pass."

"What's the hurry, driver?" The door of the carriage swung open, and Simon leaped out; a moment later he stood before Penelope, grinning. "Miss Lumley–I mean, Penelope–what a perfect treat it is to see you! Feels like a long time, and no time at all, if you follow my meaning."

"Hello!" she cried, and then said it again, since she

was so very glad to see him. "Hello!" The two of them stood staring and beaming at each other. Awkwardly, Penelope held out a hand. Simon shook it vigorously.

Penelope looked around. "And . . . where is Madame?"

He jerked his head toward the carriage he had just left. "Sound asleep in the cab. Dreaming of other dimensions, I bet. Pardon me for asking, but what are you doing out here on the road?"

She took a step closer and spoke quietly, so that the carriage driver would not hear. "Mr. Harley-Dickinson–I mean, Simon–upon reflection I realized it would be best for me to intercept you before you reached Ashton Place, so that you and I might speak in private about the reasons for my summons. I have my own carriage and driver here."

"The plot is afoot, eh?" Simon scratched his chin. "We could switch carriages altogether, but I hate to wake Madame. She was muttering the most interesting things in her sleep. I was hoping for a clue about the Great What's to Come, or a forecast for tomorrow's weather, at least."

"Your driver can take Madame Ionesco. She is expected at the house and will be warmly welcomed. You can ride back with me." She lowered her voice even more. "It may be better if we speak out of Madame's hearing as well."

He arched one of those perfectly formed eyebrows. "Right-o, then. I'll get my bag. Didn't bring much, but I wouldn't want to be without a pen and paper at a time like this. Inspiring things are bound to happen."

It took but a moment for Simon to remove his traveling satchel from one carriage and move it into the other. The coach carrying Madame was dispatched to Ashton Place. After giving the other driver a generous head start, Timothy muttered something about taking the long way back to the house so they might better enjoy the scenery. Then he chuckled and clucked the horse to a lazy walk.

Now that Simon was finally here (and sitting next to her, in the backseat, rather close!), Penelope could scarcely decide what to say first, and the whole story tumbled out in a mad rush. She explained about the Widow Ashton's arrival with Admiral Faucet, and quickly sketched her adventure with the children in the forest, in pursuit of Bertha.

"But now the admiral plans to make Bertha into a champion ostrich racer, and then, when her racing days are through, turn her into . . ." She searched for a kind way to say it, but the best word she could come up with was "Victuals. With onion sauce."

"Onion sauce!" exclaimed Simon. "What a way to go. Poor old bird."

"Not only that. He wants the children to be part of his exhibition as well, the 'Bloodthirsty Wolf Children of Ashton Place,' or some such nonsense. But without the Widow Ashton's money, he can do none of what he plans. He has proposed marriage to her in the most flowery terms, but I am sure he is only after her fortune. The widow is unsure about marrying him but seems inclined to do so anyway—unless she knows for a fact that her dear dead husband, Edward Ashton, would not approve. Therefore . . ." She paused for breath, for she had been talking nonstop. "I have persuaded her that we must have a séance."

Simon stroked his chin in that thoughtful way of his. "A séance? Ah-ha! So Madame Ionesco has been summoned to deliver the message from dead Edward, from Beyond the Veil! Dead Edward says no, the wedding is off, and the admiral can go look for another rich widow to fleece. Brilliant scheme, if you don't mind me saying so."

"I do not mind," she said, rather formally, but inside she was very pleased.

"One potential glitch, as far as I can see: What if

dead Edward says yes?"

"I have thought of that as well," Penelope replied, for this is precisely what had made her say "Eureka!" earlier. "First–and I mean no disrespect to her soothsaying abilities–but I feel it is far from certain that Madame Ionesco will truly be able to summon the shade of Edward Ashton. Do you agree?"

Simon glanced around, as if making sure no ghostly eavesdroppers could hear them. "I remain agnostic on that point. If anyone can, Madame Ionesco can, that much I will say. But that doesn't mean anyone can, does it?"

Penelope nodded. "The fortune-teller may have a true gift, but the situation is unpredictable, and we must plan for various outcomes. As Agatha Swanburne once said, 'Trust whom you like, but rely on yourself.' Therefore I propose that someone with a keen sense of the theatrical, a talent for mimicry and improvising dialogue–a playwright, perhaps?–be engaged as an understudy to the ghost, as it were."

Simon's face lit up. "Aha! So if the shade of Edward Ashton fails to appear on command, or does appear but provides an answer other than the one we require, this playwright you mention could take over the role, so to speak."

"Precisely." Penelope was so excited that she wanted to jump up and down and clap her hands, but of course this was impossible while sitting in the backseat of a carriage. Instead she smiled and said, "Simon, your gleam of genius is undimmed. Will you do it?"

"Will I? Just try to stop me! They say that Shakespeare himself played the role of Hamlet's father's ghost! I'll be walking in the footsteps of giants, and once again, Miss Lumley–Penelope–the adventure is all thanks to you. Before we met, my life was dull and boring! Tedious and uninteresting! But no more."

The carriage stopped.

"Is it the wheel?" Simon asked, ready to leap out. "I must confess, I have a knack for fixing a broken spoke. Shall I take a look?"

"The wheels are fine. Just giving the horse a breather." Which was an odd thing for Old Timothy to say, frankly, since the horse had been walking at a leisurely pace the whole time. The coachman stared straight ahead, but his words were directed at Penelope. "The young gentleman won't be staying at the house, I take it?"

Old Timothy's face was as blank as a mask. Penelope began to say something to the enigmatic coachman but stopped as the good sense of his remark sank in. She turned to Simon. "Timothy is correct. You must forgive my lack of hospitality, Simon. But given the secret role you will be called upon to play at the séance, I think it is best that you remain unseen for now. If no one knows you are here, you cannot fall under suspicion."

"There's a kind of logic in that," he agreed. "Although I hope we're not just sticking our heads in the sand about it all. Say, do you think we ought to tell Madame Ionesco about this understudy business? It's not so easy to pull the wool over the eyes of a prognosticator, after all."

Penelope frowned, for this indeed was the last and deepest mole hole in her scheme, and the one in which she feared they were most likely to step and twist an ankle, so to speak. "I would not want to insult her, of course. But if she knew what we intend, she might object to conducting the séance to begin with. . . ."

With a soft "hey-yah" from Old Timothy, the carriage resumed its slow progress. By the time they reached the edge of the parkland that surrounded the house, Simon and Penelope had reluctantly decided that it would be best not to tell Madame about their plan to have Simon step into the role, should the ghost of Edward Ashton fail to appear. Whether this would prove to be the right decision or not remained to be seen. But Bertha's life was at "steak" (if you will forgive the pun), and the children's safety and future hung in the balance as well. Much as they regretted the dishonesty, they felt they had no choice.

Without being told, Timothy turned the carriage down a side road that led to some humble farmhouses nearby. Arrangements were quickly made for Simon to stay with Jasper's family, whom Penelope recalled could use the extra help because of the new baby. The family was delighted by the visit and gladly accepted Simon as a local lad recommended by that clever young governess at Ashton Place who had worked such miracles with Lord Ashton's wild wolf children. Simon also proved to have a knack for calming a squalling infant, so he was quickly put to work. In the hubbub, Simon and Penelope had no real chance to say good-bye, but she whispered a promise to send a message later on, with details about when and where the séance would take place, as soon as it had been arranged.

Timothy drove the carriage back up to the main road and then proceeded to Ashton Place, where he discreetly stopped a short way behind the barn, out of view of the main house. As Penelope climbed out, she shyly mentioned that she hoped there would be no need for Old Timothy to mention their early-morning excursion to anyone.

He snorted in disdain and looked at her with his changeable, cockeyed stare. "A true coachman never says where he's been, miss. Or tells where he's going."

"I am glad to hear it–"

"A coachman who repeats what he overhears in the backseat of a carriage wouldn't keep a job for very long, make no mistake."

"I appreciate your discretion–"

"And I've been a coachman for a very long time. Since before you were born, and for some years before that, too. What I hear, I don't hear, if you know what I mean."

"Thank you," she said simply, for she had no wish to provoke him further. He undid the harness and led the horse away to the stables, clucking and talking softly the whole way, with promises of a good rubdown with a towel and a currycomb, followed by a breakfast of oats after the beast was cool enough to eat.

Watching him left Penelope with two very different ideas to ponder as she walked up the drive back to the house. The first was how nice it was to see someone treating a horse with such care and respect. Naturally, it made her think of Edith-Anne Pevington and

Rainbow, but to try to draw any further comparison between the grouchy, bow-legged old coachman and the fictional rosy-cheeked heroine would be absurd. "Dr. Westminster had a similarly nice way with animals," she said to herself. "Perhaps that is what I am reminded of now."

Her second thought was how odd and thoroughly unexpected it was that, of all the people she had met since coming to live at Ashton Place, it was Old Timothy whom she had come to rely upon the most. Whether that, too, would prove a mistake also remained to be seen. But there was no more time to puzzle over it, for she had already missed breakfast with the children, and although she had left detailed instructions for them about how they were to begin their morning lessons without her, even from where she stood, she could spot Beowulf leaning perilously close to the nursery window.

"Cuckoo!" he yelled excitedly as he saw her approach. He pointed at a nearby tree limb. "Cuckoo! Cuckoo!"

"Careful, Beowulf!" she called up to the window. She broke into a run. "Careful! I am on my way!"

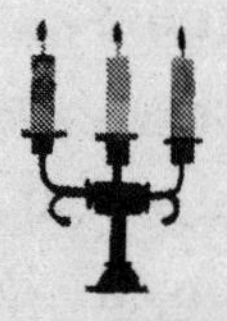

The Thirteenth Chapter

Shocking news arrives from Beyond the Veil.

Lady Constance was wildly excited about the arrival of the soothsayer and had instructed the household staff to welcome Madame Ionesco as a visiting dignitary. "Think of her as an ambassador from the Realm Invisible," she said, as if this selfsame Realm were nothing more than a midsized European nation that just happened to be populated with the spirits of the dead. There was scant time to make arrangements, but Mrs. Clarke ordered a lovely bouquet to be cut from the gardens, and a ruddy-cheeked bagpiper in a kilt was hired to play a fanfare of greeting that broadcast its nasal echo for miles around.

"What a racket," Madame Ionesco said appreciatively of the bagpiper, as she stumbled half asleep from the hired carriage and flashed her semitoothless grin. "If that's not enough to wake the dead, nothing is. What a good sleep I had! Did I miss breakfast? Some eggs and bacon would be all right. Porridge on the side. I take milk and three sugars with my tea. Keep the flowers, honey; they make me sneeze. And somebody pay the driver, that's a dear."

A hearty meal was hastily prepared and served in the dining room, although the table was only set for one, as Lady Constance had already eaten and Lord Fredrick wanted no part of this "prognosticational poppycock," as he called it. Lady Constance chatted as the soothsayer ate and pressed her for details about the séance. Should musicians be engaged to enhance the spooky atmosphere? Where should the guests sit for the best view of the supernatural proceedings? Would the ghostly visitors from Beyond the Veil require place settings for food and drink? And so on.

Instead of answering these questions directly, Madame finished her meal and announced her pressing need for a glass of sherry and a meditative

"If that's not enough to wake the dead, nothing is."

nap, so she might commune with the spirits in earnest. Straightaway she was installed in a large and luxurious guest room that Lady Constance selected especially for her. It was nicknamed the Egyptian Room because of the decor, which included a glass table held up by a pair of lifelike sculpted cheetahs (complete with painted-on spots), an antique clock that did not run but was in the shape of an obelisk, and a portrait of Cleopatra hanging above the washbasin. "Ruler of all Egypt, can you imagine? However did she find the time? Perhaps we can ask her ourselves at the séance, tee hee!" Lady Constance remarked gaily to Madame Ionesco, who nodded and yawned.

Margaret was instructed to carry Madame's small bundle of belongings upstairs and turn down the bed. She did what was asked of her, but the poor girl was so terrified of the Gypsy's mystical abilities that her knees knocked and her eyes stayed fixed on the floor. Madame Ionesco reached up and patted her on the cheek as she passed. "Don't worry, honey. Whatever the letter J means, it's all going to work out, just you wait and see." This made Margaret squeal and shriek all over again, but this time with delight, for it was well-known among the household staff that she and Jasper were on particularly friendly terms.

"But why were we not invited to greet Madame as well?" the Incorrigibles complained when Penelope finally arrived at the nursery, hauled Beowulf away from the window, and explained what all the ruckus and bagpiping had been about. Of course, she left out any mention of Simon, whose presence needed to be kept secret.

"You shall see Madame Ionesco soon enough," she assured them. "In any case, you must finish your lessons before making social engagements. Who would like to show me their morning's work?"

The children obediently took out their projects. With no time to prepare a more complicated lesson, Penelope had left instructions for them to count how many pigeons landed in the branches of the elm tree outside the nursery window while she was out and to record the figures in what she unthinkingly called a PIE chart, by which she simply meant Pigeons In Elm. That the acronym for Pigeons In Elm was the same as that for Permanent Incorrigible Enclosure had not even occurred to the distracted governess, who had been in a tizzy deciding which dress to put on, among other concerns. But the children knew nothing of the admiral's plan and had simply understood their assignment to mean that the chart should be in the shape of a pie, complete with slices.

As it turned out, the pie-shaped chart worked wonderfully well. In fact, the "pie chart" remains in use to this very day, although the Incorrigible children themselves are rarely, if ever, given credit for its invention. (Why pie charts have stayed so popular while pudding charts, cupcake charts, and even tart charts have sunk into obscurity is a mathematical mystery, but perhaps it ought not to be, for who does not like pie?)

Inspired by their success, the children were soon making charts in the shapes of their other favorite objects (although the sextant, squirrel, and chewable shoe-shaped charts did not hold a candle to the pie version). Penelope was grateful that they had found such a clever and educational way to keep themselves occupied, for she was as twitchy as a squirrel in autumn, with nothing to do but sit and count the minutes until the soothsayer awoke from her nap and the final plans for the séance could be arranged.

Even her trusty Giddy-Yap, Rainbow! books failed to distract her. All at once they seemed silly and predictable, and as she turned the pages she found herself wishing for something wildly unexpected to occur: for Edith-Anne to boldly defend the farm against an attack by cannibals, for instance, or for Rainbow to leap over the fence and gallop off with a herd of wild ponies that had never known the feel of a bit in their mouths or a saddle on their backs and that would snort in disdain if anyone tried to braid foolish ribbons through their tangled, windswept manes.

"How long could Madame Ionesco possibly sleep, after napping that whole time in the carriage?" She chewed her nails and could not stop staring at the clock. "I must think of something, anything, to keep my mind off this infernal waiting!"

Elk, elk, elk. As if in answer, the pesky refrain bubbled to the surface of her whirling brain, in time to the soft click of the second hand marching 'round the clock face. "You call this waiting?" the imaginary elks seemed to scold. "When you've already spent more than half of your life waiting for your parents to come back from wherever it is they're hiding? As the Sage Elk of the Forest once said, 'A watched antler never grows.' Stop moping and do something useful instead!"

Now, you may think it silly to take advice from imaginary elks, but good advice is nothing to sneeze at, no matter what the source. Agatha Swanburne would doubtless have said much the same thing, although the wise old founder would have put it more like this: "Busy hands and idle minds have knitted many a sweater; busy minds and idle hands have knitted many a brow."

Alas, Penelope was deep in brow-knitting mode. *Tick-tock. Tick-tock.* Once more she tried to interest herself in the sweet misadventures of Edith-Anne Pevington, who not only lived with two loving and easily locatable parents but had her own pony to boot. It was no use. In fact, she decided that the book irritated her mightily, and she shut the cover and returned it to the shelf without even saving the page.

MADAME IONESCO SLEPT UNTIL TEATIME and woke up famished. By now Lord Fredrick had grudgingly agreed to meet the soothsayer, for he had been roundly scolded by his wife. ("After all, Fredrick, it is *your* father's ghost she plans to rouse; surely you can show *some* interest!") The Widow Ashton would not join them and sent a note saying that she would prefer not to see or speak to anyone before the séance. Instead, she planned to stay in "private contemplation, out of respect for the momentous events which are about to occur."

Madame Ionesco nodded approvingly. "A smart woman. 'She who keeps her mouth shut rarely says something stupid.' You can quote me on that."

Thoughtfully she picked up a sugar-dusted biscuit and ate it in one bite. "I have communed with the spirits this afternoon. Very comfy bed, by the way! I have asked permission to Part the Veil. The spirits have answered me–like they always do!–and the answer is yes. The séance will take place tonight. At midnight."

Lady Constance nearly fell off the sofa. "Tonight? Midnight! I am afraid that is impossible, Madame. In the first place, I must be in bed by ten o'clock or my eyes will be horribly puffy in the morning. In the second place, I am planning to invite a great many people, and that will take some time, as Miss Lumley will have to write out all the invitations and, frankly, she is a bit slow. In the third place, I have ordered a magnificent gown for the occasion, made entirely of veils; isn't that clever of me? And it will not be ready until Wednesday at the earliest. Surely we can keep you occupied until then? Perhaps you would like to tell our fortunes with cards or see our love lives in the coffee grounds? No doubt your crystal ball needs polishing, after all that dusty travel." She nodded in the direction of the housekeeper, who stood placidly in a corner. "Mrs. Clarke here is in charge of everything; she will see that you have what you need."

"The séance will be tonight," the soothsayer

repeated, more forcefully this time. "We do not keep the dead waiting. Not that they have anyplace to go, but still, is good manners. Also, I have a hair appointment on Thursday in the city, and I do not wish to change it. And no guests! The spirits will appear only before people already here, in the house. Twelve people must attend, and twelve only."

"Twelve! *Only* twelve? But Lady Furbisher had hundreds of guests when *her* spiritualist was in town," Lady Constance protested. "What is the use of having a séance, if no one will be there to praise me for hosting it?"

"Reading palms, easy. Crystal ball, easy. Speaking to the dead, not so easy! To reach those on the other side, conditions must be perfect. Trust me, honey. Twelve people. Twelve o'clock." Madame Ionesco sat back and folded her arms, and her eyes rolled up in her head until they were aimed at the ceiling. It was a most impressive display.

"Fredrick, do something! Tell her!" Lady Constance implored.

Lord Fredrick pulled at his shirt collar as if it had tightened like a noose. "It's all superstitious claptrap anyway, dear. Let's do what the woman says and get it over with."

Madame Ionesco crooked a finger at Lord Fredrick. "Claptrap, you say? You should know better, mister. Twelve moons in the year means twelve people at the séance. No more. No less."

The mere point of her finger seemed to make Lord Fredrick itch. He scratched behind his ear and muttered something that sounded like "Rubbish . . . twaddle–hmm, I feel a bit of a rash coming on. . . . Probably a false alarm, but a warm milk bath never hurt anyone. . . ." With eyes darting nervously about the room, he excused himself and left.

"Moons again! I am sick to death of moons!" Lady Constance exclaimed in defeat. "And however shall we get twelve on such short notice? Very well. There will be me, Fredrick, Fredrick's mother, and the admiral. Some of Fredrick's friends have stayed on after the hunting party; Baron Hoover and his wife are still here, and the Earl of Maytag, too. That makes seven." She frowned at the soothsayer. "Do *you* count?"

"Of course I count," snorted Madame. "Who counts more than me?"

"All right, we have eight. We need four more. I can always order some of the servants to fill in the empty seats, if necessary. Not Margaret, she would become frantic, poor thing, although it would be terribly amusing to watch. How about you, Mrs. Clarke?"

Mrs. Clarke shook her head. "I'd prefer to leave the dead rest in peace, if you don't mind me saying so."

"The wolf babies make twelve," Madame Ionesco said darkly. "Bring the wolf babies. They must be there as well."

"Do you mean those dreadful Incorrigible children? There are only three of them, thank heavens—oh, I suppose you mean including their governess. Very well. Miss Lumley and the children will come, although I expect the untamed creatures will be swinging from the chandeliers in no time. Speaking of chandeliers, can we have the séance in the ballroom, at least? It will lend a sense of occasion, despite the lack of guests. Drat! I am keenly disappointed not to have a party to rival Lady Furbisher's! I suppose the wedding celebrations will make up for it, though."

In this way the séance was arranged. Afterward, Mrs. Clarke told Penelope nearly all of what was said, for Penelope had not been asked to join Madame Ionesco and the Ashtons for tea, and why should she be? She was only the governess, after all. (Mrs. Clarke left out the part where Lady Constance accused Penelope of being slow at writing invitations, which was an unkind remark as well as being untrue, and therefore not worth repeating.)

Now it was time to act. Penelope scribbled a letter to Simon with precise details about which of the house's windows opened to the ballroom (including a hastily drawn map), sealed the envelope with wax, and had it hand-delivered by Jasper himself, so there could be no mistake about which humble farmhouse to bring it to.

"Tonight you will sleep in your clothes, children," she announced as she put the children to bed an hour early. They happily complied, for they were under the impression that they would be attending some sort of late-night welcome party for Madame Ionesco. Penelope could not quite bring herself to explain the more ghoulish aspects of what a séance might entail, for then the children would never have fallen asleep at all, so she let them think what they would. After they were asleep, she paced the nursery like the captain of a lost ship, waiting for some glimpse of a star to steer by.

Tick-tock. Tick-tock.

Cuckoo! Cuckoo! Cuckoo!

The clock struck half-past eleven. It was time. She twisted her hair into a fresh bun and splashed cold water on her face. Then she roused the children, gave each head of shining auburn hair a quick smoothing with a damp comb, and helped them put on their shoes. The three stood swaying on their feet, eyes half closed, and sleepwalked downstairs with Penelope shepherding them from behind. She hoped they might stay groggy for the duration and thus be spared any disturbing encounters with ghosts and the like, but Lady Constance had a different idea.

"Boo!" she screeched, jumping out from behind one of the potted trees that flanked the ballroom's entrance. Naturally the children were startled and reacted with an outpouring of howls and barks, followed by fierce growling. Afterward, all three were vividly awake, their eyes wide with excitement and fear.

Lady Constance wagged a finger at Penelope. "Shameful behavior! Please bear in mind that I will not tolerate any repeat of what happened at the Christmas ball." She addressed the children sternly. "No matter what terrifying and bloodcurdling events unfold during the séance, you must stay perfectly still and quiet as mice. No howling! No barking! No biting!" Then, unable to resist another chance to tease, she added, "Unless wicked ghosts appear and threaten to eat us. Then I shall surely scream myself. *Eeeeeeek!*"

The three Incorrigibles looked at Lady Constance as if she were quite mad, for even they knew there was no such thing as cannibal ghosts. Then they saw the fortune-teller arrive and fell upon her with affection. Madame Ionesco greeted Penelope with a knowing smile and the children with warm, enveloping hugs.

This familiar reunion did not go unnoticed. As the doors to the ballroom were flung open and the other guests came in, the admiral sidled up to Penelope and spoke quietly into her ear. "Why do I feel certain you had a hand in this séance business, governess?"

"I am sure I do not know," she replied, which was not quite the same as denying her involvement.

"Don't you? All this nonsense about raising the ghost of Edward Ashton. I think it's your idea. I think you'd do anything to interfere with my plans."

Penelope's temper flared, but she kept her voice hushed, as the children were not far off. "Perhaps that is because your plans are all at the expense of other creatures. If not for you, Bertha would be on the African savannah right now, doing—well, whatever it is ostriches like to do. As for the children, I will never permit them to be part of your exhibitions."

They followed the others in. The ballroom was eerily empty. It had been furnished only with a long table surrounded by precisely one dozen chairs. The rest of the vast room was decorated in spooky fashion:

There were floral arrangements in the shapes of skulls and tombstones, and the floor had been strewn with dead leaves, although it was still summer. The candelabras were lit, but only half the usual number, leaving most of the room in shadow. Smudge pots of incense released plumes of scented smoke that drifted, wraithlike, along the floor.

Penelope proceeded warily through the pale, perfumed fog. The admiral held her chair for her and kept his voice low so only she could hear. "Remember, there'd be profit in it for you as well. I'd hire you to manage the wee beasties, as you seem to have a knack for training them. If you say no, I'll just find someone else. Somewhere there's a former circus employee or zookeeper who'd be grateful for the job."

"Beasties! You are referring to my pupils, sir."

"You may be their teacher, but they're not 'your' pupils. These children are Fredrick's, to dispose of as he sees fit. Once I'm his stepfather, I'll win him over to my way of thinking, mark my words."

Penelope thought of Simon, who by now must be hidden somewhere nearby. "You seem rather confident that the shade of Edward Ashton will approve your marriage plans, Admiral."

"That's because I *am* confident." He chuckled.

"Everyone has a price, governess. Even the dead."

The clock struck midnight. "Boo!" Lady Constance exclaimed, clapping her hands and whirling her skirts in the vaporous air. "Boo! Boo! Watch me, Fredrick. What fun! Doesn't this look ghoulish?"

"Raising the dead is no joke," Madame Ionesco warned. "But why take my word for it? Soon you will see for yourself. Sit down, everyone. It is time to begin."

THEY ALL HAD TO WAIT for Madame Ionesco to clamber onto her chair at the head of the table, for she was no taller than Alexander and far less spry. Once settled, she spread her arms wide. "Now is when the Veil will part, but it will not stay open for long," she intoned, looking around. "Do we have the required number?"

The Incorrigible children quickly added it up. Cassiopeia counted by twos, Beowulf by threes, and Alexander by fours, but it all came out twelve in the end. All of the expected attendees were there, and most were in merry spirits. There was Baron Hoover and his wife, the baroness, and the Earl of Maytag, who looked sardonic as ever. The Incorrigible children sat near Madame Ionesco, and Admiral Faucet took the seat next to Penelope. Lord Fredrick and Lady Constance were at the far end of the table. The Widow Ashton was dressed all in black and seated on the other side of the admiral. Her face was so somber and pale that she might almost be mistaken for a ghost herself.

The Earl of Maytag spoke in a deep voice of authority. "We are gathered here today . . . wait, that's the marriage ceremony!"

"Har har!" chortled Hoover. "Wrong funeral, what?"

"There will be a wedding soon enough, I hope." Admiral Faucet smiled toothily at the widow, but she gave him only a sad look in return.

"Close your eyes, people," Madame Ionesco ordered. "Everybody take hands. Try not to think. Let me see who's out there." She scrunched her eyes shut.

"'Hold hands and try not to think'–that's it?" the baroness whispered in scorn. "No mystical incantations? No casting of runes?"

Madame Ionesco opened one eye and glared at the baroness. "If you want to see a show, go to the theater! Now hush. I'm listening to dead people." To the widow, she said, "Remind me, honey. What was your husband's name?"

"Edward." The widow's voice wavered. "Edward Ashton."

"Edward, right, uh-huh." Madame closed her eyes again. "Okay, dead people, let's get this over with.

Edward Ashton, are you there? Your widow needs your blessing to remarry. Be a good egg and speak up. We'll wait."

The inhalations and exhalations of twelve people made a soft, sighing wheeze in the otherwise soundless room. Penelope imagined she heard, not far off, the quiet breathing of a thirteenth, unseen and uninvited, guest. Simon ought to be just outside the window by now. She wondered how long he would wait to speak.

"It seems this may take a while. Perhaps I ought to call for some snacks to be brought in?" Lady Constance whispered to her husband.

At the word "snacks," the Incorrigibles began to fidget, but Madame Ionesco shushed everyone with a finger.

"Spirits of the dead," she muttered. "What's up tonight? Come visit. It won't take long, I promise."

The silence pressed down upon them. Finally the Widow Ashton cried out, "He is angry with me, is that it? He refuses to speak to me!"

Madame Ionesco touched her fingertips to her temples. "Huh. This is weird."

"No argument there," snorted Baron Hoover, which made his wife titter.

"Is not that he will not speak." Madame Ionesco

frowned. "Is that he is not there. No offense, Lady Widow. Are you sure the man's dead?"

The Widow Ashton gasped. "Of course he is! He drowned in a tar pit."

Admiral Faucet spoke consolingly, but Penelope felt his hand clench beneath the table. "I guess the seer's vision can't penetrate through the goo. Sorry, my dear. At least now you're free to make up your own mind. Shall we turn the conversation to happier topics? Like our wedding, for instance? I think we've waited long enough."

Penelope was becoming tense herself. Where was Simon? Why did he not speak? He must be able to hear them, for the ballroom windows were open; she could see the curtains moving in the breeze.

"A medicinal tar pit," the widow repeated, as if in a trance. "But the body was never found. . . ."

The soothsayer clucked in sympathy. "A tar pit? What a mess. Sorry, honey. I cannot tell you where he is, but if I had to make a bet, I'd say he is on this side of the Veil, not the other."

The Earl of Maytag laughed. "Blast! I came here to hear dead people talking, and I'm not leaving until I do. Who else can you ring up?"

Madame Ionesco shrugged. "There are many souls

on the other side. Many more than are on this one. Not all of them wish to speak. Not all wish to be silent. Be careful who you wake."

The suggestions rang out.

"Shakespeare!"

"Cleopatra!" That was Lady Constance's idea.

"Thucydides?" Alexander said shyly, for he still had some questions regarding the causes and consequences of the Peloponnesian War, which he had recently studied, and thought the ancient Greek historian might be a good person to ask.

"How about my great-aunt Mabel?" Baron Hoover offered. "She passed on when I was a boy. Sweet old lady. Baked a lovely lemon cake."

"No offense, dear," the baroness said, "but I'd rather talk to Napoleon than your aunt Mabel."

"Well! This séance has been a tremendous disappointment so far," Lady Constance declared. "Thank goodness there were not more people here to witness it. I think we ought to ring for dessert."

For once Penelope found herself agreeing with her mistress, and not just about dessert. The evening had turned into a joke, but ghost or no ghost, it was urgent that the widow get her answer from Edward Ashton. Where, oh where, was Simon? Had he been detained or gotten lost? Had Penelope made an error on the map? She had been in rather a hurry when she sketched it.

"What kind of dessert?" Beowulf asked before his siblings shushed him.

"I believe the chef has prepared a delicious pie," the admiral replied with a smug sideways look at Penelope.

That did it. The mocking remark about pie or, rather, PIE, spurred her to act. If Simon were within earshot, he must speak now, or else all was lost. Penelope rose to her feet and yelled, "Shades of the departed! We cannot see you, but we know you are there. Who on the other side of the Veil has a message for us? Speak at once, if you please! We cannot wait any longer!"

A creak. A snap. And then:

"Mmmph! Mmmph! Mmmph!"

"Is it Aunt Mabel?" the baron asked eagerly. "Sounds a bit like her. She often forgot to put in her dentures."

Madame Ionesco jumped as if pinched. "Yow! Hmm, this is strange. I'm getting a message from someone long dead . . . someone whose name starts with the letter A . . . ah . . . ah. . . ."

"Maybe it's Aristotle," joked the earl.

"Ashton! Edward Ashton!" the widow cried.

"The name is coming, wait for it. . . ." Madame Ionesco scrunched her face until it looked like one of those ugly dolls people inexplicably make from withered apples. "Ah . . . . ah . . ."

"Ahwoooooooo!"

The howl was piercing and so close, it felt as if it might be coming from within that very room. The Incorrigibles, who had behaved in an exemplary fashion all this time, could contain themselves no more. They leaped up onto the table and threw back their heads.

"Ahwooo!"

"Ahwooo!"

"Ahwooo!"

"What did I tell you, children?" Lady Constance climbed onto her chair to scold them. "Stop that noise this instant!"

But their howling only gained in volume. They pointed into the shadows. From the dark recesses of the ballroom, two yellow eyes glinted.

"It must be their mother," the Earl of Maytag declared. "See? They are half wolf, after all. There's the proof!"

"A wolf ghost! Well, that's a new one," said Baron Hoover. "Can't wait to tell the fellows at the club about this."

The admiral rose to his feet and brandished his

"Ahwoooooooo!"

cane. "That's no ghost. It's a real wolf."

Lady Constance shrieked and tried to climb on the chandelier. "I heard the servants gossiping that some wolves had been seen near the house. One must have come in the windows. How dreadful! Fredrick, do something!"

"A wolf in the house, what? I'll deal with this." Lord Fredrick pulled a small pistol from inside his jacket and waved it blindly around the room. "Stand back, everyone."

"Mama Woof! No house! Go to cave!" But the children's cries were lost in the hubbub.

"Mmmph! Mmmph! Mmmph!"

There was a loud *thud*–followed by another *mmmph*–

"Blast–who's there?" Lord Fredrick pointed his weapon every which way, causing a cacophony of shouts and screams to rise from the assembled guests. "Is it a ghost? Or a wolf? Or a burglar? Or what, what?"

"Calm down, Freddy. And don't shoot. Let's have more light," Baron Hoover called out. The children each nimbly seized a burning candle from one of the lit candelabras and used it to light all the rest, revealing two entirely unexpected sights.

First, tipped on its side, with its four legs poking stiffly into the air, was the taxidermy wolf from Lord

Fredrick's study (the sound of it falling over is what had made the *thud*). It was no ghost, merely a gray-furred pelt stuffed with sawdust and outfitted with yellow glass eyes that reflected the candlelight in a hauntingly lifelike way.

"Say, doesn't that belong in my study?" Lord Fredrick squinted in the general direction of the wolf. "Wait a minute. Who are you?"

"Mmmph-mmph mmmph-mmph mmmph-mmph-mmph."

"It is Simon Harley-Dickinson," Penelope translated, dashing to his side. He was sprawled on the floor near the wolf. A strip of black cloth was tied around his mouth. Another bound his hands behind his back. This she began to undo at once.

"Mmmph-mmmph," he said to Penelope, in a tone that sounded much like a cheery "Hello." When he saw everyone staring at him, he nodded politely as if to tip his hat, although if he had been wearing one, it had long since been knocked off. He cast his eyes about the room and said, *"Mmmph mmmph mmmph mmmph?"* by which he obviously meant, "How do you do?"

Once his hands were free, Penelope quickly untied the gag. "He is no burglar. Simon is a friend of ours from London. And a very talented playwright, too," she added.

"Whew! That feels better, Miss Lumley–I mean, Penelope. Say, you'll never believe what happened, it's quite a tale–well, look how big you've grown, you three!" he said, for the children had jumped upon him in joy, with many cries of "Simahwoo! Simahwoo!"

Penelope anxiously scanned the room. "I am eager to hear your tale, as always, but first–who on earth tied you up like this?"

"I did." A tall man, dressed in black, emerged from the shadows. Everyone was too surprised to speak except Lady Constance, who was adamant about performing her duties as a hostess, despite that fact that she was swinging from a chandelier and had only recently stopped screaming.

"What a delightful surprise!" she cooed. She sounded as careless and charming as if she had just run into an old friend at the theater. "I certainly did not expect to see you at our merry, ghostly gathering, Judge Quinzy."

"You mean *Mr.* Quinzy." Penelope fixed the man with a hard stare.

"I'm afraid you are both wrong." He spoke in that melodic, deep-voiced way of his. "Hortense, my dear Hortense–is it possible you do not know me, even now? It is me, Edward." He stepped into the light. "Edward

Ashton. Your husband." With a half smile, he turned to Lord Fredrick and added, "Hello, Freddy."

"*Now* are you satisfied?" Madame Ionesco grinned so widely that it revealed every missing tooth. "I have to say, sometimes I surprise even myself."

The Widow Ashton floated unsteadily to her feet. "Edward–my Edward? But I thought you were–oh!" Then she fainted dead away.

The Fourteenth Chapter

One of Agatha Swanburne's less popular sayings is unexpectedly quoted.

"Bells, bells, bells, bells, bells, bells, bells." Mr. Edgar Allan Poe once wrote a poem that contained this line, and many more like it, for the poem is all about the jingling and tinkling, swinging and ringing, tolling, chiming, sobbing, and sighing of the bells. This poem (which is called, unsurprisingly, "The Bells") would have perfectly described the noisy tintinnabulation that ensued when the Widow Ashton hit the ground, for all the gentlemen simultaneously ran for help. Every bell pull that could be found was rung and rung and rung yet again, to wake the sleeping servants, call for smelling salts, find someone to run for a doctor, and so on.

The insensible widow was carried off to the nearest sofa and made comfortable there, but even after the administration of smelling salts and several stimulating spoonfuls of schnapps, she could not be fully roused. Eyes fluttering, she thrashed her head from side to side and called her husband's name. "Edward! Tar pit! Edward! Tar pit!" she moaned. When the doctor arrived, the door to that room was closed and her cries could no longer be heard, which was, frankly, a relief to everyone within earshot.

"My work here is done," Madame Ionesco announced as she slipped off her chair with thud. "I always say, it pays to use a professional. Wolf babies, come see me in the morning. I have some Gypsy cakes for you. Not too early, please." Then she retired to the Egyptian Room. The ballroom was cleared so that all the weird decorations and dead leaves might be swept up, and the rest of the séance's attendees–the Baron and Baroness Hoover, the Earl of Maytag, Lord and Lady Ashton, Admiral Faucet, and of course, the man known as Quinzy (who now claimed to be Edward Ashton himself)–gathered in a nearby parlor, for the admiral was livid and demanded that no one go to bed until all had been explained. The children fell asleep as soon as they were settled in a comfortable spot, but Penelope and Simon were not permitted to leave either.

"How peculiar this all is! I wish I had some chocolate to settle my nerves. Can I offer you something to drink, Judge Quinzy?" Lady Constance paused. "Or should I call you Father Ashton?"

"Call him a liar, if you must speak to the man at all." The admiral pointed his cane accusingly. "This is not what we agreed, sir. You were to speak in the voice of Edward Ashton and give his widow your blessing to marry me. Instead you pretend to be the man himself, risen from the grave!"

"Pretend? Oh, now I am all in a muddle!" Lady Constance exclaimed. "This is better than a show. I wonder what will happen next?"

The baroness sprawled on the divan and yawned. "Don't tell me you two are in cahoots! How cheeky. Does that mean we can go to bed now? I am quite exhausted; what a dull evening it has been."

"It not bedtime quite yet, Baroness." Quinzy, as it seemed he must still be called for the moment, held a candle to his face so he could be seen, for there had been no time to light all the lamps in the room properly. "First, my apologies to you all for the deception. The baroness is correct. Admiral Faucet and I are well acquainted. We had a prior agreement that I would impersonate the ghost of Edward Ashton at the séance. In the excitement of the moment, it seems I became carried away with the role. My apologies. Rest assured, Admiral, I will return your payment in full, with interest."

The Admiral tugged at his muttonchop whiskers in frustration. "But I planned to marry her; that was the whole point! And now you've ruined it."

Quinzy turned to Simon. "I owe you an apology as well, Simon, for seizing you from behind and tying you up as I did. I trust you are not injured! But as a man of the theater, I'm sure you can understand. After so much planning had gone into Fredrick's little play, I simply could not allow anyone to spoil it."

The admiral wheeled on Lord Fredrick. "Play? What play?"

Fredrick looked uncomfortable, but Quinzy smiled. "One with the same plot as yours, Admiral–that I would claim to be Edward Ashton. It was Fredrick's idea."

"Fredrick!" Constance clapped her hands in delight. "You had an idea!"

"Yes, yes. But it was only a joke." Fredrick sounded impatient. "I suppose it was at Mother's expense, and now that she's ill I feel a bit remorseful. But I couldn't stand it anymore, all her keening and whinging about Father. And I think it's rather stupid that he went and got himself drowned in a tar pit—a ridiculous way to expire, in my opinion. Anyway, when Constance told me about this séance nonsense, I wrote to my friend Quinzy and asked if he'd help play a prank."

Quinzy shifted the candle to the other side of his face and rubbed at his nose. "Using the stuffed wolf from the study as a prop was my inspiration; that much I will take credit for."

Lord Fredrick chortled. "Masterful bit of howling there, Quinzy. You really had me going! I thought there was a wolf in the house for sure. Lucky I didn't start shooting, what? Poor Mother, though. I never dreamed she'd fall for it. Quinzy looks nothing like Father; I've spent enough time staring at that gloomy portrait in my study to know that. How could she be so blind?"

Penelope found this an ironic remark, coming from Lord Fredrick, but it was hardly her place to say so.

The admiral sputtered in fury. "All my hopes, dashed—for a prank!"

The Earl of Maytag fixed himself a pipe. "One

schemer has been outschemed by another, it appears. Sounds like justice to me. But let us not forget: This young rogue needs to account for himself, too." He gestured at Simon. "What were you up to, sir? How did you come to be at the séance, and what mischief did you hope to accomplish there?"

"I can explain that," said Penelope quickly. "Simon was here at my request—and for good reason, too—"

The baron held up a hand. "Let him speak for himself, Miss Lumley. And make sure you tell the truth, young fellow. You are in another man's house, uninvited. There might be legal consequences, if your explanation rings false."

Simon shoved his hands in his pockets. "Well, first of all, let me congratulate you all on the superb plot twists! I'll try to add mine to the mix without getting them hopelessly tangled up." He glanced at Penelope, who nodded her permission to confess. "Believe it or not, I also was here to speak in the voice of Edward Ashton, except I was supposed to tell the widow *not* to marry the admiral. I would have, too, if I hadn't crossed paths with him." He jerked his head at Quinzy. "I climbed in through the window and slipped into the shadows of the ballroom, but once I did, I saw the wolf there in the dark. I had no idea it was stuffed! I should have been frightened, I suppose, but I have a knack with animals, plus there was a bit of sandwich left over from luncheon in my pocket. Offering a tasty treat never fails to get you on the good side of most creatures, I find. I tiptoed over and tried to make friends. By the time I realized the poor thing had already met his maker, and the taxidermist, too, hizzoner, or whoever he is, had gotten the better of me. I was trussed up like a Christmas goose before you could say jackrabbit."

The admiral spoke threateningly. "And you put him up to it, governess? To prevent me from marrying Hortense?"

Penelope stood. "I did. But only because I know you intended to squander the Widow Ashton's fortune on your ill-conceived business plans."

"Is this true, Faucet?" Lord Fredrick thundered. "For I'll not have any of that, if you please. Mother's personal affairs are her own, but the Ashton estate is very much my concern."

"Yes, it's true. But since my plan has been ruined, no harm has been done, and I will take my leave. I would have made a fortune, too. And so would my investors—but perhaps they were playing a prank as well." He shot a withering glance at Quinzy. "No need to throw me out, Ashton; I'll be gone by morning, I assure you. Give your mother my regards, if you like. But I doubt she'll even notice I'm gone, now that she thinks her beloved dead Edward is back in the picture. Good luck sorting that out."

With that, the admiral left. Everyone sat in silence, trying to comprehend what had happened—all except the baroness, who was snoring gently from the divan, and the Incorrigible children, who lay in a heap by the fire like a litter of sleeping puppies.

"Do you know what would have been *terribly* amusing?" said Lady Constance in a dreamy voice. "If, in the middle of it all, the ghost of Edward Ashton really had shown up to speak for himself? Oh, I wish he had! That would have been wonderfully spooky. But it seems Madame Ionesco is a fraud after all."

"On the other hand, maybe she was right," said Simon brightly. "Perhaps the man isn't really dead. After all, the body was never found."

Tap. Tap-tap. Tap-tap-tap. Tap-tap-tap-tap.

The noise at the door startled all who were awake, but it was only the doctor, looking pale and rumpled, as befits a man who was called to work in the middle of the night. "Is Lord Fredrick Ashton here?" he asked.

"I am," Lord Fredrick rose. "How is Mother?"

"Alive, thank goodness. But not out of danger."

The doctor cleared his throat. "My lord, your mother has had a terrible shock. She seems to think her dead husband is alive again."

"Yes, I'm well aware. It was all a misunderstanding. We'll straighten things out tomorrow."

"No, you will not–not if you want her to live. However this 'misunderstanding' came about, you must carry on as if it were true. The stress of finding out otherwise would be too much for her."

Lord Fredrick began to chuckle, but the look on the doctor's face revealed that it was no joke. "What– do you mean we ought to pretend that Quinzy really is my father? That's ridiculous. Mother will see through it soon enough anyway. Unless we take away her glasses, of course!"

"Tell her he's gone on a trip, if you have to keep them apart. But as her doctor, I assure you: She will not survive another shock like that." The doctor bowed and took his leave.

"Well, I don't envy you, Freddie," remarked the Earl of Maytag, after a pause. "You've got yourself in quite a pickle now."

"Quinzy's in a pickle as well. I'm afraid you're stuck playing the part, old chap." Lord Fredrick slapped him jovially on the back. "Pity you don't look more like

Father; we might have had some fun with it. Although you are about the right age, what? And where are your glasses? Don't think I've ever seen you without them before. Did you lose them in the dark?"

"I suppose I did." Again Quinzy's hand flew to his large and oddly formless nose, which, to Penelope's bleary eyes, seemed to be changing shape in the candlelight, and might have even slipped sideways a bit when Lord Fredrick slapped him on the back. "Given your mother's fragile condition, it seems I should do as the doctor suggested and leave on some pretense before our ruse is discovered. I will write a note to Hortense—to your mother, I mean—explaining my sudden departure. I shall do it right now, in fact. Good night." Shielding his face with his hand, he left.

Simon helped Penelope carry the children up to the nursery and put them to bed. It was too dark to give him a proper tour of the house, but he whistled in appreciation at the sheer size of it. Once the children were tucked in, he yawned and looked out the nursery windows. "Nice elm out there! Say, it's almost dawn; look how the light is changing. Wouldn't it be fun to take a walk and see the sunrise?"

Almost dawn—Penelope's hand flew to her mouth.

"It would. Simon, I must find the admiral before he leaves. There is something I need to ask him. Will you escort me to the POEHO, posthaste? I have no doubt that that is where we will find him, for that is where all his business papers are, and I know he will not leave Ashton Place without them."

Simon had no way of knowing what a POEHO was, but he was game for an adventure as always, and Penelope explained the acronym along the way. They found Admiral Faucet just as she predicted, furiously packing up the last of his architectural drawings for POEs and PIEs, his recipe for SPOTs, his plan for a chain of FOPS (that stood for Faucet's Ostrich Premium Steakhouse), and the like. Their arrival only inflamed his anger.

"Why should I speak to you, governess? You plotted against me."

"I do not deny it. But if you must be angry, be angry at that man called Quinzy. He is the one who ruined your scheme in the end."

Simon stuck out a hand. "That's right, Admiral. Whatever plot we might have cooked up never came to pass, so no harm done. Let's part on peaceful terms. As one adventurer to another."

Warily, the admiral shook his hand. "And how are you an adventurer, laddybuck? You hardly look old enough to cross a busy street, never mind Parts Unknown."

"It's in my blood," Simon said proudly. "I come from a long line of sailors. Unmapped seas and the briny deep are practically my middle names."

This seemed to put the admiral more at ease. Penelope seized the opportunity to ask, "As I said, it is the man called Quinzy who foiled your plans, not us. Will you tell me how you came to know him to begin with?"

The admiral scowled. "No reason not to, I suppose. This Quinzy fellow was my principal investor in the ostrich-racing business. He didn't put much money in to start, but he promised more once I got off the ground, and he coached me all along the way. He was the one who suggested I join the croquet club to meet rich widows—'the readiest source of capital for a dashing gent like you,' he said. The flatterer! Croquet's a bore, but he was right about the widows. Once I met Hortense, he urged me to woo her and then convince her to take me home to Ashton Place, so I could launch my business here, in England. With my ideas, plus her money and society connections, I couldn't fail. I had no idea he was a friend of the Ashtons; he never said so, although I should have guessed. He seemed to know all about them, and those wolf children, too."

Done gathering his plans, he closed his satchel.

"Double-crosser! I thought he was a businessman looking to make a profit, like me. You should have seen how excited he was at the notion of putting the children in a PIE. That was the most profitable idea I've ever had! But it seems there's something else he wants more than money. What, I don't know."

Penelope's mind raced. All along she had believed the admiral to be a danger to the children, and he was—but he was simply being used by Quinzy. Why? Why had Quinzy gone to so much trouble to bring this fortune hunter and his ostrich to Ashton Place? She thought of the children racing on wolfback through the forest, with Lord Fredrick and his hounds in pursuit.

The hunt is on. . . . Madame Ionesco's warning came back to her like a voice from some invisible dimension. This was the third time since coming to live at Ashton Place that the children had been forced to flee a wild armed mob. The first was at the Christmas ball, when the gentlemen set up a late-night hunting party to find the presumably missing Incorrigibles (luckily the children were hiding in the house all along, thanks to Nutsawoo, who had cleverly led them upstairs to a secret attic). The second time was in London, at the disastrous opening night of *Pirates on Holiday.* And now the third: the Bertha Derby, for want of a better name for it. If not for Old Timothy leading the hounds astray until she and the children had nearly reached the house, they would have been at the mercy of Lord Fredrick's wild shots.

"Yes, the hunt is on," she thought to herself. "But why?" She turned to Admiral Faucet. "One more thing, Admiral. Did you ever discover how Bertha got loose to begin with?"

"A funny business, that. The latch on the cage wasn't damaged at all. It'd simply been opened, and I know I closed it up properly." He shrugged. "Someone must have let her out."

It was too late for Simon to travel back to the farmhouse to sleep, so he bunked with Jasper in the servants' quarters, where he was able to get an hour or two of rest, at least. Penelope scarcely slept at all, for her mind was whirring with all that had happened, and she wondered how all the pieces of this strange puzzle might fit together. Eventually she drifted off out of sheer exhaustion, and did not wake again until Margaret tiptoed into her bedchamber with a jug of fresh water for the washbasin. Quinzy was already gone from Ashton Place, Margaret told her, and the admiral was, too.

As planned, Penelope, Simon, and the children met Madame Ionesco in the Egyptian Room for a late breakfast of Gypsy cakes and tea. The cakes had been carried from London and were a bit crushed, but even in pieces they were delicious, and the crumbs would make excellent treats for Nutsawoo, not to mention the pigeons, warblers, nuthatches, and other creatures that were likely to come by the nursery windows later on for a taste.

The children found the cheetah statues amusing and busied themselves doing math problems with the spots. Madame Ionesco was still aglow with pride about her ability to summon Edward Ashton back from the dead. Penelope did not have the heart to tell her that it had all been a trick, but she and Simon exchanged private, knowing looks. "I've outdone myself this time," the soothsayer crowed. "Never had one actually come marching through the Veil before! Wait'll this story gets around. I'll have to double my price."

Tap. Tap-tap. Tap-tap-tap. Tap-tap-tap-tap.

"Who's going to turn up next–Cleopatra?" the Gypsy merrily and rhetorically cried. But it was not the ruler of all Egypt, nor any other long-dead person knocking on the door. It was the Widow Ashton, looking very much alive. There was color in her cheeks and a serene expression on her face. She had shed her mourning dress and wore an attractive powder-blue gown. Instead of a black veiled cap, a sprig of fresh flowers was tucked into her hair. The sparkle in her eyes made her seem ten years younger than before.

"Try some Gypsy cake?" Alexander offered politely.

"Sorry. Only crumbs." Beowulf sounded apologetic, but held out the plate.

"Yum yum crumbs!" Cassiopeia insisted, dribbling some into her mouth.

"No, thank you, children. I do not mean to interrupt your breakfast. I simply came to offer my thanks to Madame Ionesco." She turned to the fortune-teller with shining eyes. "Once I finally regained my senses, all I could do was think: What if I had remarried, only to discover later that Edward was still alive? It would have been a tragedy beyond imagining. I am so grateful, dear soothsayer! You have saved me from a gruesome fate, indeed."

Madame Ionesco grinned her semitoothless grin. "I'm glad you're happy, honey. I have to be honest; I was worried. Crossing the Veil is not done so often. I was afraid that husband of yours might evaporate."

"He has, in a way." The Widow Ashton held up a letter. "He is already gone; he took his leave early this morning, before I could see him again. But he left this letter for me. In it he tells me things I have longed to hear for many a moon. Finally, my heart is at peace. My Edward is alive—and someday, I know, he will return."

Gently, Penelope asked, "Forgive me, my lady, but are you certain it was your husband? He appeared so briefly, and the room was so dim. . . ."

"There is no doubt in my mind." The widow smiled and pressed the letter to her heart. "In these pages, he says things that only my Edward would know. And I would recognize his eyes anywhere. That is why I fainted last night when he suddenly appeared. Oh, to look into his eyes once more! Madame Ionesco, for that alone, I can never thank you enough."

"Don't worry about it, honey." Madame Ionesco patted the widow's hand. "But take my advice: Leave the prognosticating to professionals. What the future holds is anybody's guess. Even if your husband does come back, he may not be the same Edward who left. People change, darling. People change."

Penelope and Simon glanced at each other. Did Madame Ionesco know more than she was letting on?

The widow just smiled. "I'm sure you are wise, Madame. But I prefer to live in hope. The day will come when he finally appears at the door. What a happy reunion that will be!"

"Maybe happy, maybe not. Keep an open mind! You know what they say, Lady No-Longer-Widow. No matter how big the egg, don't count your ostriches before they hatch, eh?"

Penelope gasped. "If I am not mistaken, Agatha Swanburne once uttered the very same words, but it was certainly not one of her more popular sayings. Wherever did you hear it?"

Madame Ionesco rose from the table. "During the séance. Remember when I said I was getting a message from someone long dead? Whose name starts with the letter A?"

"That was it?"

"That was it." Idly she tapped the obelisk clock with the handle of her teaspoon. There was a soft *whirr* as the hands of the ancient clock spun 'round and 'round; they did not stop until they told the exact right time (which was quarter past ten, to be precise).

Tick-tock, tick-tock, tick-tock, said the clock, as if it had been running perfectly all along.

The fortune-teller licked the spoon and dropped it into her purse. "Interesting woman, that Agatha Swanburne. Will you look at the time! Better call the carriage for me now, darlings. I have a train to catch."

SIMON HAD A TRAIN TO catch as well. "Wish I could stay longer, but I received some urgent news about my great-uncle Pudge just before I left London. He's not in good health, and he's been asking for me. I'll ride with Madame to the station and catch the train in the other direction."

As Penelope already knew, Simon's great-uncle Pudge was very old and had been a seafarer in his youth; now he lived in a home for old sailors in the city of Brighton, near the sea. "I am sure he will appreciate the visit," Penelope said warmly, but in truth she was sorry that Simon had to leave so soon; she felt there was something important she had forgotten to tell him in all the excitement, but she could not think what it was. At her request, Old Timothy readied the big landau carriage and took them all for a ride to Ashton Station, so that she might spend at least a little more time with her friend. But with Madame Ionesco snoring in the opposite seat, and the children climbing over them and pointing at the scenery on either side of the road, all she and Simon could do was sit in silence and smile shyly at each other now and then.

Once at the station they walked Madame Ionesco to the platform. Simon lifted the fortune-teller's bag onto the London-bound train, and Penelope finally worked up the courage to pose the question that had been taking shape in her heart for some time now.

"Madame Ionesco, if a person–two persons to be precise–are not actually dead, but merely absent, would your soothsaying powers still enable you to send them a message?"

The wizened lady patted her cheek. "Messages to the living? That's what the post office is for, honey. So long, wolf babies! Come visit when you're in the neighborhood."

The Incorrigible children hugged the fortune-teller and danced in and out of her countless billowing scarves as they caught the puffs of steam from the awakening locomotive like so many wind-filled sails. Penelope watched the children play with a fond heart and considered the Gypsy's reply. She could write a letter to her parents, but where could she send it? To the Long-Lost Lumleys, care of Alpine Scenery, Somewhere in Europe? Even the London General Post Office, which was the swiftest and most reliable postal service in the world, would be flummoxed by that address.

Madame Ionesco's train departed right on schedule. Simon's train waited on the opposite platform. Once aboard, he secured a window seat so he could continue to wave many highly theatrical farewells to Penelope and the children. In fact, he was hanging so far out the window that Penelope could not help but think of Beowulf and the warbler. How could she ever have thought it was a nuthatch? "Distracted by a book," she thought wryly. A silly book about a silly pony contest that she knew from the very first page Rainbow would win, for Rainbow always won. If, just once, something wildly dramatic could happen to Edith-Anne and Rainbow–something truly unexpected, like an attack by cannibals–

"Cannibals!" she exclaimed. Penelope reached up and grabbed Simon's hand, which dangled just within reach. "I meant to tell you: I found an unusual book in Lord Fredrick's library, written by a cabin boy," she said in a rush, for the conductor had already shouted "All aboard!" and closed up the doors, which meant the train was ready to leave. "It has to do with cannibals, but it is so smudged with age and seawater I can barely read a word of it."

"Cannibals?" Simon laughed (although of course, there is nothing particularly amusing about cannibals). "That's funny. Uncle Pudge is always talking about cannibals. Claims he met some once, when he was only a cabin boy. Something to do with a shipwreck."

"This book deals with a shipwreck, too." She felt suddenly lightheaded, and would not let go of Simon's hand.

"What's it called?"

"The title is *An Encounter with the Man-Eating Savages of Ahwoo-Ahwoo, as Told by the Cabin Boy—*"

Whoo whoo!

Whoo whoo!

The train whistle blew as soon as she started to speak, and she was drowned out.

"Didn't get any of that," Simon yelled over the rumble of the engine. "Say again?"

She coughed from all the steam; when she found her voice, she yelled, "*—and Sole Survivor of a Gruesomely Failed Seafaring Expedition Through Parts Unknown: Absolutely Not to Be Read by Children—*"

Whoo whoo!

Whoo whoo!

Once more she was drowned out by the whistle's blast. "Never mind," she shouted when the din stopped. "It is a long title. But it is definitely about a cabin boy. In a shipwreck. With cannibals."

Whoo whoo!

Whoo whoo!

"A cabin boy in a shipwreck, you say?" Simon was

shouting now, too. "That'd be a funny coincidence. If it were the same shipwreck, I mean."

"It certainly would. Yet I think I would have noticed if the author's name was Pudge. Unless I was distracted." Penelope shivered, for that slippery, icy feeling was trickling down her spine again. "Is Pudge your great-uncle's real name?"

He grinned. "I doubt it. Who'd name their child Pudge? But it's the only name I've ever known for him. I'll ask him when I see him. I do remember the name of the island where this shipwreck happened, though; he's told me the story many times. It's—"

Whoo whoo!

Whoo whoo!

The train began to move, and Penelope was forced to let go. Simon shouted, and she tried to read his lips. But the train whistle hooted and the engine roared, and a thick, rolling fog of steam blanketed the station platform. The train lumbered off, slowly at first, and then gained speed.

"Stay there, children!" she shouted, breaking into a run. "Do not move!" Penelope raced along the platform, neck and neck with the train, until it pulled ahead and she could not keep up anymore. Through the fog she saw Simon's head craned out the window,

Simon shouted, and she tried to read his lips.

mouthing the name of this mysterious island in time to the train whistle:

Whoo whoo!

Whoo whoo!

"Ahwoo-Ahwoo," she whispered to herself. "Of course."

Epilogue

In the words of Agatha Swanburne, "Many are happy to give advice; few are happy to take it." As usual, the wise old founder was right, for most people tend to trust their own opinions far more than they should and are stubborn, recalcitrant, unyielding, and even obstinate when someone helpfully suggests that they wipe the fog off their pince-nez and have a good look at hard truths that have been staring them in the face all along.

Of course, there is such a thing as bad advice, and

not every pithy nugget of wisdom is worth stitching onto a pillow. Consider the old saying "Out of sight, out of mind," otherwise known as OOS, OOM. OOS, OOM absurdly suggests that things that cannot be seen are quickly forgotten, but nothing could be further from the truth. Objects that are out of sight are rarely out of mind, and things unseen can be more present than that which is right in front of one's nose. Just ask a long-grieving widow whose husband drowned in a medicinal tar pit, or a plucky young governess who spent more than half her life wondering whether she might someday see her parents again.

To put it bluntly: OOS, OOM is poppycock, balderdash, rubbish, and nonsense. Even the clumsy, unattractive, and bad-tasting dodos have occupied people's thoughts far more in extinction than they ever did when they were alive.

And speaking of dodos, and tar pits, and things unseen: Edward Ashton had long been thought dead, or even very dead, but apparently he was not as dead as a dodo. Thanks to the skill of a soothsayer, the scheming of an impostor (or two), and the optoomuchstic hopes of the woman who loved him, Edward Ashton had become, not quite living, but somehow less dead than before.

Penelope was up to her elbows in suds, but her mind wandered, as minds tend to do, and the topic of Edward Ashton was where it settled. "He is still lost, one could say, but not long lost," she thought as she poured a pitcher of fresh water over Beowulf's head.

"Ow," said Beowulf, squirming in the tub. "Soap in eyes. Rinse again, please."

"Ahoy, shipmates." Alexander popped up from beneath the bubbles. "Sunken treasure!" He offered up the washcloth, which he had just retrieved from the bottom of the tub.

It was not their usual bath night, but the Incorrigible children had been itching and scratching with increasing frequency since their adventure in the forest. At first Penelope panicked; she thought they might have somehow caught the strange moon sickness endured by Lord Fredrick Ashton, but the true explanation was simpler: The children had fleas. Within days the whole nursery had become infested. The rugs were brought outside to be swept and beaten on the lawn; the children's bedding and clothes were laundered; and everything in the room was scrubbed by hand in hot water and strong soap, including the Incorrigibles themselves.

Cassiopeia was done with her bath and had slipped

on her nightgown, but her long auburn hair was still very wet.

"Careful, Cassiopeia–use a towel, please; do not shake–oh!"

It was too late. Cassiopeia put her head down and shook her wet hair vigorously, like a dog that has just come out of a lake. Water droplets flew everywhere and needed to be mopped up. This task finally tore Penelope's mind away from her ruminations about how many degrees of dead there might be, and back to the bright, cozy nursery and the extremely lively children who lived there.

Afterward, the children asked for a chapter from one of the Giddy-Yap, Rainbow! books. Penelope agreed, but even in performing this happy task, a note of melancholy crept in. The book pleased her, of course, but it pleased her in a different way than it had in the past. It pleased her because it made her think of how much she had always loved these stories, all the many times she had read them over the years. It pleased her because she liked feeling, just for a while, like the girl she was when she first met and loved Edith-Anne and Rainbow. It made her remember how sweet it had been to curl up among the hand-stitched pillows in the window seat at the Swanburne Academy (she would scarcely be able to fit into it now, of course) and imagine that she herself was a character in the books–a character who was partly Edith-Anne and partly Penelope, too.

She would always find these books delightful; of that she had no doubt. But after her recent thrilling adventures, and in light of the somber questions that now flooded her mind at odd moments, demanding answers, the Giddy-Yap, Rainbow! books did not seem to offer quite the right range of experiences to be of practical use to her anymore. All except the one about Edith-Anne and Albert, of course. That one continued to fascinate.

It was much like the way small children can devour head-sized mounds of cotton candy with sticky-handed glee one summer, only to discover that by the time summer rolls 'round again, the notion of plunging one's face into a glob of spun sugar has lost much of its appeal. After that happens, there is no turning back: the love of such gluey, toothache-inducing treats will soon give way to an appreciation for bittersweet chocolate and tarte Philippe, onion sauce and strong, ripe cheese (not all at the same time, of course).

Whether this shift in taste is a gooden thing or a baden one is a matter of opinion, but that it happens is a fact of life, and no amount of burying one's head in the sand will make it otherwise. Penelope was just beginning to understand this, and frankly, she was not sure how she felt about it. In the words of Madame Ionesco, "People change, darling. People change."

When the children were sleeping and she was alone in her room, Penelope once more took out the curious volume about the cannibals. The pages were warped and brittle from having been soaked again and again in seawater and then, she imagined, laid out to dry in the sun. The ink had run; the text, where it survived, was written in enigmatic verse, and the centerfold map was almost completely obscured with smears and blotchy stains.

Penelope closed the covers with care, but even this small movement caused the yellowed pages to crackle. Could this account really have been written by Simon's great-uncle Pudge, when he was a cabin boy so many years ago? "One of Lord Fredrick's ancestors was an admiral, known for his seafaring adventures," she thought. "If they were on the same voyage, it could explain how this book ended up in the Ashton Place library. If only I could make sense of it!"

But it was no use. Perhaps Simon would learn

something interesting from Great-Uncle Pudge himself, at the old sailors' home in Brighton, and send news. Of course, any news at all from Simon was good news, and what could be more interesting than that?

THE NO-LONGER-WIDOW ASHTON SOON DECIDED to return to the Continent, but not to mourn. She said she wanted to see her friends, to devote more time to croquet ("I have long wanted to improve my jump shot," she explained, "but until now I was too sad to apply myself properly to the task"), and, of course, to wait for Edward's return.

Her son treated her kindly enough, but once she was gone Lord Fredrick was visibly relieved. "If I had to hear one more word about dear old Dad risen from his gooey grave, with his dreamboat eyes like the dark side of the moon . . . why, it's enough to bring on a headache. Blast! Has anyone seen my almanac?"

Lady Constance cooed fondly and falsely over the children while her mother-in-law was watching, but that too changed the moment the lady was gone. "Fleas! How disgusting. More and more I feel you should have left those wild, filthy creatures in the woods, Fredrick. To think your mother prefers them to the idea of us having children of our own! Well, we shall see about that, won't we? Babies are a dreadful bother, of course, but I cannot stand being told I cannot have something, even if it something I do not particularly want. . . . Fredrick? Fredrick! Are you listening?"

Bertha seemed happy enough in the POE, for now. But Penelope resolved to write to the director of the London Zoo and see if there was some way to return the big bird to Africa, so she might live out her days in her native habitat, among others of her long-leggèd, dim-witted kind. In the meantime, the children kept her company and took occasional rides on her back, but only when she was in the mood.

As it happened, Nutsawoo and Bertha got along quite well, for they possessed similar levels of intelligence (although Nutsawoo may have had a bit of an edge). Bertha liked to race with him around the POE, and the shining-eyed, bushy-tailed squirrel learned many new tricks to earn himself tasty bits of SPOTs, all of which he frantically buried, for the summer was drawing to a close.

It took some weeks for the opportunity to present itself, but eventually Penelope was able to sneak into Lord Fredrick's study and get another look at the portrait of Edward Ashton. The burly man whose likeness stared down at her would never be mistaken for Quinzy, at least at first glance. One was tall and big bodied, the other was tall and trim. One had a thick head of silvery hair; the other had a thick head of ink-black hair. Both had dark eyes, but that hardly proved they were the same eyes, did it?

"The Widow Ashton was convinced they were, but after wanting and hoping and dreaming about it for so long, the poor woman could easily be convinced of anything." Penelope kept her gaze fixed on the portrait, so that she would not have to face the glassy stares of all those dead, stuffed creatures. "What a tragedy, to spend one's life waiting for a loved one who may nevermore return. Nevermore!" she could not help adding, although there were no peas nearby to toss in the air.

Yet the very thought made her blush scarlet, for how many heavy-hearted hours had Penelope spent longing for just such a reunion? Was she, too, living in a haze of hope? Was she so lost in the fog of wishing that she could no longer see what was right in front of her, as plain as the nose on her face—or the hair on her head, as Old Timothy had once, enigmatically, remarked?

"Almost done, miss?" Margaret squeaked nervously from the hall. The reluctant girl had been persuaded to serve as lookout. She would not dare set foot inside the study herself, of course, because of all the dead animals.

"In a minute," Penelope murmured. "The nose on his face . . . the hair on his head . . . what am I failing to see?" She stepped closer to the painting. There were the pale, long fingers. The slight, contemptuous curl to the lip. And those eyes—black they were, and bottomless as tiny twin tar pits.

Penelope was not a playwright, like Simon, but she had once attended nearly all of the first act of a show in the West End, so she was no stranger to stagecraft, either. (The title of the show should be on the tips of the tongues of those of you who have been paying attention to this point and therefore need not be mentioned here; no doubt you recall that the plot had to do with pirates.) "If he lost a great deal of weight," she thought, "and blacked his hair with dye, and wore glasses to conceal his eyes, and covered that distinctive sloping Ashton nose with putty, of the sort actors use to change their appearances . . . the sort that might get sticky and soft if the wearer stood too close to an open flame . . ."

It was all quite improbable and unbelievable; unlikely and implausible, too. And yet, hypothetically, it was *possible* that "Judge" Quinzy, who might not really be a judge, was actually the long-dead Edward Ashton, who might not really be dead, despite Quinzy's claim that he was only pretending to be Edward Ashton—which could, of course, be a lie.

"But if that were so," Penelope thought, once she had wrapped her mind around it all, "why would Edward Ashton fake his own death? And why would he turn up now, so many years later, and lurk around his former home in the guise of a judge?"

And what did the Incorrigible children have to do with it all? For by now Penelope was quite sure it was Quinzy, or Ashton, or whoever he was, who had set Bertha loose to begin with, and all as a way of getting the Incorrigible children back into the woods, where Lord Fredrick's hunting party might find them, and where they might come to some dreadful harm, accidentally or otherwise. If not for Old Timothy . . .

"The hunt is on, Mr. Quinzy-Ashton-Whoever-You-Are," she whispered to the portrait. "The hunt for answers, that is. But from now on, I shall be the hunter, and you shall be the one pursued. I wonder where you will turn up next?"

Despite all the precautions taken, it soon became evident that Miss Penelope Lumley had acquired some fleas of her own. "It is just as well," she thought ruefully, as she worked a fresh coat of Miss Mortimer's poultice into her hair. "For I am overdue for a treatment of this mixture, and Miss Mortimer has made it quite clear that she intends for me to use it regularly. Her package has arrived just in time."

And it had: At long last, Penelope had received a reply from Miss Mortimer, complete with a fresh supply of the hair poultice, some picture postcards for the children showing animals from the various zoos of Europe, and a letter to Penelope as well. Now that the poultice had been applied and her head wrapped firmly in a towel so that it might set there for an hour before rinsing, Penelope sat down to read her long-awaited correspondence.

My dear Penny,

Well! After many weeks of travel I have returned to a towering pile of mail, much of it from you! Once again, family business has caused me to go abroad. No doubt any questions you posed to me in your earlier letters have long since been sorted out, so I will not waste ink and paper answering them now.

I hope you have found time to enjoy the great outdoors during this fine summer weather. Book learning is all very well, but as Agatha Swanburne liked to say, "If you want fresh ideas in your head, get some fresh mud on your boots." I am sure I hardly need to remind of you that.

Do you recall meeting Miss Swanburne? I expect you do not; you were so very small, and she was in the final months of a long and highly satisfactory life. (She was always a bit cagey about telling her age, but we thought she might have been ninety-six when she finally entered the Realm Invisible.) You had just arrived at school, four or five years old at most, and were feeling a bit sad and lost, as little girls do when away from home for the first time. Even in her frail condition, Miss Swanburne took a special interest in you. "That," she said to me after you had gone, "is a true Swanburne girl. She has the look."

Speaking of Swanburne: Your alma mater soldiers bravely on, although there are struggles. Books and pencils and porridge oats get dearer by the day, and the girls go through embroidery floss at an alarming rate. The trustees have begun to solicit donations to help pay expenses, with mixed success. You may be interested to know that, while I was abroad, a certain Judge Quinzy was appointed to the board of trustees. It is unusual for a gentleman of his means and influence to show such an interest in the education of poor girls, so when he contacted the board and offered his services, along with the promise of a generous donation, they welcomed him with open arms.

In his letter he mentioned that he belongs to the same gentlemen's club as Lord Fredrick Ashton. It is a small world, is it not?

Warmest regards, from your loyal friend,
Miss Charlotte Mortimer